ASHES OF RAGING WATER

BOOKS BY MICHAEL J ALLEN

<u>Blood Phoenix:</u>
1. ASHES OF RAGING WATER
2. RULED BY TAINTED BLOOD
3. VENGEFUL ARE THE DROWNED
4. RISE OF THE EXILED LADY
5. RAZING THE LAST BASTION

<u>Scion (Original):</u>
1. SCION OF CONQUERED EARTH
2. STOLEN LIVES
3. HIJACKED
4. UNCHAINED

<u>Bittergate:</u>
1. MURDER IN WIZARD'S WOOD
2. THE WIZARD'S BANE
3. FORGE OF WAR
4. SCYTHE OF ILLUSIONS

<u>Guns of Underhill:</u>
1. FEY WEST

<u>Dumpstermancer:</u>
1. DISCARDED
2. DUPLICITY

<u>Delirious Scribbles:</u>
(SHORT STORIES)

- WYRM'S WARNING
- SCRAPING BOTTOM
- CRIMINAL JUSTICE
- DREAMS OF TREASURE
- DESPERATE
- THE BOTTOM LINE

COMING SOON:

<u>Binarai Online:</u>
1. STORM REFUGE
2. ROGUE PLANET
3. POWER BREAK

<u>Wayman Chronicles:</u>
1. CROSSWAYS

<u>Guns of Underhill:</u>
2. METTLE KINGDOM

<u>Dumpstermancer:</u>
3. DECOY

<u>Scion Rising (Remaster)</u>

Ashes of Raging Water

Blood Phoenix Chronicles: Book One

Michael J Allen

Delirious Scribbles Ink

Delirious Scribbles Ink, Inc.

Copyright

Delirious Scribbles Ink, Inc.
4519 Woodruff Road
Suite 4, #108
Columbus, Georgia 31904
www.deliriousscribblesink.com

Interior Layout ©2022 Delirious Scribbles Ink, Inc.
Cover Design ©2022 Delirious Scribbles Ink, Inc.
Cover Art ©2018 Andrea Fodor

ISBN 978-1-944357-38-2 (intl. tr. pbk.)
ISBN 978-1-944357-38-9 (hc.)
ISBN 978-1-944357-40-5 (epub)
ISBN 978-1-944357-73-3 (large print)

Printed in the United States of America
10 9 8 7 6 5 4 3 2 1
Ashes of Raging Water / Michael J. Allen. — 1st ed.

For Tina, an inexhaustible fount of help and support.

For B, B & E, J, S & J, and L.

Delirious Scribbles Readers Group

Like free stories?

How about curated deals for Science Fiction and Fantasy books?

Get your first benefit—a FREE story sent right to you—by becoming a member of the Delirious Scribbles Readers Group.

Begin your journey, just scan this image with your phone camera!

Content Advisory

In order to provide my readers the best possible experience as well as be responsive to reader requests, I've created a reader-curated content advisory on my website. If you are sensitive to certain kinds of fictional representations, please check this book's listings before reading.

I hope you enjoy this story...

— Michael J Allen

To visit the advisory, just scan this image with your phone camera.

Chapter One

Incursion

Quayla

Someone's unbridled need for morning coffee nearly cost my life. Dying isn't normally the end of the world, but this time it really was the beginning of the end.

A green Humvee rocketed onto the exit 252 onramp and whipped across my lane in a mad dash for the empty shoulder. The maneuver required two ninety-degree turns that at least should've put the behemoth up on two wheels, but only amounted to a pair of reckless slides.

Deprived of a clear path, the Humvee's driver cut back across the off-ramp, forcing the minivan in front of me to slam its brakes and jerk left. Slick concrete betrayed the van's traction, transforming its overcorrection into a spinning slide through my lane and down the embankment into rush hour traffic.

I wrenched my Johammer motorcycle around in a tight, full-throttle circle inches ahead of the Ford pinball paddle. Praying heightened reflexes and Caelum's modifications to my baby sufficed to save my tail, I jerked my pearl white jelly bean with wheels to a jarring stop.

Squealing brakes cut short a relieved breath and brought my

"

attention up to oncoming traffic, certain my escape had been a hollow victory thanks to drivers more focused on phones or applying makeup than me and my bike.

I beat the odds.

The rush of adrenaline lifted a smirk onto my lips. A pickup slid to a halt rather than splatter me under its huge tires. My smirk died when its headlights ended up close enough for me to count the bug carcasses.

All the cars behind me managed to stop without hitting anyone.

A snarl launched from my lips toward the Humvee. "Selfish, hell-blighted wafer!"

Anima's voice emerged from the tiny bronze archangel mounted just beyond my handlebars. "Shield Quayla? Do you require assistance?"

Dread welled up to fill my throat. Pleading with our Shield's automata had taken considerable wrangling. If she chose to back out and read the other shields in on my operation, I'd lose my one chance. "Ani, you promised. This is just between us girls."

"Might be best if I notify the Shieldheart," Anima said.

"I need to handle this myself."

With a cringe, I checked the angel. The figurine wasn't Anima, merely a way for the automata to communicate with us in the field. The angel itself stretched arms toward the heavens. Outstretched wings braced the figure like a feather shield version of see no evil, but it didn't otherwise appear disgruntled by my not-totally-unwarranted outburst or my departure from protocol.

"Okay, but please keep me up to date," Anima said.

Dread exited in a single exhale. "Thank you."

Warranted or not, neither my outburst nor curse were fair to the wafer in the Humvee. She knew nothing about where I was headed or the lives that were at stake.

Nor should she.

Truth was, I'd screwed up and my mistake had cost hundreds

of mortal lives. If I didn't redeem that selfish choice, I was dead—really dead, like couldn't be reborn again True Death.

I couldn't blame the last few decades of increasing everyday selfishness for my mistake. I'd made my choice and caused all those deaths over a century ago on another continent. I'd tried to save myself and cost others their lives—something I'd tried to make up for every day since the Shieldheart had let me off probation and out of our sanctum.

Even though humanity had grown more selfish in my time sequestered, they were still worth protecting. Of course, when weighed opposite their great potential for goodness and caring, such blatant disregard for each other threatened to exceed disheartening on the way toward nauseating.

Today's shining example blared her horn when a car in front of her blocked a path the Humvee driver felt entitled to have to herself. It would've been more fitting if the vinyl family on the Humvee's back window made rude gestures. Instead a vinyl dog, two cats, four children, a mom and a decapitated dad with his head stuck to the window between his legs offered only innocent grins.

My Johammer had a lot of power—certainly more than provided by the manufacturer, but the motorcycle offered little protection against the herds of selfish drivers and their metal behemoths. It did, however, let me flow through traffic along paths of least resistance—just the way I liked it.

Leaning right, I slipped between a timid SUV and the sidewalk onto Howell Mill. The Humvee following my example, jock-eyed across a gap left by an instant's too-slow reaction to the sound of blaring horns. She mounted the sidewalk and cut across my path.

A blonde girl in pigtails waved through the window as her mother made a desperate dash through oncoming traffic toward the Starbucks.

Great plan, orphan your family to get that so-called green monstrosity into the drive-thru for some burnt coffee.

Thumbs tapped my handlebars as I gritted my teeth.

Gentle ponds. Babbling brooks.

I took a deep breath.

Shields served the light. No matter how self-centered a wafer was, no matter how ignorant they were of the other cherished souls surrounding them in the great plan, we did not levee punishment upon the untainted.

A phoenix has to do what a phoenix has to do if she wants to avoid probation.

Yeah, phoenix. Five of us comprised my Shield—part and parcel of a cosmic Plan B. We'd each been created from the essential energy of a given element, including a fire of course—his name's Ignis. If we died protecting humanity from the Sidhe Courts, we could be reborn from the enchanted essence of our individual elements.

Or if we get mowed down by a caffeine-deprived soccer mom.

Our Shieldheart had a real grudge against me. Maybe he didn't like water. Maybe he disliked girls. Maybe he just couldn't be bothered to look up from his books and train a younger shield, but most likely, it was because of my history. Whatever his reason, I was pretty much our Shieldheart's whipping girl.

Caelum—our air phoenix—maintained that I was overreacting, but I *knew* our Shieldheart was collecting evidence to prove I deserved True Death.

Luckily, he wasn't the real boss, just the boss's old pal. That's where stopping the incursion alone came in. Faeries from both of the major Sidhe Courts had been breaking through the Veil inside animal shelters, killing and stealing the animals. My mission was about more than just saving a bunch of waggy-tailed puppies and precious little kittens. I had to stop the incursion and figure out what the Sidhe were up to before humanity caught them in the act and our whole fragile world—yours, mine and ours—went to hell in a djinn's lamp.

I had to stop the incursion, save the animals and figure out the Sidhe's plan without the others along. If I succeeded, there'd be no way for our Shieldheart to give credit for the mission's success to one of the others.

Save the world, rescue some furbabies, and redeem myself enough to save my own feathers in the process—no pressure.

Stop-and-go morning traffic, navigating commuters with delusions of supremacy, and the crazy low speed limit the angel on my dash made me follow knotted my shoulders. I tapped my thumbs harder and checked the horizon. Dawn lurked just behind the impending birth of morning twilight. Cleanup had to be complete before wafers started arriving for work.

Come on. Come on.

A narrow gap in oncoming traffic converged with my destination's driveway. A self-conscious glance shot to the angel's stern expression. I licked my lips and thumbed the booster Caelum had added to my bike. The engine's electric hum intensified to a banshee's shriek.

Horns blared as I whipped onto a side street and into the Humane Society.

"Get out of the way, lady!"

I didn't return the mortal's rude gesture—I swear.

I pulled to a hard stop under the animal shelter's guest awning. The required-by-law helmet I didn't need mussed my hair as I yanked it free. One hand sorted my hair, and the other hung the helmet on the bike's handlebars.

The angel glared at me over folded arms. I tapped its head, "I'm here, Anima."

The finger rings of two Karambit knife hilts stuck out from the custom sheaths mounted at opposite angles just behind the handlebars. I grabbed both and leapt off my baby.

Excited barking rose over the sounds of angry traffic.

I flipped the knife hilts around on their finger rings, tucked the bladeless knives into my jean's belt loops, and scented the already muggy, early morning wind.

More dogs barked beyond the building's attractive facade. Mournful howls escaped dark, windowless metal buildings, twisting my heart even more than the scent of so many animals kept too close together. My pulse rushed as images of imprisoned puppies and kittens flashed through my mind.

I forced away righteous indignation and rising disgust.

Focus. I'm here to stop an incursion, not lecture wafers.

I inhaled deeper in search of dark faerie taint. I circled the unlit building, sniffing for faeries and scanning for a tear in the Veil from a Sidhe court.

Wish Caelum and his nose were here.

I berated myself. We all had our gifts, standing around and whining profited no one—especially not the lives caught in this newest faerie machination.

But why are they risking exposure to steal a bunch of animals?

Exposure could've been the goal. We kept a lid on Sidhe existence the best we could, but once in a while they got to a mortal, offered a seemingly good deal in exchange for granting mortal desires, and stole, enslaved or perverted the wafer. Still, the Sidhe seldom played a simple, straight forward game.

A change in barks sent me running back around to the front of the building. I hooked a hilt out of my belt. With a deep breath, I tightened my hand around the hilt's ridged grip and pushed on my center.

Frothing water slid out the hilt's heel, solidifying into a forward curved blade of glistening blue. I swept my essence knife up the seam between doors, severed the lock, and charged in.

An alarm console chirped.

Dammit.

I considered going back and using my helmet to conceal my face, but the haloed angel Caelum had painted along its surface for me was unique and readily identifiable. I bent my face toward the ground, freeing my hair from an aquamarine hair tie to hide my face as I concentrated. My wavy black hair took on the wet blue-brown appearance of Atlantic waves. Strands of living water flowed around my head, coming together in an undulating mask that only resembled hair at a first, distant glance.

I charged inside and through the administrative area, eyes scouring everywhere for trouble. A frame wrapped in black ribbon brought me up short. The picture displayed a mousy, bespectacled woman holding a humongous orange tabby almost as big as her torso. A label included birth and death dates too short to apply to the cat's owner.

I wasn't allowed a pet, but several strays I'd kept fed had died on me. In light of the crisis, the itch behind my eyes had to be pushed aside, but I allowed myself an instant's sadness for her loss before continuing toward the panicked barking of living animals in need of my help.

Movement flashed in my peripheral vision.

I slid to a halt on paw-printed linoleum and threw open the door to the kitten cages.

Two waist-high grendlings whirled. The diminutive faeries clutched kittens to their molding-blueberry chests and spat like angry cats through needle teeth.

My nose rebelled. The stench of dank mold seldom teamed up with rotting meat, but together the potent miasma overpowered shelter smells of litter box and Lysol. The stink nearly overwhelmed my gag reflex even through a filtering mask.

So glad I don't have Caelum's nose.

Pinching my nose offered immense appeal, but I toughed it out and drew my second hilt.

"Put those kittens back." I pushed my essence out of the end in shimmering blade. "Breakfast hours are officially over."

Dropped kittens skittered everywhere, mewing their objections.

The grendlings gibbered insults at me in Wyldfae and drew knives from behind their backs. Shaped troll bone throbbed with magic so dark green it was almost black. While the acidic magic's primary purpose lay in subduing the regenerative abilities within the troll's bone pressganged into a weapon, the acid and magic also combined to arm the primitive blades with poison and agony.

The pack hunters circled me, one moving slower to position

themselves on either side for best advantage. Their extended bat ears twitched eagerly forward.

That little shit lied. He told me the raiders were Unseelie.

I relaxed into a fighting stance, sweeping my feet in smooth circles. I clinked my hilt rings together, keeping an ear on the sound.

Grendlings weren't goblins.

They possessed the same intelligence and mentality, but grendling tribes dwelled in caves rather that settling in forests or ruins. Grendlings maintained fierce independence from other faerie and prided themselves on the mold colonies cultivated on their skin.

They rushed me from either side.

I sought the room's acoustic center and pitched my voice to boom like the legends of Hera on high. "By the Undying Light, I command you to surrender."

My echoing voice folded the grendlings' ears against their heads, stealing a vital battle sense—equivalent of dropping a flash-bang in front of an eye-stalker. I used their disorientation to slip between them, body flowing around their strikes quick as class six rapids.

My blades sliced across the shorter's leathery skin, parting its spotty blue hide to expose even darker flesh. Sidhe taint rippled nausea up my blade and into my gut. Black blood glooped from the cut like a month-old blood pudding.

His partner thrust for my heart. An upward sweep decapitated his blade and a downward counter sliced across the shorter's side.

The other grendling's broken blade bit into my thigh. Denim protected me from the worst of the damage, but the shallow cut burned like cuddling a welding torch. I punched the grendling, finger ring breaking teeth from its mouth.

The shorter hurled his knife and scrambled for the door.

A fluid weave escaped the blade's path.

The other grendling caught the blade, reversed it and thrust once more for my chest. I slid downward, doing a split. My head snapped back, turning to follow the blade mere eyelashes from my nose. My attention whipped back to my opponent as my shimmering Karambit sliced upward. Empowered essence focused to a razor's edge severed the grendling's arm at the elbow

Disgusting black blood splattered my face.

I gave up a surprise wake-up massage for this?

I turned away.

The armless grendling sank teeth into my extended arm and shook it like a terrier. I cried out and cut its head off with my other knife. The thing's jaws didn't release in death, if nothing else they bit down harder. I tried to shake the stubborn thing away so that I could pursue the shorter grendling but was forced to saw open the still-locked jaws from my arm while the other grendling escaped.

I sucked the water blades back into my body, partially filling bite wounds.

I scooped the kittens away from the blood before they could lick it up. I rubbed their purring little heads against my cheeks and cooed reassurances.

Dylan's fingers are fantastic, but this is rewarding too.

It would've been nice to bask in their purring adulation, but I rushed them back into their cages and bolted back into the hall.

Black blood trailed away from the frantic barking, crying, yelping tumult. The roar pounding in my ears like surf on sand demanded I chase down the little bastard, but I couldn't turn my back on the heartbreaking sounds coming from the main kennel.

I cursed and let the grendling escape.

I'll hunt him down after.

My first glimpse through the kennel door's window stole breath from my lungs. Dozens of grendlings—enough for several tribes—swarmed the kennels. A winter-deadened tree dominated the play space between runs, stretching up from a crack in the concrete floor until its dark limbs scraped the ceiling.

Two decoratively armored grendling chieftains braced either

side of a foul portal. They disdained each other, the larger's muscles poised to fend off his one-eyed rival as they paid less attention to the raid than their one up man's contest of posture, glower and stance.

Dark magic throbbed through the whole tree, as if the heavy breathing of some carnivorous tree from a dark forest. The skin-crawling throbs worsened, shooting nausea through me as each grendling fed a stolen animal to the tree's dark, gaping maw.

The grendlings and their prey disappeared the moment they touched the seemingly two-dimensional cartoon tunnel, transported into the Unseelie realm—or perhaps in the case of wild grendlings, Faery's Wyld Wastes.

My fingers wrung the grips of my Karambit hilts. I squeezed harder on my essence, forcing more of myself through the veined handles until it formed into curved blades. Considering the fight ahead, I ratcheted up the pressure from uncomfortable to the edge of painful in order to extend guard blades across my knuckles from the finger rings.

I took a breath, centered myself and threw open the door. "In the name of the Undying Light, I order you to cease this unsanctioned action, return the stolen animals unharmed to their kennels and surrender."

Not being the brightest of faerie, several grendlings just blinked at me—one biting the head off a Chihuahua. A nervous giggle escaped the grendling nearest me.

The one-eyed chieftain's dark chuckle filled the room. "You're outnumbered, little bird."

His confidence infected the others, spreading the malicious laughter through the room.

"A couple of grendling tribes aren't enough to worry a shield."

The other chieftain, Muscles, cracked his knuckles and added his own laugh. "Our two tribes might not, but how about the six raiding the other rooms?"

Hell's gates!

Muscles eyed his opposite. "We'll deal with this one. Sound the retreat before the rest of her Shield arrives."

Grendlings around the room pressed their ears against their heads.

One-Eye drew a bone and silver horn and blew a note to make any lighthouse proud.

Another grendling pushed open a back door and blew a similar horn. Half the room's grendlings drew trollbone knives and clubs. The other half increased their pace, dragging the animals into the dark, gaping crack in the tree's trunk.

"Oh, no you don't." I whirled to the wall behind me. I leapt onto it, spearing blades into drywall and climbing several quick arm lengths. I threw myself backward off the wall atop the row of chain-link kennels. My landing ended up slightly off balance, but I recovered and raced across kennel tops toward the central play area.

Grendlings shimmied up in a swarm, but I cut through three in short order in my rush toward the tree. I like high ground—it's a bird of prey thing—but I needed to destroy the Arch.

I somersaulted off the kennels nearest the tree, whirling to face the two chieftains. Muscles and One-Eye met me with nasty swords honed from troll leg bones. I flipped over One-Eye, drove a blade into his skull, spun to deflect Muscle's blow and kicked him in the face. The little faerie flipped end over end once, then slid across urine wet floors.

I didn't want to, but I turned my back to him to deal with the Arch. Two slashes of my water-essence blades sliced a gleaming X into the portal's surface—disrupting the magic and cutting the faeries off from escape. The effect was all but immediate. As grendlings howled outrage, the tree shuddered then shrank away, smearing odd orange chalk marks on the concrete as the shrinking gateway connecting Creation and Faery took its death stench away with a pop.

Muscles bellowed his best Minotaur imitation and charged. I

slipped around his blow, following up with a counter that missed him by a few bristly hairs.

More grendlings poured out of the adjoining kennels—too many more.

Blighted hells!

Muscles charged again. I slid under and behind Muscle's blow then took off his head with a scissor cut. Taking up a defensive stance, I started a slow fluid dance that oozed confidence and menace far beyond what was truly warranted for a single shield against such daunting numbers.

The horde swarmed me.

They raced up between the runs.

They leapt at me from atop the kennels.

They circled the cages to attack from behind.

In the center of the seemingly endless sea of violent, violet monsters, I just tried to stay focused on the forms I'd learned. One after another, I flowed through dodges and punches, weaving and slicing as each opportunity presented itself.

My Karambit blades flashed like schools of silverfish through the tide of attacking Wyldfae. But each slice of my razor-edged essence through tainted grendling blood nibbled at my strength. I fought to purify my essence as I also fought for my life, but so much taint overwhelmed my ability to counter.

Troll weapons sliced and stabbed through holes in my guard.

Poison and dark magic burned away my strength even further.

Grendlings died, but at the cost of my blood. The tide of oncoming grendlings never abated. They poured into the room, dead or panicked animals in their filthy-nailed clutches.

I forced more essence into my blades, pushed until that pain rivaled my injuries. All the effort only added a few inches to the knives' maximum lengths.

Despite my grace, despite the slippery defensive nature of my fighting style, there were just too many grendlings.

Their weapons struck at me from enough angles to take

advantage of vulnerable openings. Acid magic and troll poison burned through dozens of slices, invading my veins like liquid fire.

I knew stopping the incursion was about something bigger than just the animals, but the soft brown eyes and tucked tails and whimpering puppies needed someone to save them. I'd chosen to handle the incursion myself instead of calling backup.

I could've retreated. I could've fought my way clear, escaping to my bike to call for help. If I did so, the faeries would open another Arch. More animals would suffer and die to fuel whatever Machiavellian plot the Sidhe had hatched to plague humanity.

I can't let that happen, I just can't.

I decapitated another faerie and kicked the severed head into the grendling behind. "I won't! I will not let you use these innocent animals, not again, not today, not ever."

Dark laughter and darker insults proclaimed their derision.

Heavy impact atop a chain-link kennel drew my eye. A larger —well, he wasn't exactly a grendling, but I'd never seen anything like him. Splotchy mold grew over bulging muscles several shades too light. He gripped a trollbone sword so large it had to have been carved out of flesh of a greater troll.

Demi-grendling? Greater grendling?

"Too young, too alone." His tongue slid along pointed teeth. "Too delectable to resist."

Sudden terror squeezed my heart tighter than any grip I'd ever used on my essence until the hammering organ lodged in my throat.

My blades kept striking, but my eyes slid along the horde to imprisoned dogs. Some faced off against the little faeries with hackles raised and teeth bared. Others cowered in their own urine with ears pressed to their heads.

I squeezed my insides harder to mimic the condition of my heart. I compressed it with all of my will in preparation for one last desperate choice.

Anxiety squeezed back even harder. I couldn't breathe, frozen on the brink of making the same choice that once murdered countless mortals.

Ignis's training held up transmogrification as a valuable tool in our arsenal, but changing into my true form in public had led to burnings and torture. That mistake had cost me my first family. It had landed me ostracized, on probation, and justifiably terrified my next mistake meant True Death.

I considered attempting a shield, but not only was it not a skill I'd honed, a makeshift barrier would waste my potential arsenal.

My gut writhed, wrestling with faerie taint and the ramifications of choosing to change.

I'm not afraid of dying, not this time. This is about stopping this incursion, saving these innocents. Changing is the correct tactical choice.

My eyes shot to the web cameras mounted around the room.

Please, God, let no wafers witness my change this time.

I dropped into a crouch and forced my essence to condense into a tiny, throbbing star.

Grendlings mobbed me.

They abandoned their weapons. Grendlings sank teeth into my flesh, laughed and licked their bloody chops like they were at a Labor Day barbeque.

I drew in my hair, forsaking my mask to push as much essence into my center as I could. My core became a black hole, drawing all water in from around me.

Urine puddles slithered across the concrete.

Water bowls around the room spilled horizontal water falls.

The greater grendling's much smaller ears twitched forward.

Hose spigots burst.

Supply pipes exploded.

Hissing sprays filled the air, converging on me like time-lapse fog.

He bellowed urgently, dancing side to side looking for an opening. "Kill her, now before she—"

I exploded out from within the mob.

Graceful, sweeping wings threw grendlings back in all directions. I shot upward on wide, outstretched wings of shimmering liquid a dozen feet wide—a great bird of prey. Wing beats sent a torrent of storm-scented wind whirling through the building. Despite my flapping wing, my lithe, natural form floated rather than flew.

Their leader dismounted the kennel behind the cages as he called his lessers to the front lines. "Swarm her! Quickly!"

Grendlings leapt from atop kennels at the whirling phoenix that was the true me. My talons caught some, shredded others. High jumpers felt the wrath of my beak.

Feathers—some purposefully shed and others carved from me by trollbone—tumbled away like fall leaves, glistened in a hundred shades of bluish-white. Shed feathers controlled and connected by instinct and will swirled around me in a spiral of razor edges.

I'd killed so many among their horde, shed so much blood, the little faeries were driven into a mindless blood rage abandoning all thoughts of retreat. They threw themselves at me above and below. They stabbed up at me. They hurled knives and clubs.

I kept the largest of my feathery blades going in a whirlwind orbit. Dark grendling blood coated their edges. I dissolved the smaller castoff feathers into thin razor-wire ribbons of glistening, hardened water—a translucent thresher crafted by a vindictive but masterful glass blower.

The frenzied grendling mob threw at me anyway. My watery Cuisinart shredded them into foul, sun-rotted, purple coleslaw.

Wholesale slaughter proved insufficient to stem the entirety of the faerie tide. For every few I killed, they landed a strike that cost me essence. The tainted blood coating me leached away strength.

Another large grendling charged in from the other kennels, his lanky frame bedecked in feathers. The new chieftain assessed the carnage and screamed at his minions. "Retreat!"

Anima had to have already sensed my transmogrification. She'd summon others to save me, but they would be too late this time. I was going to protect these innocents and stop this incursion even if thwarting the Sidhe schemes cost me everything.

My vengeful shriek echoed off the walls. All ears—faerie, canine and feline—pressed tight against skulls. Every animal, even the bravest Chihuahua, cowered in fear. Grendlings froze, my cry somehow flipping some primal terror switch that bought me a moment's respite.

I forced more and more of my essence into the assault. I robbed my wings to fill out a solar system of spinning feathers. Watery tinsel trailed off the jagged planets like orbital rings.

I let out another screech, hoping additional hesitation might add just one more feather to Justice's scale and doom my prey.

They bolted instead.

I spun in the air in a rapid pirouette, unleashing my assault. Layer after layer of razor water sliced outward in every direction.

A few of the shelter's animals leapt at the grendlings, terror overcome by instinctual response to fleeing prey.

I held onto control of the aqua kinetic assault for all I was worth, screeching once more with the effort to either avoid dogs or soften sections of my weapon to keep from hurting them. Rapidly exhausting my ability to stay aloft, I drove dwindling wings down for a quick climb then dove at the greater grendling.

Talons shredded his flesh as his sword filled my body with searing agony.

My beak snapped at his throat. Dying heartbeats thundered in my ears. The putrid flavor of rot filled my mouth an instant before the sound and sensation of his snapping spine reached me.

I'd done it. I'd stopped the incursion all by myself. Rather than spit his foulness from my beak with my last breath, I smiled.

Then I died.

Chapter Two

Internal Trouble

Vitae

An agonized shriek drew my eyes up from my morning read. I draped a silk ribbon between the vellum pages of my mentor's copy of the Iliad and set the twenty-five-hundred-year-old book in my lap. I turned toward five pedestals arrayed atop an unlit river stone hearth. A phoenix cast in blue-white crystal tucked its head down between folded wings.

My eyes fixed upon the statuette, tightening in time with my jaw. My youngest shield had died again. "Light save me, Aquaylae, what have you done this time?"

My concern didn't center over her fate so much as the circumstances of her death. I didn't need her habitual carelessness rekindling the fires of another witch hunt.

There'd only been one shriek, but I checked the other four statuettes as I rose from the comfort of my fine leather chair. Each figurine held its head high and its wings outstretched, the intricate detail of their crystal feathers illuminated from within by a mote of each phoenix's magical essence. My eyes lingered longer on the milky, yellow topaz of my other young shield, but Caelum's likeness showed no signs of distress.

I moistened lips and pressed them back together.

She went alone. Why won't she learn?

I set my book reverently on my side table, turned off the antique lamp so as not to bleach the cover and strode from my study.

The march up mahogany stairs to the penthouse's second story doubled back halfway up toward twin metal doors covered by paneled oak. My patent leather shoes made no sound on the wooden stairs on or off the runners despite the heat in my chest.

"Anima."

The one word to our sanctum automata was enough. It knew to open up the biometric scanner Vilicangelus had mandated. Using technology less than a century old to secure the second most vital room in our sanctum seemed foolhardy. New, unproven tech ripe for modern day piracy didn't deserve so vital a role, but then again the contents of the room were no more deserving.

My hand upon a biometric scanner started the entry process. Considering any death would change my hand and require recalibration just proved its faulty nature. The next lock opened by recognizing my voice, another variable element that the technology didn't take into account. I spoke my access code in Ancient Babylonian, my best effort to ensure the doors unlocked for me rather than a faerie counterfeit.

Foot-thick doors parted to either side.

I strode into the control room, lights and monitors flickering to life around me. "Anima?"

An airy, angelic voice greeted me. "Good morning, Vitae. How may I serve you today?"

"I need a location on Aquaylae." I massaged the bridge of my nose, trying to relieve the tension headache often brought on when dealing with our Aqua. "Better contact our Praefectus, too. Inform him our Shield has experienced a death."

The map of Atlanta shifted on the main screen and zoomed. Aquaylae's icon appeared at the Howell Mill Humane

Society. Anima narrated the shifting view. "One of Quayla's seeds indicated another impending Veil breach at an animal shelter."

A blood vessel throbbed in my forehead at the sound of Aquaylae's shortened name. Before I could correct Anima, it revealed even more irritating news.

"A Seelie contact confirmed portents of probable action."

"What is *Aquaylae* doing fraternizing with a Seelie, and why didn't she see fit to call in?"

"She notified me but considered the incursion to be low threat."

Of course she did. Youth constantly overestimates their abilities.

"You didn't think I needed to be notified that our least experienced shield intended to face a breach alone?"

"Quayla didn't want me to disturb you. She felt the incident was well within her capabilities," Anima said. "I was about to notify you that I'd sensed her transmogrification."

"Aquaylae isn't qualified to make such judgements. You need to inform me even when she requests otherwise."

"Acknowledged, Shieldheart."

I nodded my satisfaction. I didn't wholly trust the new automata, but at least it took orders. "Were there any witnesses?"

"Dogs and a few felines."

I frowned. "Probably not an issue. Please display the others' location."

The map pulled back. Three other icons blinked around the metropolitan area. Roadways highlighted with traffic levels and accident locations. A small red circle identified hot, fresh Krispy Kreme donuts available at the marked location.

I tensed, glaring at the foreign marker. Modern companies frequently found ways to insinuate their market hawking into technology, but this instance seemed more likely a case of internal piracy.

Caelum. These two are becoming problematic. I'll address that tonight and reprogram that nonsense out of the sentry net later.

"Iggy is second closest, but he's on duty at the fire stati—" Anima's voice cut off.

The undignified nickname for our Pyri sent another throb into my head. "*Ignis*. Traffic will prevent Ignis from arriving in time. We—"

"Vitae, the Isaac advises technological eyes watching Quayla. He is still ascertaining if any mortals witnessed what the eyes observed."

A reprimand stopped on the threshold of my lips. Aquaylae had been witnessed by mortal electronics. "Convey this development to Vilicangelus. Anima, we must address this displeasing display of informality."

Even for a programmed computer automata, her tone grew defensive. "I serve the shields protecting the Atlanta territory. If a shield asks me to refer to them in a certain way, I am expected to comply."

I glowered at the technological eye mounted atop the largest monitor. I couldn't reprimand her for performing her programmed functions, but warmth still pricked the underside of my jaw below each ear. Laziness permeated the mortal world, but I'd be Destroyed before I would allow such weakness into my Shield again.

"Unacceptable. Add this topic to the evening's schedule and prepare a report of all instructions you've recorded that were not given by Vilicangelus or myself."

"Yes, Vitae."

"Meanwhile, I'll go clean up after Aquaylae once more. Please include my intentions in your update to Vilicangelus and lock down the garden."

"Vilicangelus shall be notified. Be careful, sir."

Another throb stiffened my shoulders. I aimed my displeased scowl at the room in general. "I'm just as capable of handling an incursion as the others."

"I offered warning, not insult, Vitae. One phoenix has fallen to whatever threat breached the Veil. Protocol requires caution when investigating a death regardless of the shield's skills or capabilities, particularly when only one phoenix is available."

Anima wasn't a living being capable of offering offense. Though I didn't fully trust the technology that had replaced the viewing pool and oracle of centuries before, taking offense where none was offered remained a choice of perception. I'd chosen to transfer my irritation with Aquaylae to the harmless machine.

"Your caution is correct. I offer my apologies."

Chapter Three

Rebirth Pains

Quayla

Awareness flared as the prepared waters of my nest rose above the basin, reforming my body cell by cell. A curse escaped my mouth the moment the essence finished coalescing into a full body.

My voice sounded strange, but the tiny mirrored alcove caging my nest always distorted sounds just as it always reflected the glowing silver runes etched into my basin's stone rim.

I grimaced, running my tongue across my teeth to scrape away the memory of grendling blood from my tongue. I pushed open the alcove's doors.

A teardrop sapphire embedded in my chest sparkled with magical essence. Blue ripples cradled the jewel, seemingly tattooed to compliment the gem.

Two of the mirrored walls swung away to reveal a complex glyph. The glowing symbol matched a teardrop sapphire embedded in pale white skin high over my heart and the complimentary blue ripples cradling the gem with sparkling magical essence.

My touch triggered the essence locks. They dimmed, energy

no longer drawing the two symbols together like electromagnets. A counter mechanism took advantage of the missing attraction to slide apart the bookshelves hiding my nest.

Sunlight filtered through gossamer curtains, filling my clothes-strewn bedroom with rose-tinted light.

I turned my back to the room and raised my arms toward the chin-up bar suspended above me.

I cursed again.

My new arms no longer reached the bar.

Damn it, Dylan's going to be so pissed. He loved my long legs.

I closed my eyes, squared my metaphysical shoulders and directed my gaze downward before opening my eyes once more. Held breath exploded from me in response to my relief.

I have breasts, they're much smaller, but I have them.

I looked lower, fighting a cringe.

Thank God, I'm still female.

Each rebirth created my fellow shields and I anew. I'd never actually heard of a phoenix being reborn hermaphroditic, but each new body was formed from the full spectrum of human possibilities. Anything and everything could change with a new body.

I'd hatched female, but big picture, my gender had never really mattered. I'd always focused on the contents of another's heart rather than what parts did or did not dangle. Dylan hadn't so much changed that, but bathed the possibilities involved with rebirths in desperate anxiety.

A chance meeting with one of Dylan's ex-boyfriends during a night out early on in their dating informed me of his bisexual tendencies. The revelation had been one of the supporting reasons I'd ultimately decided to trust him with the truth of what I was. He'd listened, and once the initial shock faded, chosen to stay with me.

Even so, this is the first time I've died since we started dating. Who knows how he'll take this.

An itch took up residence high on both cheek bones. I tried to squash my concern, but Dylan's reaction could make or break our relationship. Dying offered a litany of troubles enough without borrowing trouble with Dylan. In the modern age, changes of appearance or gender meant my identity died when I did.

Just lucky that financial transactions aren't exclusively dependent on fingerprints or facial recognition yet.

Even with all the other troubles queued up in my day, I had trouble pushing Dylan from the forefront of my thoughts. I should've been more worried about Vitae and the fallout from yet another failure, but Dylan was one of the few parts of my life that was distinctly mine. To make matters worse, I'd seen other phoenixes with mortal loved ones in my first Shield deal with the ramifications of a death.

If the mortal hadn't been trusted with the secret of the phoenix's true identity like I'd trusted Dylan, that phoenix died—forced to watch their loved one grieve, move on and eventually surrender to old age.

Probably why Ignis and Terrance don't date.

If the mortal was in the know, they faced the shock involved in loving someone suddenly possessed of a wholly new body.

In this case, Dylan's bisexuality should make things easier. He shouldn't care which parts I possess after a rebirth.

My heart ached with a dread I couldn't seem to shake.

The simple truth was it didn't matter how well Dylan had taken the initial revelation. Some relationships simply didn't survive that first death.

I leapt up to the chin-up bar, hanging by my arms while my essence dripped from my toes back into the basin. As shed tears dripped back into my all-too-empty nest, I really studied my reflection. Tight curls of plainest brown replaced the long, black hair that'd formerly framed my face.

I groaned.

In summer humidity, my hair's going to be a frizzy disaster.

My face hadn't changed much, though more so than the previous death and gender change. My new legs were definitely shorter and a bit thicker, but still athletically toned. I'd lost all the tan I'd worked most of the summer to get for Dylan—not that he'd been so shallow as to request I sunbathe.

I shrugged to no one in particular. Dylan complimented me on my tan when we first met. Squeezing sunbathing time into my busy schedule hadn't been easy, but the tiny gesture pleased him.

Hopefully enough to tip his heart in my favor today.

The new breasts beneath the mark of my birth element had been reborn at least two sizes smaller.

Great, bra shopping.

My expression brightened.

Guess it's not all bad. I won't have as many back aches, and my overall fighting balance will probably improve—once I learn it.

Ache crept down my arms. I swung back and forth, trying to hurry clinging tears back into the basin. I reversed my grip, swung a few more times and launched myself out of the nest. I hit the ground wrong and stumbled.

I turned, reached out to the bookshelves and noticed the water level of my nest. A tingle along my spine solidified into a knot of unease. I knelt beside the basin. Scrutinizing my remaining essence wasn't encouraging.

Barely enough for one more death.

"Ani?"

"How may I serve you, Shield Aquaylae?"

My mouth quirked into a frown. I'd asked the automata to call me Quayla. A sudden realization explained the change, Vitae had overridden me...again.

"Who's headed out to the humane society?"

"Vitae."

This day isn't improving.

"Do you suppose he'd be willing to collect any of my essence he can mop up?"

"He is away from his vehicle, so I am unable to contact him. Could you simply call him to ask?"

I stifled a scream. "Ugh! I transmog'ed my phone!"

"That complicates things," Anima said. "I am sorry. I'm sure you would've liked to retrieve any essence with as low as your nest is at the moment."

Anima was somehow able to sense the levels of our nests. She'd no doubt inform Vitae how much I had left, bringing on another lecture from the inconsolable life phoenix.

Just after my catastrophic mistake and subsequent relocation to the Atlanta Shield, my new Shieldheart had seemed cold, distant and disapproving. I'd deserved his scorn and the probation for what I'd done, but I'd tried everything to prove myself, to earn his respect.

I simply could not manage to find any traction with him.

It wasn't fair.

I'd tried working hard.

He'd criticized everything I did.

I'd tried backing off and giving him space.

He'd accused me of being inattentive to my duties.

I took a deep breath and exhaled. "Thanks, Ani."

"It is my pleasure to serve, Shield Aquaylae."

I crossed to my vanity and set a hand on a small alderwood box inlaid with tarnished silver. I touched the gem in my chest with the other hand and closed my eyes.

"In service onto death I swear this life unto the Undying Light."

Each word sent a tingling thrum through my new skin. The box vibrated beneath my touch. The glow died within the little chest as my eyes reopened. I lifted the lid to find a silver-dipped feather hung like a pendant on a matching chain.

The necklace had been lost with my death, but while everything else—like my phone—remained behind, the angelic token from the Shield's divine could always be called into the box shaped in whatever form I desired.

I pulled the chain over my head and hurried into my closet. I glanced at the door's mirror as I passed, noting my new dimensions for fitting purposes. A small stool from the closet floor helped me bring down emergency clothing shoeboxes marked by size and gender. The paisley designs on the correct box knotted my stomach.

I drew out granny panties obviously purchased during a drunken stupor. A set of rhinestone-studded bellbottoms and a tie-dyed smock added insult to injury. The smock went over a shaking head before my whole focus shifted to struggling my way into the pants. The jeans proved too narrow for my new hips.

I jumped up and down, yanking until I reclaimed enough fabric to mostly close my pants with a belt and several safety pins.

At least the smock kind of covers everything.

Pink flip flops topped the insult sundae.

I rushed out the door, only to stop short and growl. I hurried back to my MacBook and sent Dylan an instant message. "Honey, I need a bit of help."

"What's wrong?" Dylan asked.

"I lost my phone. Can you order an Uber for me?"

"Do you want me to call your phone so you can find it?"

"Lost isn't the right word so much as destroyed?"

"How did you destroy your phone?"

"I kind of died. Could you please help?"

He didn't answer for several moments. Each short, silent breath hollowed out my gut a little more. A thought bubble with three dots replaced his silence.

I held my breath.

The three dots disappeared.

They reappeared delivering more unease.

When I couldn't take his silence any more, I sent another message. "Dylan, baby?"

"Where are you going?"

"Humane Society on Howell Mill. Is everything okay?"

"It's on its way." A second message followed. "We'll discuss this later."

He signed off of the messaging system.

I pinned a quivering lip with my teeth.

I rushed to the sink, turned on the water and listened to the water's sound as I took a few calming breaths. Atlanta water was horrible stuff, and a running faucet wasn't the babble of a flowing stream, but I needed my calm sooner rather than later.

When I felt in control of myself once more, I hurried down three flights of creaky stairs, holding the railing to keep my unfamiliar body steady. A shadow appeared through glass ovals of the foyer's front doors.

A smile blossomed on my lips only to die under a deluge of apprehension. I grabbed the door anyway, letting an overflowing shopping cart and my aged landlady into the three-story walk-up.

"Thank you, Quayla."

"You're welcome, Mrs. Cox. Can I help you with those?"

"No need, dear." The tiny, grey-haired woman looked me up and down with a steadily growing frown. "Dear, what possessed you to get a perm in all this humidity?"

Despite the changes to both body and voice, Mrs. Cox proved mostly oblivious to the changes. The phenomenon stemmed first from the tendencies of mortals to only really look at a person once —relying on subconscious mental algebra to adjust for changes of clothes or hair. An additional aspect of our nature discouraged mortal eyes from completely fixing on my kind. Instead, mortal eyes tended to slide away, distracted by one thing or another.

I deflected the perceptive question with casual, good-humored laughter. "Something just came over me."

"That handsome boy talked you into it, didn't he? Please tell me he's not trying to rope you into some cult that wants to bring back disco."

"No," I looked down at my clothes and offered her a chagrined smile. "Couldn't find anything else to wear—laundry day."

"You should plan ahead, young lady. Speaking of which, when are you two getting married?"

"He's mad at me at the moment," I said.

Mrs. Cox patted my hand. "You stick to your guns, dear. He'll back down—especially after you got that horrid hairdo for him."

A car horn sounded outside the building.

"I've got to run, Mrs. Cox, we can—" I froze in the doorway, gaping at a jacked-up Cadillac Escalade with Uber and GrubHub, Lyft and Waitr decals augmenting an eye-searing Florida Gators paint job.

Just not going to be my day.

Quayla

I asked the Uber driver to drop me off a block away from the humane society. I left him and his NASCAR bobble heads nodding to some twangy woman singing about slitting car tires. The moment I came even with the street leading to the Humane Society, visions of renewed probation loomed out of a dozen flashing lights. I slid through a growing crowd of gawkers toward the police line.

Vitae stood tall and lean in a black suit, suitable for nineteenth century England rather than modern day Atlanta. The island of space surrounding him had nothing to do with his attire. His personal bubble somehow forbade the pressing wafers entrance. A glowing aura emphasized the subtle sheen of perspiration coating his skin.

Formal clothes in this heat? What is it with him?

I never unintentionally sweat, but even so my too-tight jeans made an alliance with a sweltering early morning to overheat me.

A vitality colored Vitae's radiant, olive skin that didn't inhabit either stance or expression. He aimed robust, furrowed brows toward me. An emerald gleam backlit large, brown eyes.

He gestured to the phone at his ear.

My heart leapt.

A shutter sound aborted my grab. Vitae lowered the phone. "Update it immediately, Isaac. Thank you."

Vitae turned his back on me.

I followed his scowl to a paramedic team dragging a gurney of poorly-concealed grendling bodies.

Vitae slid the phone into an inner pocket. "You left bodies."

A well-dressed woman stuffy-looking enough to be Vitae's type stopped the EMTs and raised the sheet. Her soft features hardened.

"I died, Vitae."

The detective turned away, receiving a stack of paper from a rotund woman in bone-decorated lavender scrubs. The officer split the stack, handing them out to uniformed cops.

"You're the one who chose to ride in on a stallion, six guns blazing, setting off alarms and leaving *faerie body parts* in your wake."

"I was still in Europe during the start of the wild west era, Vitae. When later I came here, you put me under house arrest, remember?"

A cute uniformed cop pushed a printout in front of Vitae, addressing him in an authoritative soprano. "Excuse me, sir, have you seen this woman?"

My eyes shifted from the officer's firm legs and athletic frame to a grainy picture of my last, partially masked face.

"I do not see a lot of women with plastic bags over their faces," Vitae said.

My hair doesn't look like a plastic bag.

The printout left me cringing.

My liquefied hair did, in fact, resemble a cheap plastic bag in the poor resolution printout. My gaze came up to find beautiful blue eyes narrowed in my direction under a frame of lustrous hair.

"Miss?" The officer scrutinized me. "Do you know this woman, a relation maybe?"

I shook my head. "Sorry, no."

The young cop seemed unconvinced but moved down the

line. I watched her, trying to ignore a lovely profile made even more enticing by the gun belt and handcuffs on her hips.

Vitae cleared his throat. "If you're done considering another improper relationship, we must address the mess you've caused."

The woman officer glanced back at us several times. The cop's interest remained professionally suspicious.

I don't know why he's so mad at me. It's not my fault new bodies are always so anxious to test all of their new parts.

I sighed. "Do you expect me to march in there and take the corpses away from them, Vitae?"

Red spots appeared under his jaw. "You are a shield, a servant of the Undying Light. I want you to focus on your duty rather than sensations and experiences like some hell-tainted *faerie*."

A rush of gooseflesh raced over me and my scalp tingled like my hair had decided to levitate away. I pressed my lips into a thin line.

"Furthermore, you will advise me of possible incursions, stop going off solo and for the love of the Light, cease embarrassing us among the other Shields. Thanks to you, we're a laughingstock."

I bristled again. "Bull, but even if it wasn't, how's that my fault?"

"How many rebirths does your nest hold?" Vitae asked.

Anima must've got ahold of him.

I checked my fingernails clean. "One?"

His lips pressed together as he massaged the bridge of his nose.

"I've been busy," I said.

For a moment, power flashed behind the stoic phoenix's eyes. He turned his back to the tableau, hiding his reaction and lectured in lofty tones. "Copulating with mortals does not excuse you from fulfilling your duties Aquaylae. They may have free will to choose carnality over propriety, but you are not one of them. You need to fulfill your purpose, not emulate their laziness or perversities."

"I'm not lazy and I don't spend all my time in bed with Dylan."

"Whatever you are doing that is interfering with your duty must stop immediately. Do we understand each other?"

I understand you, but I doubt you've bothered to understand me.

"Do we?"

"I understand, Vitae, I'm not a hatchling, but I deserve time for the things that are important to me too."

Vitae whirled, his expression darkened despite his glowing eyes. "No, Aquaylae, you serve the Light. Your life is not your own. You were created to serve. That is all there is. I think it would be best if you—"

A cleared throat turned us around. A very tall, blond man looked down his hawkish nose at us, dressed much the same as Vitae save his centuries-newer, golden-white suit.

I couldn't help an involuntary gulp.

Vitae bowed slightly.

Our Praefectus gestured to where the young officer I'd ogled pointed the well-dressed detective our direction. "This discussion must cease."

"You have our deepest apologies, Vilicangelus. I'll address—"

"I will address it, Vitae, at your evening briefing. For now, you and I shall fade while Aquaylae deals with the approaching shield."

"She's one of us?" I asked.

"She is a mortal shield, but a servant of justice nonetheless." He placed a hand on Vitae, dragging him a step backward as they both faded into transparency.

Their unexpected vanishing act took my breath away.

How?

"Excuse me, miss," the detective said. "I'm Detective Sabrina Foxner. I need a moment of your time."

Chapter Four

Too Much History

Vitae

Vilicangelus and I watched Aquaylae's interrogation, a layer of Light separating us from the real world much as the Veil kept Creation and Faery apart.

Aquaylae's stance remained defiant, and her answers practically begged the detective to mark her as a suspect.

It's almost as if she wants the attention.

I gestured toward Aquaylae's behavior. "She needs to be transferred somewhere lower profile, especially in light of this incident."

"I see no reason to relocate her. The Isaac will see to the surveillance."

"This is Headingham all over again. It's almost as if she's addicted to mortal attention."

Vilicangelus raised an eyebrow. "Perhaps she does crave attention. Even so, I think perhaps your memory is too long, my old friend. Dare I also suggest that your neck has not relaxed with age?"

While the Shield's automata couldn't offer offense, my old friend's evolution to divine hadn't robbed his memory. He knew

"

where to stick the knife. He remembered too well my first days in his Shield, unsure and awkward in the presence of so many elders.

"Vitae, she's been in this jurisdiction for over a century without a major incident. She's doing her best. Forgive a little."

"Her best." I couldn't help the snort. "All I see is an addictive penchant for exploring mortal nethers."

"Neither Terrance nor Ignis have complained about her willingness to learn," Vilicangelus said.

"She doesn't learn. The Isaac said she transmogrified in view of live interweb cameras."

"He'll purge the webcam feeds."

"That isn't the point. He shouldn't have had to purge the feeds. She should've arrived with others, taken out the cameras in advance, but she just doesn't think things through."

I straightened my suit, taking the moment to quench heat bubbling up in my soul. "Her insistence on handling this alone, her thoughtless transmogrifying in front of a broadcasting camera, it's the same story over and again." I turned my disapproving expression on Aquaylae and the human shield. "Do you enjoy chasing down mortal witnesses? Can you really afford her sloth instigating more murders? Another mass witch hunting?"

Vilicangelus's expression soured. "Together or alone, the Isaac would have had to purge the feeds of grendlings and animals traversing an Arch. Using her true form in that situation, under such heavy assault, doesn't seem thoughtless to me."

"It only takes a single witness to bring about another inquisition or mass burnings. You know how corruptible mortals have become. Fear and superstition rampaging through the streets hunting witches is nothing compared to what could befall humanity if her carelessness transmogrifying revealed the faeries to mankind."

"There are plenty of possible ramifications, but a mass burning—especially on the scale you suggest—seems unlikely. Yes, Aquaylae made a mistake coming alone. No, it wasn't her first, but even so I've looked into her past, spoken to her former divine."

"None of that matters, Aether! Mortals died—"

Light flared around the divine phoenix. "Mortals died because the Sidhe intervened. They took advantage of her mistake and turned her village's superstition into a murdering frenzy before their divine could step in. As for your other concerns, the Isaac is Watching."

I lowered my head. I hadn't meant to call Vilicangelus by his former name. The mistake had been disrespectful, and it shamed me. "Forgive me, Divine One, but I still want her out of my Shield. She's embarrassing—"

"Pride, Vitae?" Vilicangelus's jaw tightened in an eerie echo of his former face. "Is that what this is about?"

It took an effort to meet my former brother's hard eyes. "This is about my duty to ensure this Shield follows the strictures laid down to ensure the proper protection of His Creation against the hell-blighted Sidhe."

"And toward that noble goal, I replaced your fallen Aqua."

"Yes, we needed an Aqua, but not this one, Divine One. You shouldn't have sent her here. This one should've been—"

Vilicangelus's temper simmered just under the flaring waves of Light that washed over me like a tide. "Vitae, Phoenix of Life, why would you suggest I separate Aquaylae's soul from her essence and send her on? Is not life about growth, new chances?"

The tide of our argument had turned against me, but I had to make Vilicangelus understand. Aquaylae needed to go. She acted more like Sidhe than a shield. She just wasn't cut out to be a shield. "Yes, of course, but—"

"You needed a new Aqua or have you forgotten Mare's True Death so soon?"

Screams and images lunged out of darkest memory, swarming my mind's eye. Mare's specter fell over my core, darkening the life spring tied to my soul and sending shivers through me.

I would never forget beloved Mare, never—no matter how often Aquaylae's similarities made a mockery of Mare's memory.

For a moment, whispered memory of long gone fingertips stroked the jewel embedded in my chest. Gooseflesh rippled outward, not a thousand little fearful bites but the tingle of anticipation from a long absent touch.

"Aquaylae made a mistake, Vitae. She'd never died before, and to be burned to death—she acted out of fear. Do you even remember the terror of your first death? The uncertainty?"

I licked my lips and closed off my face from all emotion. "I felt no such fear, Vilicangelus. I had faith."

Vilicangelus snorted. "Faith? Or was it that you'd seen me die and be reborn several times before you fell?"

I folded my arms. "Faith—though you did die an awful lot."

Vilicangelus laid a hand on my shoulder. "Aquaylae's response to that event has made her special, little brother. It gave her a passion for all Creation that so many of her elders have outgrown."

I gestured at the gawking crowds. "That passion got us into today's situation, Divine One."

The Praefectus's smile grew indulgent. "Vitae, Quayla's heart remains like a hatchling just quickened—if not even more so. Such passion is as rare as any True Birth."

I opened my mouth to correct his use of her nickname, but stopped. I set my shoulders. "I am sorry, but you are wrong, Vilicangelus. She needs to learn duty. She needs to learn to obey—"

"You?" Vilicangelus asked.

"Him, His Divine, the tenants of Aquaylae's creation and caution in the public eye."

"She's still young and headstrong. She needs to prove herself to you—the only authority figure in her Shield who treats her as unworthy of personal attention or training."

"My library is stocked with all the knowledge she needs. If she invested herself in the books as much as she invests herself in spreading her...passions—" I shook my head. "Some hawks never take to the hood no matter how skilled their handler."

"She remains in this Shield, Vitae, but while we're discussing your library, the Beijing Shield has agreed to an exchange if you are willing to pen the copies."

"What did they wish in return?"

"A copy of your Shieldheart's Guide to Nests."

"I'll begin copying Nests once I've dealt with this, but it may take a few weeks to copy and return their volumes."

"I'm sure that will be acceptable for books in your fine hand, but have you ever considered using print-on-demand technologies to speed the process?"

I snorted before I'd mastered myself, even so a hint of derision leaked into my voice. "Not even lifting voice to the possible ways doing such might leak information to the mortals, glued wood pulp would never prove itself against the passage of time."

"Plus, you love hand illuminating and binding the books."

A self-conscious smile escaped my mask of propriety for only a moment. "The scent of leather and vellum are satisfying."

Vilicangelus chuckled.

"I've already contacted the Isaac. He will update Aquaylae's driving license and other public records as well as purge her social media of all former pictures.

"Efficient as always, Vitae."

"Thank you, but I failed to act quickly enough in regard to the vehicle she left parked in front of the building."

"I dispatched Summus—"

"Summus?" I asked.

"Summuseraphi, your new Praefectus."

Creation seemed to drop away like a mortal rollercoaster. I did not wish a new Praefectus. Even if he no longer had time for the occasional game of chess, I was loath to relinquish a voice of wisdom—even if sometimes incorrect—from my earliest days. I opened my mouth, but Vilicangelus spoke first. "We will handle introductions this evening. Suffice to say he relocated Aquaylae's vehicle prior to the arrival of the local authorities."

A throb behind my eyes coaxed my brow to furrow and lips to turn downward. "If you aren't concerned by her actions, why were you watching her?"

"We're always watching." Vilicangelus smiled as Light stole him away.

Without the Praefectus's veil, I faded back into the reality Aquaylae had turned into a hornet's nest. Nearby, the detective's dubious expression resembled a hunting dog. Aquaylae wouldn't be able to break away soon enough to clean up the bodies in the morgue. She'd be too late to prevent medical examination, and in any case her entrance into a monitored government facility while the mortal shield scented Aquaylae for guilt risked exposure.

Maybe I should let her go anyway. Such exposure might help me convince the new Praefectus, it might force his hand and we could replace her with a dutiful Aqua.

I rubbed the bridge of my nose.

I don't get out often enough as is, and I won't conveniently forget my duty just because it becomes onerous. Thus, I shall don a forgiving countenance and once more, clean up after the less dutiful of my Shield. We are not individual. We are a Shield of the Light, created to serve.

I took a final look at Aquaylae before retreating to await her.

We five are one, strengthening each other's weaknesses for no one of us is strong enough to Shield this shire alone. Thus is it so, and thus shall it ever be.

Chapter Five

Acting Normal

Quayla

I endured Detective Foxner's questions, trying not to show the growing itch of impatience. I needed to get to the city morgue. Cleaning up the corpses inside the humane society hadn't been an option while I was returning, but I wasn't going to leave the task of clean up at the morgue to anyone else in the Shield.

It's my mess, I'll clean it up.

Foxner treated me exactly the same as I might've treated a faerie suspect. I wasn't fond of being on the receiving end. It'd been a hard morning—not that I could fault the detective for rattling her suspect. I wasn't about to risk lives to get my coffee fix, but some tea or hot chocolate sounded like a great way to calm my nerves.

My drifting attention pressed Foxner's rosebud mouth into a hard line. Her eyes flashed and color tinged her clenched jaw. A trained expression almost covered her feelings, but what slipped through proclaimed that the mortal shield distrusted every word that escaped my lips.

I wasn't lying to her—not exactly. I wasn't her perpetrator.

Her so-called thief had died, leaving a puddle rather than a corpse. It wasn't my fault she was convinced I was lying through my new teeth.

"All right, Miss Buckler, I'm going to need your home address," Foxner said.

An itch assaulted my nose and my eyes tightened. My nature allows me not to cry just like I don't have to sweat, but inwardly I did as I rattled off my address. The Isaac had probably purged my memories with Dylan from the internet the moment I died, but it fell to me to clean our apartments. I'd have to destroy all the evidence linking me to my former life, every special moment Dylan and I had shared over our relationship.

Maybe I should pick up chocolate croissants from the DeKalb Farmers Market on the way to the shop.

"I'm sorry, I expected you to give me your address by way of your ID."

"You didn't ask for my ID."

"May I have your ID?" Foxner asked.

"I don't have any on me."

Foxner scrutinized me once more, looking me up and down.

I spun slowly, lifting the smock only while my back was turned to the detective. "No wallet, see."

"What about a purse?"

"Don't carry anything when I jog."

"You're jogging in that?"

"Laundry day," I said.

Foxner made no attempt to hide her disbelief. "I see. Do you remember your driver's license number?"

"Sorry. Can I go?" I asked. "I'm going to be late for work."

"Fine, just give me a phone number."

"Don't have one anymore," I said.

Foxner scrutinized me once more. "Everyone has a phone."

"Then I must be lying." I offered her my sweetest smile. "Where do you think I'm hiding one?"

"Bra?"

"Not wearing one, besides, it would get all sweaty." I grabbed the hem of my smock. "I can prove I'm both braless and phoneless if you promise not to cite me for public indecency."

Foxner leaned closer. "I don't appreciate your attitude, Miss Buckler. Someone broke in, ransacked the place, got their jollies assaulting animals and stole a bunch more. My gut tells me Officer Quarles is right, you're involved somehow."

I closed the distance, temper rising like a raging river. "What's that supposed to mean?"

Foxner gestured at my clothes. "You're all dressed up like some liberal hippy flower child, the exact opposite type to our perpetrator. Maybe you are...innocent, just out here gawking in the heat because it's somehow arousing."

"But you don't think so?"

Foxner held the printout up and lowered her tone. "I know you look a lot like our perp. I know someone attacked innocent animals with stink bombs and paint." She stabbed the photo with a finger. "I *know* this woman is the kind of depraved, low-life degenerate who thinks they're smarter than the cops, someone who thinks they can hang around a crime scene to watch the aftermath without getting caught."

She's goading me? Really?

The detective seemed bright, dedicated and very good at her job, but she was way out of her depth. I liked her moxie even if she was starting to piss me off.

Memories of dappled pools helped focus me enough that I could offer the detective enough cheerful delight to annoy her. "Of course animals are more important than people like you, detective, but really, what liberal hippy would hurt the poor, little furbabies imprisoned here?"

Foxner's eyes hardened.

I gave the detective a cheery little wave before flouncing away out of pure vindictiveness. My cheer faded when I realized the police had impounded my baby. I had no way to work but the taint-stained MARTA trains and buses. I headed for the bus stop only to see Vitae leaning against his Mercedes.

No, thanks. I'll take stinky people and public transit over another lecture.

Vitae's expression darkened in answer to my own. He pointed. I followed the gesture and a little bubble of joy buoyed me up. My Johammer and helmet had been moved under a shaded parking spot a half block away. I flashed Vitae a smile and mouthed my thanks.

Vitae cleared his throat, dangling my spare keys.

I crossed the distance and reached for them. "Thank y—"

"I will handle the morgue, Aquaylae. I can't take a chance of you screwing up again."

I opened my mouth to insist upon cleaning up after myself, but Vitae talked over me.

"We will discuss this later."

My bubble deflated. I wanted Vitae to accept me, to treat me like the other shields. Rather than show him how much his disapproval hurt, I covered by rolling my eyes. "Yes, *Dad*."

Vitae's jaw clinched, but he let go of my keys.

I hurried away toward my Johammer in desperate need of some dark chocolate.

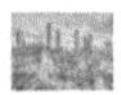

Quayla

The drive through Atlanta dragged on, particularly under the disapproving glower of the bronze angel. I tried to flow between the traffic, but too often jockeying drivers blocked the easiest paths.

When I'd been younger, the challenge of flowing through traffic without getting stopped had been something of a game. Drivers of that era hadn't cut each other off for another car length. They hadn't been anywhere near as impatient or egocentric. Road rage hadn't even been some writer's nightmare rather than a fact of life that had mortal governments writing laws to limit the bloodshed.

The DeKalb Farmer's market hadn't been any more polite than Atlanta byways. It'd taken me twice as long to stock up on fruit and chocolate croissants because the woman in front of me refused to surrender her position in line while she sent children running for last minute items.

I pulled into a parking lot separating Ponds de Leon Flowers and Camp Woof—a doggy daycare run by a fabulous old man who'd have made a perfect match for quirky Mrs. Cox if he hadn't been gay.

Pete's one of the good ones, a shining example why we should protect humanity from the Sidhe.

The bell over the door jingled as I entered the flower shop and inhaled the mixed perfumes. The sweet symphony wasn't quite as wonderful as the garden back at headquarters, but it was definitely my second favorite olfactory happy place.

"You're late." The petite Korean college student's glower worsened. "Ugh, you ruined your hair. What *are* you wearing?" She flipped up a hand and looked away. "Never mind, I don't care."

"Morning, Judith." I grimaced at my reflection in the mirror behind the counter. "I don't like it either, but I haven't had time to fix it."

"You should be shot for visual affront of the public." Judith picked up a small clutch and pushed past me toward the door.

"Where are you going?" I lifted my flower-covered reusable shopping bag. "I bought the mango raspberry croissants you like."

"I need *decent* coffee. I couldn't go get some because you didn't bother to show up at a reasonable hour." Judith turned a flat stare at me. "How do you get away with always being late, anyway? Owner should've fired you by now—if he ever actually came into the shop. Never mind, I don't care."

"There's tea in the back." I smiled. "Besides, you could've picked up coffee on your way to work."

"I did." Judith marched out of the shop. The door's bell jangled her displeasure.

Judith's anger wasn't the worst thing that had happened that day, but it reminded me of how Dylan had replied or not replied when I'd asked him for help ordering an Uber.

The weight on my shoulders doubled.

If things went badly that night, I might have to call Vilicangelus to erase Dylan's memory. Clearing out all the pictures made me want to cry, but the prospect of erasing the man I loved so that no memories of us even existed shriveled my soul.

I open the bag, ripping aside cellophane to let me at one of the chocolate croissants. I chewed. The pastries the farmer's market sold were wondrous, but all I tasted was pencil shavings.

I needed to talk to someone who wouldn't lecture me or tear out my heart and stomp on it. I rushed out the front door not even bothering to lock it. Neither of us made food, but Camp Woof and I often exchanged treats so I'd bought extra pastries with every intention of delivering them next door.

I just hadn't planned on delivering them on the brink of tears.

A scruffy-looking man in clothes worn to the edge of indecency came up the block, turning to approach me directly. "Excuse me, miss? Could you help a veteran hard on his luck?"

I glanced skyward, thanking Heaven for reminding me how much worse things could be and how I could still improve lives. I dug out a package of croissants and offered it.

He took it with an uncertain expression. "Thank you, but," he lifted the hem of a ratty shirt. "I was hoping you could help me with some money, so I can go to a salvation army for another shirt."

"Oh, yes." I reached into the too tight pocket for the last of the cash I'd kept stashed in my Johammer. I handed it all to him.

His eyes lit and warmth blossomed inside me.

"Thanks." He waved and continued down the street.

I entered Camp Woof to the sound of barking dogs. The pet daycare ran by the amazingly warm old man definitely wasn't an olfactory treasure, but playing with the animals always lifted my spirits.

A thin woman with short brown hair smiled up at me. "Quayla!"

"Morning, Mara." I lifted my package. "Croissants for a hug?"

She eyed me for only a heartbeat before rushing around the counter to wrap me in her arms. Her warm reassuring embrace offered the slice of solace I needed.

"Your hair isn't that bad." She released me. "I'm sure your Dylan will love it."

I dug a package of her favorite strawberry and cheese from the bag to hide the gut shot she'd just delivered.

Mara tore open the packaging, grabbed a pastry and took a bite. She rolled her eyes in delight, licking a dab of strawberry puree from the corner of her mouth. "Oh, you are a rock star."

I forced a small smile and set out the other packages I'd bought for their crew. "I have to get back."

"Sure," Mara mumbled through full cheeks. "I'll tell Pete you came by."

I retreated out the door only to stop short.

Across the street, the homeless beggar got into a Lexus, put on designer sunglasses and drove away.

"Quayla? Everything okay?" Mara asked.

I inhaled, fighting for calm to forestall the surge of anger and disgust that gripped me like a rope in a giant's tug-of-war. I hurried back to the shop without answering her. Despite the surrounding beauty and quiet, the day's events met me in the shop, circling my subconscious like vultures.

I'd died that morning.

True, I'd stopped an incursion, but I hadn't arrived fast enough to save all the animals. Worse, I'd failed to stop the faeries without exposing their existence to the mortals.

Vitae'd insisted upon handling my cleanup, unwilling to trust that I could do the job without endangering Creation.

I can't even say his anger's totally unwarranted.

Worst of all, my screw-ups threatened to take Dylan from me —the only thing outside the florist shop that was truly my own.

It'd been over a century since my first, cataclysmic screw-up. I'd tried so hard to make up for that, tried so hard to do everything right.

None of that effort mattered to Vitae.

He wouldn't even listen long enough for me to prove I'd done everything right.

My Sidhe informant, Grynnberry, had warned me of more impending attacks on animal shelters. So, I'd hit up a Burlington Coat Factory for a slew of small desktop fountains that trickled water over what the box description had called river stones. Sure, short notice forced me to dip into my nest for essence, but I'd worked tirelessly to distribute the seeded fountains to Atlanta's various shelters as gifts.

I hadn't had time to replenish my essence. I couldn't reach out to the faerie that made the really good fountains I normally used to seed our sentry net until the Goblin Market reopened.

Not to mention Vitae would give birth to little vultures if he knew Sidhe helped build my seeds or that I'd let Grynnberry meet me at my apartment when he had intel to trade.

Until that morning, all the animal shelter seeds had remained quiet except the one a gangly young man had knocked off its perch. The no-kill shelter had been surprised to see me return and twice as surprised I'd known something had gone wrong with her fountain.

At least I didn't have to call on Vilicangelus to rewrite the wafer's memory.

After the urgency of Grynnberry's warning, the long span of quiet left my nerves on edge.

If I had known I'd have so much time, I'd have visited the faerie craftsman as usual. Ralein's sturdier, custom fountains contained my essence inside the base—protected against spills and wafer foolishness—instead of exposed.

When the attack came, they were grendlings. Why grendlings? What do Wyldfae want with all those animals?

I cringed.

Other than snacking.

The Sidhe breach opened Atlanta up to Faery, tainting the little seed of my essence hidden in Howell Mill's stress fountain with me mid traffic jam. Nowhere near my nest, my only option for informing Anima was via the statue's connection to the angel network. I hated using the network because the sanctimonious bastards monitoring delighted in tormenting us.

I glanced out the shop windows at my Johammer.

Like when they blew up my motorcycle's batteries to punish me for speeding.

Unfortunately, Vitae had forbidden Caelum from connecting Anima's systems to cellular networks or the internet. So, I'd had to talk Anima out of informing Vitae under constant threat of the bored old buzzards telling him just to spite me.

I needed to focus on something other than my woes, so I turned my attention to the shop. I wove my way through the storefront, checking the water levels in all the live pots. Judith might complain a lot, but I found no low vases. None of the plants left out on display showed any signs of dying.

Judith having taken care of the front, I headed into the back, busying myself checking and filling orders. Caelum had put in a big order for another one of his corporate events. Unlike a lot of customers, he left the arrangement to me. It wasn't a vote of confidence as much as his disinterest in anything as boring as flower arranging. Since I'd already planned out how to arrange his table displays, all I had to do was go through the motions.

Despite my intentions to bury the morning's disaster by keeping busy, my thoughts drifted back to it. I'd been expecting a small sortie of Unseelie forces and had intended to take at least one alive to question. Instead, I'd faced several grendling tribes working together.

Probably better that they were Wyldfae. Vitae would've thrown a fit if I'd killed some vassal connected to one of the powerful Courts.

I'd never encountered so many grendling in one place. Tribes seldom worked together, and they almost never breached the real world in concentrated areas of Seelie-Unseelie conflict.

That Arch practically thumbed their noses at Vusolaryn and Mariena—the local royals of the Seelie and Unseelie Courts. Why make themselves a target of the two more powerful Courts? There were less contentious places to hunt.

Whatever drove the Wyldfae to assault the humane society had cost me a life and all that came with a rebirth. The more technology progressed, the harder it became for my kind to re-enter the world. We had to be circumspect about what we said on phone conversations. We had to guard against agencies like the IRS or INS investigating renters with no apparent income.

I wasn't as old as Terrance or Ignis, but I knew enough to hide caches around our territory in case of calamity or death. Unlike my previous Shield, Atlanta's protected a huge metropolitan era. I'd been relocated to Atlanta just after some huge fight between the older shields. Ignis, Terrance and Mare had apparently overruled or ignored Vitae's objections to taking personal residences and joining the workforce.

The stodgy life phoenix seemed ill at ease close to the mortals, preferring his books and his lofty tower to the life teeming on Atlanta's streets.

He even dresses almost a century out of vogue.

Terrance had helped me found Ponds de Leon Flowers—his joking suggestion for a name—just after I'd arrived in Atlanta. I'd changed the shop's ownership over to a shell company a few decades prior in response to several deaths. Current official records designated Quayla Buckler as just a random employee, not even the official shop manager.

I'd never met or even spoken with the Isaac. To the best of

my knowledge, none of the others had either except Vitae. The idea of a phoenix with hacking skills of the Isaac's level didn't sit right, but Vitae was unlikely to trust anyone outside our kind.

Regardless of his identity, the Isaac had never failed to rebuild one of us after a death. He'd do his computer magic. By the end of day, new Quayla received a new life all her own, and old Quayla vanished as if she never existed.

Except to Dylan.

I bit my lip to keep it from quivering. I didn't want to lose him. Despite centuries of longing, I'd resigned myself to a loveless existence of duty and sacrifice like Vitae wanted. Neither Terrance nor Ignis had dated in centuries, though they did defend me when Vitae went after me for what he saw as unacceptable fraternization.

Meeting Dylan had been an accident, an act of God—or so I insisted on believing.

He fits with me in a way I can't explain. He makes me better.

Anytime duty grew heavy or selfish wafers made my resolve waiver, I need only picture his face to remember why it was so important that they protect humanity.

If dying isn't enough to send him packing, enduring Detective Foxner's looming inquisition is likely to seal the deal. Can't really blame either of them. If I were Foxner, I'd be digging into my world right now—not to mention turning upside down every life connected to mine.

A lot of things bothered me about the morning's assault, certainly not least of all the loss of life—the animals more than mine. Unfortunately, no matter how much I tried to puzzle out whys and wherefores surrounding the incursion, the coming confrontation with Dylan kept intruding.

Not even dread over Vitae's coming inquisition could push aside the possible end of my relationship.

Sweet and smart, compassionate and caring about the environment—few lovers had fit me so exactingly. It was as if we were the same person, separated only—momentarily at least—by gender.

Tears I knew I should save dripped from my nose into the table arrangements.

A tinkling of bells and the wafting aroma of over-sweetened coffee announced Judith's return. She joined me in the back, frowning. "Quayla?"

I opened my mouth to ease Judith's concerns, but the young woman filled the silence first.

"Did you stop wearing lifts or something? You seem shorter. That or you got extensions before that stupid perm."

I frowned.

I might have to fire her if she looks too close.

"Never mind." Judith snatched up a pair of shears and set to scissoring plants with dour viciousness. "I don't care."

Maybe it'll be all right. Even the most perceptive wafers seldom bother giving someone they know a thorough second look.

I imagined Judith's reaction if I walked into the store with a new Magnum PI body.

I can almost hear her.

<Did you forget to bleach your mustache? What's with the flowery shirt, aren't there enough flowers here? You know what? Never mind, I don't care.>

I smiled through the tears.

Chapter Six

Aftermath

Vitae

I marched off the elevator into the city morgue's lowest basement. Mortals had been created with near limitless possibilities. Most of the populace exercised this potential watching cat videos on the interweb.

Over recent years, laziness and convenience had become humanity's goal. It didn't matter if living five minutes closer to something cost a whole forest and the wildlife dependent on it. The forest came down and newer, closer homes went up. Greater convenience trumped all other concerns.

Proof positive we can never let them know about the faerie.

The current trend for shirking personal responsibility while micromanaging other's lives had expanded government oversight considerably. Such meticulous administration thrived on mortal functionaries comfortable wearing blinders while they jockeyed for little caches of power rather than thinkers interested in embracing the truth. These regulators of everyone else's business had no room in their lives for introspection or evidence that might shatter their petty little world views.

Creation might've been better gone to the dogs.

Examples dangerous to humanity's carefully crafted ignorance ended up in Basement E.

"By the gods...," an eager young voice escaped the far examination room. "This is incredible, just incredible!"

I pushed open a heavy door and stepped into one of the medical examiner's room. Chemicals and death hit my nose in a barrage as taint rubbed against my flesh like an insistent cat.

A red-haired youth with a lip-mold mustache and a medical coat stared down at an exam table. His teeth pinned a lopsided half grin. A scalpel in his hand deftly scraped a nodule of flesh away from a trollbone blade. Delighted eyes brightened. He bounced on the balls of his feet, a titter escaping his lips like a toddler amazed by a trick for the hundredth time. He cut away another nodule with another bounce, glancing from the regrowing spot and the little growing balls of troll flesh.

I cleared my throat.

The medical examiner glanced up, his expression changing to that of a guilty child. "Who're you?"

I folded my hands behind my back. "I intended to inquire the same thing."

The young mortal put down the trollbone and extended a gloved hand. "Bradley."

The room's potent taint disqualified the exuberant youth of being Fae Kissed. I'd rather not have touched him, but a gentleman's greeting—even if unearned—could verify the mortal's condition. Still I resisted, paying attention instead to the faerie weapon.

The rate at which the small exposed spot regrew the rest of its missing body appeared too slow to offer an immediate concern. Unlike the bone, the numerous flesh nodules weren't limited by magical acid. They grew outward in all directions without the constraints retarding growth on the trollbone weapon. If I didn't intervene, the childish mortal's little experiments might soon grow out of hand into a hungry horde of trolls.

I raised my eyebrows.

Bradley glanced down, blushed and passed a small blow torch over the chunks. He set the torch down, strategically charring the growing section of bone. He rubbed a hand against his pants and extended his hand once more. "Doctor Bradley Sky, junior assistant coroner. What did you pointedly avoid saying your name was?"

Interestingly astute.

The filthiness of modern mortals didn't cause my reluctance to shake his hand. Truth be, I'd lived through much dirtier eras—though current humanity's trust in new and trendy chemical technologies left them more vulnerable to germs they assumed the chemicals eradicated. I extended my hand, listening for my fingers to mark the boy as a source of the thick taint. "Vitae Illuceo, Mayoral Public Relations Adjunct."

He surprised me with the firm grip of an honest man right before he insulted me.

"Huh, I guessed right. Had you pegged as useless." Bradley frowned. "Did your parents hate you or teach dead languages or something? Wait, were they sorcerers? Is that why they named you Life Illuminated in Latin?"

I cleared my throat and forged into the business at hand. "I've come regarding an incident at the Howell Mill Humane Society."

Bradley rolled his eyes. "Of course you have."

His response took me aback. I blinked at him, head canting to one side. "What do you mean by that, sir?"

"I heard the stories. Government types like you strong arming Gus, insisting he keep quiet about the weird stuff we get down here while calling him delusional in his official record." Bradley picked up the trollbone knife. "As if anyone with any sense could ignore the truth stabbing them in the eyes."

"I know not what you mean, young man. You are the doctor of course, but the Mayor's office does not want word of a bio-engineered mold causing a public—"

"Troll."

"I beg your pardon?"

"Troll." Bradley waved the knife between them. "This is bone. This bone is regrowing flesh, not mold, which stops growing when burned. The bone also seems to be treated by some sort of acid. It's troll."

Astuteness aside, the boy reminded me forcibly of Aquaylae, spouting whatever she believed like there could be no other truth. His being correct only worsened things. A throb behind my eyes beckoned my fingers. I rubbed to bridge of my nose. "How exactly did you come to this fantastical explanation?"

"Dungeons and Dragons," Bradley said matter-of-factly. "I had a +9 troll-slaying knife. I sure wish I had one now, if they were real."

I took a deep breath and calmly removed a silver cigarette case from my inner pocket. Cracking open the case allowed brilliant light to spill out.

Bradley leaned in, eyes narrowed at the tiny glowing feather.

I whispered to the light. "Vilicangelus. Vilicangelus."

"Vilicangelus?" Bradley asked. "Overseeing angel?"

"Vilicangelus," I finished, snapping the case shut.

A winged-being appeared in a blinding flare of light.

"Holy shit, a real archangel!" Bradley said.

The light faded, revealing a divine phoenix. It shifted shape, rearranging into a younger, almost naked man with sweeping white wings. The wings folded, fading out as clothing faded in once more.

Light save me, I didn't think Aether would be replaced until tonight.

I fear my shock was greater than that of the mortal, or at least he recovered more quickly. I'd called for my old friend and gotten in exchange a counterfeit not much older than Caelum.

Why in Heaven's name would they elevate a phoenix not out of his first eon?

Heat flashed through me.

If anyone should replace Aether, it should've been me.

"I've never met a real archangel before," Bradley snatched the cigarette case from my fingers, opened it and reached for the feather.

I took it from him before he could sully Vilicangelus's feather and bowed to the newcomer—though I did not pay him the same level of deference I might Vilicangelus.

He hasn't earned it.

"Thank Heaven and her Creator for sending you, Summuseraphi of the Divine. May I ask where Vilicangelus might be?"

"Vitae, right?" A thick accent placed Summuseraphi's last shield somewhere near Australia. Summuseraphi's gaze shifted away. "Not great with names."

Of course he isn't, leaving me to make lemonade from unripe lemons. Perhaps his youth will make him more easily persuaded to remove Aquaylae.

"You are correct, Divine One."

Bradley pulled a phone and started circling Summuseraphi. He beamed, whispering excitedly to himself. Summuseraphi's brows rose. He turned with Bradley, examining the medical examiner with equal interest.

"Um, yeah, Vilicangelus is dealing with a problem in England. Winter Court is re-enacting the Battle of Five Armies with the tourists starring as the refugees being slaughtered fleeing Dale."

The throb returned. I massaged the bridge of my nose. "As you see, we have a difficulty here too."

"All right, let's try this."

Summuseraphi reached up and placed his hand on my head.

Alarm shot through me.

Try?

Summuseraphi closed his eyes. "See for me, Vitae, show me true."

A surge of energy shocked me. I jerked involuntarily, but Summuseraphi kept his hand in place. A tingle wrapped me like raw cotton, lifting me like a gentle thermal. I seemed to float on the gentle air as morgue events replayed across my thoughts.

Unease filled me.

Is he seeing my thoughts as well?

Summuseraphi withdrew his hand and cocked his head at Bradley who hadn't stopped filming. "You're a queer little wafer, aren't you?"

"Wafer?" Bradley asked.

"Never you mind, Mister Sky." I shook his head, trying to clear the lingering clouds. "If you have no objections, Summuseraphi, I will see to the faerie remains."

"Fairy?" Bradley asked.

Summuseraphi beamed. "Be my guest. This is my first reality edit. I'd rather not have an audience."

I focused on my duty, not letting my dismay reach my face. It wasn't bad enough the young shields under my wings undermined our efforts to control the Sidhe, we'd somehow acquired the greenest divine phoenix in creation.

I inhaled, seeking the sources of the tainted, sour faerie tang beneath death scent and chemicals. I made my way from source to source, collecting all the evidence which need be destroyed. Once I'd collected all the grendling parts from drawers, I sought more with my eyes closed.

A moment's focus allowed me to revert my body from human flesh to swirling crimson essence. Nearby taint tickled the surface of my essence, but I ignored the sensation to maintain focus. Crimson liquid blazed to sudden light, my body becoming a living sea of scarlet and gold energy.

Fully converted to the energetic plasma of life, my senses came alive under attack from the intangible yet antagonistic auras of faerie creatures. Maintaining plasmic form required my supreme focus, particularly when treading upon solid surfaces without causing them damage. Still, the form allowed me to suss out faerie parts in air-tight bins. I added trollbone weapons and other recovered artifacts to the extensive pile of faerie remains. It seemed the detective that had given Aquaylae such trouble had sent everything from the scene to Basement E for examination.

Saving me a trip to her precinct.

In the background, Summuseraphi circled Bradley with his wings extended, mantling the young medical examiner like a hawk might his meal.

Bathed in Light, the mortal walked backward through several previous hours' worth of actions. Bradley paused mid step, stood frozen a moment, then resumed forward motion. Around the mortal, Summuseraphi's projected reality played out like a silent, yet full color film—rewriting Bradley's life.

Bradley froze.

Summuseraphi turned to me. "I think that should do it. Do you have everything?"

I examined the dazed junior assistant coroner. "Yes."

Summuseraphi approached the pile. He rolled his shoulders, swinging arms back and forth. "Here goes."

I fought not to display my inward cringe.

Summuseraphi's hands came together with a thunderous clap. Divine fire shot out between them, swirling around the piled objects and burning them to a fine golden ash. Summuseraphi twirled one hand while pulling a small clay pot into creation with the other. The golden dust spiraled up and into the pot.

He handed it to me, beaming with pride. "For your garden, friend of Vilicangelus."

If Summuseraphi had been able to read my thoughts, he gave no outward sign of taking offense to their contents. I offered him a respectful inclination of my head and took the pot. "My thanks, Divine One. Do you need a ride to our meeting?"

"Sure. Could I drive?"

A hard throb stabbed the back of my eyes.

"I'd really appreciate it," Summuseraphi said. "I don't get to actually live like a wafer much anymore."

I fought to keep my discomfort concealed, leading the way toward the elevators to keep him from seeing my face. I managed to unclench my teeth enough that my words escaped unmarred. "Of course, Divine One, whatever you desire."

"Great...oh, damn."

I turned to find my new Praefectus in full cringe, shying downward with a placating hand raised toward heaven.

"Sorry! Sorry." Summuseraphi relaxed, turning toward me after a smiteless moment. "Sorry, Vitae. I forgot to bring him out of the fugue. You go ahead. I'll catch up."

I smiled, inclined my head and exited the morgue.

I hate letting anyone drive my car.

Chapter Seven

Queueing the Music

Quayla

Caelum's order kept me cutting, wrapping and preparing arrangements until long after Judith closed the shop on her way out the door. I intended to leave early enough for a shopping trip to replace my clothes, but Judith managed to infuriate an already upset customer. Dealing with the inconsolable woman cost me hours.

I considered leaving the order unfinished and returning that evening. If things went the way I expected with Dylan, I'd be in no state to do anything beyond cry into my nest. So, I kept at it until the very last bouquet.

Heading out of DeKalb toward downtown, my speedometer edged over the speed limit. I glanced at the angel for some sign of disapproval. A screech of brakes served as my only warning. I squeezed my brakes and whipped up the quickly-narrowing strip between the offender and another car. The gap closed before I could flow through it. I braked as hard as I could without throwing myself forward over the bars.

I pushed myself back into a sitting position. My heart careened around inside my chest like a superball.

The angel on my console wore a self-satisfied smirk.

"Are you kidding me? You caused an accident to punish me for speeding?"

The angel's expression didn't change.

"Vindictive pricks! It's no wonder He doesn't let you run around creation any more."

"Are you in distress, Quayla?" Anima asked.

I growled.

"I do not recognize this language."

"Fine. I'm fine, Ani, but I'm probably going to be late."

"I will inform Vitae."

"Stop," I lurched toward the angel. "Don't tell Vitae. If by some miracle I make it on time, I don't want another unearned lecture about tardiness."

"Vitae was most displeased that I did not inform him of your actions this morning. He ordered I inform him even when you order me otherwise."

"All right, but this morning I was investigating an incursion, something potentially far more dangerous than being stuck in Atlanta traffic."

"Very well, I will do as you ask."

Gratitude flooded me. "Thank you, Ani."

Even at the tail end of rush hour and employing the Johammer's ability to slide through clogged roads between cars, crossing Atlanta into the city center enforced a maximum possible speed of twenty miles below the limit. My thumbs tapped the handle grips with barely-restrained frustration. Vitae often complained about their complacency, citing it as evidence that knowledge of faerie in mortal hands could end Creation. At their core though, wafers were good people capable of so much.

Just wish they didn't revel in being infuriating.

By the time I reached the parking decks for our building, the constant thumb pummeling cracked a small split down my handlebars' grips. The lights above my reserved spot were out, but I parked in the resultant shadows anyway.

Maybe some misguided wafer will jump me, and I'll be able to help them see both the error of their ways and just how great a blessing painkillers can be.

I leapt off of my Johammer and bolted for the elevator. The doors opened to my call, assaulting my temper with languid, sleepy notes. I turned to the floor controls and cursed.

"Hold the elevator!" Caelum jogged down a concrete ramp in khakis and a violet shirt, short brown hair waving in the breeze. He flashed me a wide smile and stepped into the elevator—his hair arranging itself neatly.

Smarmy bastard.

Don't get me wrong, Caelum is pretty great. He doesn't treat me like an invalid and he's often the first to spout off some distracting comment when Vitae sinks his teeth too far into me.

"Died?"

He just has to ask the stupid questions...and he's not even out of breath.

I glared.

Even his questioning expression didn't distract from his play-boy, pretty boy aura, if anything his looks improved. "And why aren't we moving?"

"No keycard."

Caelum laughed. "Right."

He slid a security card from his wallet, held it against the reader and pressed the penthouse button. As the car rose, eyes the grey of a storm-filled sky and glinting with inner lightning slid up and down my body. "Too short to get noticed now so you're going to lash out with disco?"

"It's all I had that fit." I jabbed the button again and again.

The elevator continued its ascent.

"Oh. Why not go shopping?" Caelum asked.

"Someone put in a really big order for tomorrow."

"Great, you're working on it. Everything ready? This one's a big one—CEO's attending."

I closed my eyes and concentrated on the music.

"Quayla?"

"Yes. Your order is ready. Thank you for your business."

"Wow, that almost sounded sincere." Caelum laughed. "Maybe if you dressed more professionally, I'd have taken you seriously."

I tapped the elevator door. "This door may save your life, Caelum, if it opens soon."

"Ouch, whitewater warning. You do realize Walmart is always open, right?"

"Yes, Caelum."

"Stays open all night for insomniacs, antisocials, dark faerie in need of discount baked goods, and superheroes." He struck a pose. His smile flickered. "I thought I hacked in and purged all this sleepy time music."

"Vitae."

Caelum grinned. "Enough said."

The elevator doors opened to a marble foyer two stories tall.

Caelum patted himself, then kissed the doorframe. His words were breathy. "Thank you, you saved my life. We should get together sometime."

I rolled my eyes to hide my amusement. "I don't think the elevator door feels that way about you."

Caelum looked taken aback. A moment later his startled expression cleared with a shrug. "Oh well, even the best relationships have their ups and downs."

The horrid joke reminded me of Dylan's sense of humor. My lip quivered.

Caelum wrapped an arm around me. "I'm sorry, little sister. I was only trying to make you feel better."

"Good job," I sniffed.

"This is about Dylan? I thought you told him what you are."

I nodded.

I had died. I'd died doing my duty, but I had no idea how Dylan would react to our relationship's first encounter with death. Up the stairs, Vitae awaited, ready to whip me for any of a thousand things I'd done that didn't keep order with his perfect world and the perfect slave he wanted us all to be.

I was walking into a beating I had to accept quietly. Worse, without a distraction, seeing Dylan that evening—maybe for the last time—consumed my attention.

The whole world pressed in on me like a garbage compactor. My chest squeezed painfully until I couldn't breathe let alone speak.

Caelum's normally flippant expression sobered. He let out a deep breath. "You're going to have to brace yourself then. Everything might go fine, but if not, it's going to hurt."

"I love him. He loves me. Shouldn't that be enough?"

"It should," Caelum shook his head, "but sometimes it isn't."

Heat flashed across my skin and a roaring waterfall filled my ears. "What would you know? All your encounters are quick flings and sport sex."

Caelum's jaw tightened. "*Because* I know. I lived through a similar situation. Shelby and I were inseparable, pieces of the same puzzle...at least until I died.

"She said everything was all right, that she didn't mind me as a male instead of a female." Caelum studied his hands. "That's the great thing about finding wafers with fluid sexual tastes. An unexpected gender change doesn't interfere with the love you feel for each other in your hearts. It's compatible souls that matter."

"Right."

Caelum pinned his upper lip in his teeth. "Right. That's how it should be, just...sometimes it isn't. Sometimes they can't get over the loss of you even though you're standing right there."

"Caelum? Are you all right?"

Caelum flashed me a trademark grin that was just so much stage makeup. "I'm fine, and no matter what, you will be too."

"Vitae is waiting for you both," Anima said.

"How are you, Ani-doll? I've been thinking we should program you a boyfriend. A babe like you shouldn't be singl—" Caelum's expression filled with horror. "Oh, hells, Quayla..."

Quayla

I took the mahogany stairs two at a time, leaving Caelum as far behind as possible. I knocked into a side table on the switchback, teetering the planter balanced there. My rush carried me to the upper landing and through the outer balcony doors.

Anima opened the heavy doors at the opposite end of the short glass hallway before I crossed the distance.

"I'm glad you made it in time," Anima said.

And yet Vitae's waiting on us?

I stopped short.

My eyes clamped shut and tightened almost as much as the fists digging nails into my palm. The pressure I'd thought vanquished, ambushed me as if the short glass tunnel had squeezed everything going on into an overwhelming dread.

A perfectly balanced perfume of growing things breathed cool air on my face. Water tinkled from the garden's fountain. Their combined siren song invited me into my favorite place in our Shield, but this time the sweet melody hid false promises and savage teeth. The garden's sirens summoned me into peril and conflict.

I'm not sure how much more I can take.

Vitae cleared his throat.

My eyes snapped open.

"Aquaylae, you're blocking the entrance." Vitae scowled from the garden's center. "Your hair is untidy. Fix yourself."

I pushed long curled locks from my face.

A stone archangel loomed over our life phoenix, wings and arms outstretched from the fountain's center to the ceiling. Intricate stonework surrounded the angelic statue with a crowd of winged, infant trumpeters often misnamed as a cherub. Water streamed from each putto's horn. Pure, glistening streams of water flowed from the trumpets into the wide basin, circulating water that Quayla had enchanted like Mare before her and Mare's predecessor if one existed.

The fountain hadn't been crafted by someone familiar with the putti. I had seldom encountered them myself, though thankfully never so ill-attired. They were brilliant crafters, but ill-suited to transporting water which needed to arrive clean.

Tougher than Sidhe dwarves, a statuary depiction as guardians over the small, depressed alcoves between their sandaled feet suited the putti's nature. Each of five putti stood astride an egg larger than any an ostrich ever laid and more valuable than any other single treasure on Earth. A jeweled ovum to shame Faberge's greatest creation nestled within a shallow recess ringed with angelic runes.

The nearest egg—my egg—had been formed of sapphire and celestial silver. The life invested within glowed in time with my heartbeat. My egg drew me with more intensity than the other sirens—enough force that if my nest ran empty, the egg would summon me away from the threshold of True Death once.

I glanced up at Vitae.

His gaze darted to my egg and back. His palpable disapproval said everything. Terrance had shared the story with me just after my assignment.

True Death had claimed Mare.

None of the others, not even gentle Terrance, would explain how both Vitae and Mare had ended up without an egg. After True Death claimed Mare, an unexplained shortage forced the Atlanta Shield to go without a water shield for decades.

A disgraced phoenix lucky not to be sent beyond—me—had replaced beloved Mare shortly after the Headingham incident.

Vitae had been more than happy to hold Mare up as the penultimate example of duty and sacrifice. Mare had died saving the region in general and Vitae in specific. He'd made it abundantly clear that I was not, and would never be, Mare's equal.

Not even if I Died for the Shield.

I gathered myself to face whatever Vitae had in store.

"Terrance!" Caelum's greeting made me jump. "How's the DMV?"

"Rude, but necessary."

My eyes followed the deep baritone to the bald, thick-bodied Moor. His smile blossomed like white orchids.

"In other words, perfect for you." Caelum whispered into my ear. "I am sorry for before."

I stiffened, not acknowledging his apology and crossed to Terrance's wrought-iron bench. He took my hands, and I realized Terrance had somehow drawn me across the garden without speaking. "Hello, Quayla. You look beautiful."

"Of course she does," Caelum said. "Her skin's even got that newborn smell."

"Enough, Caelum," another voice said.

"Geez, chill out, Iggy," Caelum said. "Always so testy."

Ignis slid fine-boned hands onto my shoulders. "I'm sorry for your loss, little sister."

I looked over my shoulder into slanted eyes the color of dying coals and cupped his hand. "Thanks, Iggy."

"Will this cost you Dylan?" Ignis asked.

I bit my lip to prevent it quivering and held back the world's returning weight. "I don't know. It shouldn't, I mean he knew, but..."

"But do they ever truly understand?" Ignis asked.

"Come to order and praise the Undying Light," Vitae beckoned.

We rose, each bowing to the fountain's statue. Blazing light filled the rooftop greenhouse. Two divine phoenixes coalesced from the light, shifting from great bird to winged man to a pair of businessmen.

The assembled bowed to one knee and spoke in unison, "Vilicangelus."

"Genuflect and acknowledge Summuseraphi," Vitae said.

They repeated their bow, uttering, "Summuseraphi."

"Summus has earned elevation," Vilicangelus said. "He

bravely defended the New Zealand Shield when all his brethren fell. When the mantle of Divine One was thrust upon him, he rose to the occasion and put down the remaining Sidhe insurrection."

"His *whole* Shield fell?" Caelum said. "Even their *Divine*? I thought—"

Vitae shut Caelum up with his expression, a mean feat since Caelum never shut up. He gestured for Vilicangelus to continue.

"Summus shelters under my wings, so you now shelter beneath his. For his next century of training, all communications channels that reach my ears with reach his as well. I remain this Shield's Praefectus, but Summus will handle the year-to-year oversight." Vilicangelus inclined his head toward the younger archangel.

"Um, thanks. Obviously, I'm Summus—still getting used to the name—"

"What was it before, Summy?" Caelum asked.

Vitae scowled.

"Lympha," Summus smiled.

I froze, staring at Summus, unsure how to feel. An aqua not much older than myself had been forcibly changed, not to a different body or gender, but to a completely different kind of phoenix. Questions spun out of control in my mind.

Why did the divine—may his soul rest gently—have to elevate someone else? How could a divine fall so many times that their nest was empty? Do they even have nests or eggs? What if Lympha didn't want to be elevated? Did she even get a choice? Why did she become a he? Are there no female divine?

Vitae glowered at me, pointing at Summus and demanding my attention.

Right. We don't get any choices. We aren't human. Our free will is a counterfeit. We're just eternal soldiers never allowed rest.

"There's been a death in this Shield, though thank Creation not a True Death." Summus turned to me. "Mistakes were made. I know, it happens. You should've seen the mess Vili had to clean up from my first moments Divine. Even so, mistakes must be addressed—"

"Summus," Vilicangelus said.

Summus's eyes flitted to his superior.

"You've more than exhausted your introduction." Vilicangelus gestured to Vitae. "The Shieldheart will conduct the briefing while we observe, quietly reserving our wisdom until the end."

Summus's expression grew sheepish. "Oh. My apologies, Shieldheart, pray continue—can I say pray?"

Vilicangelus smirked.

Chapter Eight

Come To Vitae Meeting

Quayla

"First and foremost, this Shield has displayed a shameful lack of respect. Woolgathering in the presence of not one, but two Praefectus!" Vitae's eyes blazed green at Caelum, then shifted to me.

I fidgeted, lowering my eyes.

Vitae straightened his attire. "This Shield serves a vital function. Not only do we *discretely* protect humanity from supernatural interference and police the Fae Kissed who make deals with Sidhe who slip through the cracks, our jurisdiction abuts royal enclaves from both Sidhe Courts. We are protectors in diplomatic as well as physical regard.

"Are you dressed or groomed as dignitaries? Do you carry yourself with dignity?" Vitae's disapproval drilled into me, squeezing my heart. "No, you're slovenly embarrassments to our Praefectus and our Creator."

"Vitae," Vilicangelus said.

My Shieldheart forged on, emphasizing every few words by slapping the back of his hand into an empty palm. "We *must* maintain clean, *professional* appearances while walking as if on rice paper. We *must* come and go like a breeze. We must *never* leave behind evidence we exist."

"Like Men in Black," Caelum said. "I call Agent C for my codename."

Vitae's displeasure shifted, lifting the building weight of accusations off of my chest.

I took a breath.

Thank you, Caelum.

"Anima is concerned about the growing gaps in our sentry net. The faerie continue to remove the seeds of your essence planted through the city faster than they're being replaced, blinding us to mischief and worse, stealing souls from Heaven by converting mortals into Fae Kissed. This cannot be allowed to continue." Vitae focused on Ignis. "Your seeds in particular are heavily depleted."

"What do you suggest I do, Vitae?" Ignis asked calmly. "The wafers—"

"Mortals," Vitae corrected.

"Right, we had no reason to expect the Sidhe would do something to actually help the mortals. Their awareness campaign demonizing the perils of ingested smoke came out of nowhere."

Caelum snorted. "Out of thin, smoky air as it were."

Ignis rolled his eyes. "The faeries don't even have to remove my ashtrays; the mortals are doing it for them."

"Find a new way to seed your essence throughout the city," Vitae said. "We must be able to feel faerie movements, or we risk ending up with full scale covens of Fae Kissed."

Caelum snorted.

"What exactly do you find humorous?" Vitae asked.

"That you can't dress in this century, but we've got to be politically correct instead of calling them what they are," Caelum said.

"Names have power, little brother," Terrance said. "You know better than to risk summoning their attention."

"A Pyri in my last Shield opened a chain of open grill kebab stands," Summus said. "She added to our web, and we got to eat what didn't sell. They were delicious."

He's not as stuffy as Vili. Maybe a younger Praefectus will set a more relaxed tone—maybe even get uptight Vitae to back off.

Ignis smiled. "Tha—"

"Thank you, Divine One." Vitae cut across Ignis. He cleared his throat. "However, this Shield's failings will not be solved by adding more frivolous activities."

I stared at Vitae.

"Um, you're welcome." Summus smiled uncertainly, glancing at Vilicangelus. My hopes the new Divine One would offer us a reprieve from Vitae's unreasonable, inflexible adherence to the rules died in Summus's quiet mumble. "Her stands never interfered with her duties...you know, before she died."

"We are honored by her courage and praise His mercy that her egg stood between her and final death," Vitae bowed his head and we all observed silence with him. "Perhaps our Ignis could consult her once her regrowth completes, and she hatches in a century or so. In the meantime, Ignis will need to find other ways to satisfactorily perform his duties."

Ignis' expression remained passive, but tiny glows escaped clenched fingertips.

"Caelum, your seeds are the second least," Vitae said.

Caelum spread his hands. "I've got a lot of things on my plate. The city beautification program Summer 'encouraged' has the wafers—"

"Mortals," Vitae snapped.

"Yeah, them—they're removing my tags all over town."

"These excuses are unconscionable." Vitae's accusing finger swept the garden. "Faerie are running amuck because you are failing at your duties, yet all I get is finger pointing. They're exploiting the holes in our sensor net and tormenting our charges." His finger stopped on me, reinforced by a dark expression. "Your little hobbies—"

I stiffened. "They're not hobbies. Our jobs keep government agencies off our backs."

"If these jobs distract from your duty, then they will be forbidden."

An early winter washed through my essence.

I can't lose the shop. It's the only place that's mine.

Summus raised a finger.

Vilicangelus shook his head.

"How do you expect us to pay our rent then?"

"You will relocate into headquarters," Vitae said. "Rededicating yourselves to your duties rather than frivolous pursuits."

Thermal vents lazed my essence to the brink of boiling.

"Move in here with you, Dad?" Caelum asked. "No thanks."

Vitae whirled, but Terrance cut across him. "Caelum and Quayla are correct. Moreover, protecting Creation requires we stride its byways. You lost this argument when populations grew larger than could be easily monitored from a high perch, and those numbers have only grown. Your feelings aside, things are not as they once were. We must adapt."

I stared at my brothers, my own head of steam waning as they stepped in one at a time to defend me.

"We have to be part of Mortal civilization," Ignis said. "How many times did Mare cite a need to live with mortals so that we can understand them?"

Vitae's jaw tightened. Spots under his jaw colored, and he turned his anger toward me. "You don't have to understand them to protect them. You certainly don't have to engage in fornications."

"No, but it is fun," Caelum said. "You should try it, maybe replace that stick up—"

"Caelum," Ignis snapped. "Shut up already. You're not helping."

Part of me wanted to quail under Vitae's glare, but the support of Ignis and Terrance bolstered my confidence enough to speak my mind. "What are we supposed to do, Vitae? Be like these putti? Unfeeling stone perched on rooftops? No offense, Terrance."

Terrance smirked.

"Not unfeeling, impartial," Vitae said.

Now that the words had started, the flow didn't abate. I shoved an accusing finger at Vitae. "You might be happy sitting up here in your ivory tower reading books and trusting the sentry net, but we actually care. We like the wafers. We know they're not two-dimensional, not vinyl figures. They're living, breathing, dynamic individuals, and we need to be near them, close enough to keep up with their rapidly-changing technology with an ear to the ground for trouble."

"You were created for a duty!" Vitae thundered. "You are not supposed to be weakening our defense, by spreading your nests—and legs—throughout this city."

Caelum placed a restraining hand on me before I'd taken a second step toward Vitae. I didn't recall my first, nor him moving.

Vitae ignored my expression and kept speaking. "Your petty indulgences are endangering our existence and our secrets. How many more mortals must burn at the stake for you to learn—"

A waterfall roared in my ears.

"Vitae," Vilicangelus's tone hardened. "Take care."

"All she had to do was let them burn her," Vitae said. "She'd have been reborn in her nest without costing who knows how many mortals their lives? We are *not* individuals. We are a Shield, singular, an extens—"

I shoved Vitae. "You think we don't know that? I died—"

Vitae backed up to the fountain but kept his feet. Contempt tainted his words. "You jeopardized everything to protect some filthy strays."

"God's creations!" I said. "Aren't you the phoenix of life? All life? Besides, I was stopping Wyldfae from killing His creation and exposing their existence to the wafers."

"Mortals."

Caelum drew me gently back away from Vitae and the fountain.

"Whatever—you know what, that's the problem too with your little picture of us as gargoyles," I said.

"Can we use Batman instead of Gargoyles?" Caelum asked.

I elbowed him.

"Fine," Caelum backed away, hands raised in surrender, "but that cartoon was horrible even with all the Star Trek actors."

I resisted the urge to further accost my unfeeling elder and took my temper across the garden to Vilicangelus. "If God is about love, then why are we kept separate? We have souls because He realized without the ability to connect and love the wafers, we'd go the same way as the previous Angelic Host. We'd objectify those around us, think of them as fixtures to be moved on a whim. Why else would He give us souls but that He wanted us to love and be part of Creation—yet we don't even have names of our own."

Vitae interposed himself. "That's enough, Aquaylae. Your actions prove the reasons why. You've let the self-important vanity of this generation corrupt our ideals. It's bad enough your sloppiness has required Vilicangelus to take time out of his busy—"

Vilicangelus held up a hand. He stepped around Vitae and set the other on my shoulder. "Aquaylae, beautiful, caring child. You were created with a duty."

Vitae glowered down his nose, folding arms across his chest.

"Duty alone would drive you to serve to the best of your ability," Vilicangelus said. "He gave you a soul, knowing with it you would go above and beyond your best. You would love Creation with His heart, willing to give absolutely everything in you for it —willing even to face Destruction as Mare did."

Vitae's face grew wooden.

"We must avoid Lucifer's path," Vilicangelus said. "We must not become too full of ourselves. We limit such vanity by being mindful of the purpose of our power without abandoning empathy. It is a delicate balancing act helped by keeping us both part and apart."

"Okay, that's enough heavy philosophy for one meeting," Caelum said. "Let's all gang up on Quayla for screwing up her hair."

Caelum's attempted distraction failed to protect me from Vitae. He made an example out of me, as usual, waving my mistakes as the banner for lectures on procedure. He berated us all, but even with all the others attempting to deflect Vitae's anger, I felt more beaten by Vitae than I had by the grendlings.

Summus offered the group ineloquent encouragements, and Vilicangelus took Summus and Vitae to one side.

I seated myself on the fountain's edge, fingers traipsing through the water. I sprinkled my silently singing egg, the droplets of water on the egg tingling my skin.

"You all right?" Caelum asked.

I nodded.

He smirked. "You need a good party...in fact. Hey, guys?"

Terrance and Ignis joined us.

"My company's throwing a huge picnic party out at Stone Mountain on Labor Day in two weeks. You're all invited. What do you say?" Caelum said.

"No," Vitae snapped.

"You weren't invited," Caelum chuckled. "Well, at least not yet."

"That weekend is DragonCon," Vitae said.

"He's right," Ignis said. "The Courts relish exploiting the power boost from all those dressed up like the faerie."

"They always exploit the power boost," Terrance said.

"I'm talking about Monday," Caelum said. "Most everyone's gone by then."

"No," Vitae said. "The Courts will be up to mischief. This Shield will maintain high alert the whole weekend—including Monday."

Caelum's expression turned sly. "Fine, fine."

We followed Caelum out, but Vilicangelus stepped between me and the garden's exit. He lowered his voice. "May I have a moment, Quayla?"

A surge of dread wrapped crooked fingers around my heart. "Please, don't relocate me. I know Vitae isn't satisfied with me, but I'm doing my bes—"

The divine phoenix placed soft fingers across my lips. A corner of his mouth curled up. "I am not removing you from this Shield or your paramour."

My breath caught in my throat. Ideas circled my mind in a swarm of ravens and vultures.

"You made some mistakes today, but I am well pleased with you," Vilicangelus said. "Pets and children are the ultimate innocents, precious in His eyes, and you were right to defend them."

Tears leaked from the corners of my eyes.

He wiped them away. "No matter where your journey takes you, follow your heart. The one given you is precious."

Light flashed, forcing me to blink away spots and the tears still clinging to my eyes.

Our Praefectus had praised my choices. He'd reinforced that I made mistakes, but he hadn't belabored them. He expected me to work them out if I hadn't already. He treated me like a shield.

The encounter buoyed my spirits, though not enough to totally eclipse my impending meeting with Dylan. I took a moment to wipe my face and square my shoulders before heading out.

A vice clamped down on my bicep. "You and I are not done."

Vitae glowered at me, eyes blazing with essence.

"Please let go of my arm," I said.

He looked at his grip and eased open his fingers. When they moved away, white handprints lingered a few minutes longer.

"Pack your things," Vitae said.

"I thought we'd settled that. We need to live with the mortals."

"You're leaving this Shield. I will not have such a disgrace endangering our charges."

The thermal vent opened back up. "I'm not a disgrace."

"You are. You're selfish, unthinking and careless. Your refusal to follow procedure is going to cost more mortal lives, and I won't have you killing our charges.

"You've proven yourself time and again to be nothing but a maverick, a lifelong disappointment. I don't want you in this Shield. I've demanded you be relocated or Destroyed."

I gaped at him, nothing but a soft hum in my mind.

"We need a real shield as our Aqua. Someone who will help protect Atlanta," Vitae said. "You've got no business here. You could never replace Mare."

The heat rose, drying out even a desire to cry. "I'm a shield...part of the Atlanta Shield, and I'm not going anywhere. Vilicangelus even said so."

He snorted. "He'll change his mind, and if not, it won't be hard to convince the new Praefectus. You're barely better than a Sidhe."

My finger jabbed so hard into his chest, pain lanced up my arm. "I am a full shield, Vitae. I'm as good as any Aqua, I can prove it."

I stormed away before the rising current roaring in my ears rose too far. Vilicangelus had praised me, told me I was staying. He wouldn't lie, so either Vitae was trying to motivate me or lying or some other misunderstanding was afoot.

It didn't matter.

I would not willingly leave Dylan.

I would prove myself to Vitae in such a way that no one could ever question my dedication again.

I would figure out why the Wyldfae attacked the shelters. I would unravel their game and then I would stop it.

I am Aquaylae, Shield of the Atlanta shire in service to the Undying Light.

Caelum

Quayla emerged from the garden and stomped to the top of the stairwell. From her expression, whatever Vitae and Vilicangelus had said to her hadn't been nice.

Caelum wasn't sure the best way to help her.

Terrance and Iggy just said to support her, but I'm not sure that's enough.

He'd tried to ease her fears, tried to help brace her for the possible loss of her mortal love. A knot around Caelum's heart tightened to a tourniquet. He missed Shelby.

The love of his life, the woman that had rejected and nearly destroyed him was eighty-four, a great-grandmother not long for the world. He'd kept an eye on her, at first just to protect her from faerie reprisals, but later he'd found he couldn't walk totally away.

Mortal intoxicants hadn't worked on him—not even a whole tavern's stock. Drugs hadn't worked either—mortal or faerie. Carnal pleasure distracted him, but never dulled the edge.

They couldn't, not while he watched Shelby age alone, abandoned by children too weak to stand by her while age ate away at her body and her mind.

"Deep thoughts, little brother?"

Caelum turned toward Terrance's deep voice.

"It's been a day for them," Ignis hoisted a smile as Quayla descended the last few steps.

She tried to smile back, but the results looked brittle, on the edge of shattering.

Caelum pushed away thoughts of Shelby and trotted over to push the elevator call button. He offered the room a rakish grin, waggled his brows and lowered his voice conspiratorially. "You know, we can be on high alert from the picnic."

"I'm afraid Vitae is right in this, Caelum," Terrance said.

Caelum deflated, his attempt to raise Quayla's spirits a bust.

Tension clung, a palpable pressure like the thick humidity just before a summer storm. Each phoenix's body language echoed his own muscled shoulders.

Ignis set a hand on Quayla. Terrance followed suit a moment later. She closed her eyes.

"What did they say?" Caelum asked.

Her voice didn't break, but it did crack. "Vitae asked that I be relocated or Destroyed."

Lightning flashed through Caelum's chest, burning long, hot lines up and down his body.

"I have spoken for you with Vilicangelus," Ignis said.

Her eyes opened, latching on Ignis with obvious gratitude.

"I, too, have praised your service," Terrance said. "Vilicangelus will do neither."

"I-I know. He said so, it's j-just...," her eyes sought us each in turn. "I need to prove myself, on my own."

"Screw Vitae," Caelum said. "You don't need to prove anything to us."

Terrance scrutinized her. A sigh escaped him as his head began to shake. "She needs to prove herself to Vitae."

"Why?" Caelum asked.

Quayla looked up, eyes glowing a glistening blue. "I just do."

Vilicangelus

Vilicangelus stood at the edge of the garden hidden behind a curtain of Light. He watched the four departing shields through the Watcher's eyes and listened to their conversation.

Worry ate at his essence. Atlanta's Shield was fractured.

Still broken by Mare's sacrifice. It's essential I do something to fix this before things become irreparable—no matter how much pain that requires.

Vilicangelus eased himself back into reality. He didn't bother to seek Vitae. There was no need. His old shieldmate would regret seeking out Vilicangelus soon enough.

Vitae stormed across the garden like an Aero clouded in temper.

Summus took a step to either intervene or join them.

No, Summus, let this conversation be between Vitae and myself.

<Shall I listen?>

Not this time.

"She has to go," Vitae snarled.

Vilicangelus didn't return his shout. "No."

Vitae balled his fists, his body vibrating. "You're wrong. She's destroying this Shield. I demand you remove her."

A corner of Vilicangelus's lips quirked upward pushing up the matching eyebrow. "No."

"She's selfish, obstinate and disrespectful of me and her duty."

"Then you should be glad, shouldn't you? Do not those qualities make her less like Mare?"

Fury bent Vitae's features into something nearly demonic. "Aquaylae is nothing like Mare. Nothing."

"And yet they are so similar."

For a moment it seemed my old pupil would strike me physically. He shook, eyes ablaze behind a halo of barely restrained tears. "She has to go."

"No."

Vitae snatched up a nearby bench, roaring like a maddened bear cornered by a circle of spearman. He hurled the wrought-iron furniture into the greenhouse glass.

"Shieldheart?" Anima asked.

Vilicangelus held up a hand. "Not now, Anima. Let him rage."

The Shieldheart locked eyes on Vilicangelus. A cold iron mask snapped into place as he straightened his suit lapels. Only the tears betrayed the calm as illusion. "She has to go. I cannot do my job with her here."

"What is your job, as you see it?"

"I am the Shieldheart. I must protect and perfect this Shield, see to it that this Praefecture is protected from the Sidhe."

"We've had few Fae Kissed and fewer still diplomatic issues with the young leaders placed here by the two remaining Queens. It seems this Shield is doing the job admirably."

The violent head shake set several tears free. "We're spread out. We're weak. Holes riddle our net and the Sidhe mock us."

"The Sidhe mock often. You'll have to do better than that."

Vitae purpled then returned to his normal color in turns. Words poised behind lips pressed so tightly together they all but disappeared.

Vilicangelus watched Vitae struggle with guilt and rage and countless other emotions. The life phoenix had been bottling them all by sheer, unconquerable will.

If that cork doesn't burst soon the pressure may become too much. Maybe it would be a mercy just to rewrite him and swap him into another shield.

Vilicangelus's stomach turned at the thought.

No, I couldn't inflict so unjust a punishment on Vitae, certainly not after all he's accomplished here. He must grow beyond this.

"Fine," Vitae spun on his heel.

"When you first came here, I'd never have imagined you a coward." Vilicangelus shook his head. "Do your books allow you to hide from yourself as effectively as you hide from your duty?"

Vitae whipped around, heavy suit fabric fluttering around him like a dark flame. "I've done all I can to perform my duty while that lazy, incompetent Aqua sulked in her chambers watching the city grow. She has to go. She will not cause me to fail."

"Again."

Vitae swung, his rage so complete that he nearly telegraphed the move with holographic foreshadowing.

Vilicangelus slipped out of the way.

Summus lurched forward.

No, Summus, stay clear.

Vitae swung again.

"Admit it, Vitae. Own it."

"Own what?" Vitae's voice broke. "That I failed? That the Sidhe played me like a fool?"

Vilicangelus's gut twisted, but Vitae's willful wall of denial was cracking. The divine snorted. "That's hardly all that was your fault."

"What else do you want from me, Aether?" Furious, shameful tears burned golden-red lines down Vitae's face. "You want me to admit that I led this Shield into the middle of a fake war meant to give the Sidhe sport and take our lives? I admit it."

"That's not the whole of it."

Vitae swung at Vilicangelus. The divine phoenix caught the blow and twisted Vitae's arm into a painful lock. "Admit it, Vitae. If you're not a coward, then face it like a shield and own all of it."

Vitae transmogrified into swirling gold and scarlet plasma, reversing Vilicangelus's hold and throwing him into the greenhouse glass after the bench.

"Fine! I let my pride get the best of me and I cost Mare her—"

True Death. Did you ever even confess your feelings for her?

Vitae whipped aside, seizing a planter box and shattering it against the floor. "Never again will I let this Shield fail. Never again will an undeserving shield in my care be Destroyed, not even if I have to ride them night and day to His absolute perfection."

"Life isn't about perfection, Vitae." Vilicangelus rose, dusting himself off. "Neither is perfection His will. That's why He gives forgiveness."

"If I need His forgiveness, then I failed...again."

"You need to forgive Aquaylae."

"She has to go."

"No." Vilicangelus locked his hands on Vitae's shoulders and matched gazes with his hurting friend. "You need to forgive yourself and forgive Aquaylae for not being Mare."

Eyes locked together and skin touching, Vitae's thoughts

slammed into Vilicangelus's mind with furious clarity. *<Never. This Shield will become the best in Creation if it costs me True Death.>*

Vilicangelus dropped his eyes and let go of Vitae. He couldn't bear to watch his millennia-old friend destroy himself for Mare's death. He'd relinquish the duty to Summus. Maybe without their shared history, the new divine would be able to lead Vitae out of his self-made hell and back into the light.

Chapter Nine

Lies & Turncoats

Quayla

We split up when the elevator deposited us in the parking deck. The warmth my brothers offered me lingered even though their touch had gone. Caelum didn't understand my need to prove myself, but Ignis and Terrance did.

I hadn't been as close to the Terra or Pyri of my first shield. Without Ignis's and Terrance's support, I wasn't sure how long it would've been before Vitae's accusations started to feel like truth.

I sighed. My trials weren't over. Dylan awaited across town.

Traffic clogged the highways, dragging out my dread.

In Atlanta, bustling wafers filled the roads early morning to late evening, tapering off only in the darkest times of night. Stores and corporations ran all night around the city in little islands, but for the most part, wafers hid in their caves when darkness descended—an instinctual or perhaps genetic memory warning them of the things darkness hid.

Like faeries coming out to play.

I pulled off the interstate, taking a moment at the red light to reach my senses out to my seeds. Anima monitored the web around the clock, but that didn't absolve me of my duty—something Vitae had practically screamed into my face during the group meeting. I felt no taint upon my little pools other than the faintest itch of residual magic and air pollution.

A car honked.

I glanced into the side mirror at another huge SUV practically driving up my back wheel. I eased into traffic, the driver whipping around me with a rude gesture. I shook my head and tapped my thumbs. I pulled off the main thoroughfare to a small apartment building. The sight of Dylan's car in its parking space seized my chest and squeezed.

My Johammer fit in the space Dylan had left between his bumper and the curb. I glanced at the archangel talisman.

Neutral and unfeeling, a good soldier like Vitae wants—just like he wants me to break up with Dylan. Might get his wish.

I entered my three-story walk-up. Each step seemed to echo like the final, condemned strides of someone marched across a platform to be burned alive. I opened my apartment door. Dylan reclined, asleep on the couch with a tech magazine on his chest. I watched him from the doorway, memorizing his soft, sandy hair, rugged features and blue eyes hidden behind Harry Potter glasses.

"Just going to stand in the doorway?" His eyes widened. "Quayla?"

My teeth kept my lip from quivering. "Yes."

He rose, looking me up and down.

"I told you this could happen," I whispered.

"I know, and I've seen you come home injured, but I guess I never really...even your voice is different."

"It's a whole new body."

His cute little dimpled smirk appeared then fell away. "We need to talk."

I can fight dark faeries hand to hand, I can face this.

I squared my shoulders. "You're angry."

"I was. I was in the middle of an important meeting, and you tell me you died like you were asking me to pick up milk at the store."

"I had to hurry back."

"You had to hurry back? To your corpse? To the people that killed you?" Dylan asked.

"Yes, there are certain—"

He turned his back on me. "Don't you care about me at all?"

What?

He turned watery eyes back to me. "I worried about you before, but you *died* today. No warning, no nothing—"

"I don't generally plan on dying."

Dylan paced, hands gesturing away his agitation. "You just tell me you're dead, and now you're telling me you didn't take time to explain because you had to go back and try to get yourself killed *again*."

"It's...my job."

"Quit."

"I can't quit being what I was created to be."

"Have you ever tried?" Dylan asked.

"No, but it's not like that. I only appear human."

His expression soured. "You're not human?"

"I am, sort of, I shape shift, okay. I told you this."

"You told me you became a phoenix, not that you were a...a bird changed into a human."

I closed the distance, looking up into his face from a much lower perspective. "Dylan, please, I'm still me. I still love you."

"Damn, you're short."

I cast my eyes to the floor. "I knew you'd hate that my legs are shorter."

"I hate that you died. I hate your job."

"We can't change what I am."

He frowned. "Is it a work visa kind of thing? Must you do the job to stay in this world?"

"Not exactly."

Dylan took my hands and drew me close. "Marry me."

What?!

So many emotions shot through me, I felt as if I were caught in a riptide and a whirlpool all at once.

"If we get married, you become a citizen, you quit risking your life and we can live happily ever after," Dylan said.

"It doesn't work like that. For one thing, you're going to age and die. I'll look like this long after you're rotting in a grave."

"Unless you do something stupid to get yourself killed again."

I bristled. "I didn't do anything stupid, just couldn't beat that many grendlings alone."

"Why didn't you call for help? Didn't you say there are four more of you?"

"There was no time."

"So, you what, saved a school bus full of children?" Dylan asked.

"Animal shelter."

He pushed me away. "An animal shelter? You died for a bunch of strays?"

"They're God's creations too. Besides, it's my job to stop incursions."

"So what, some little gremlin vampire wants to snack on an alley cat, you're just going to throw your life away?"

"Animals are living, breathing, feeling creatures. They have every right—"

"To be food."

"Dylan!"

"That's what God created them for, to be part of the food chain."

I opened my mouth to argue, but hesitated. Technically he had a point.

That's not a good enough reason to let him win this argument.

"God created them to be companions. They're the ultimate innocents, created to be part of our families."

"No, we did that."

"So, you're happy if I die saving children, but not kittens?"

"I'm not happy with you dying at all!"

"I don't do it very often. We've dated almost four years with only one death," I said.

"Great, every four years I can look forward to a new president and your job killing you. Why won't you even try to quit? How many times can you come back, anyway?"

"I can't quit. My body can be reborn an infinite number of times as long as there is enough essence in my nest."

"How many rebirths does your nest hold?" Dylan asked.

"Right now, one more...I think."

"You think? Are you going to stick close to home until your nest is full?"

I shook my head. "Can't. Filling the nest will take too long."

"Aren't there any faster ways?"

"Yes, there are faster ways but they hurt."

"Death versus pain," Dylan rolled his eyes up as if he were thinking. "I'm going to go with pain."

"*You* are going to go with pain? It's me that has to chop off limbs."

"You're exaggerating."

"No, I'm not."

"Can't you take vacation or something?"

"You don't understand. I can't just hide. I need to find out who attacked the shelter."

Dylan threw up his hands. "It's just a bunch of animals!"

"No!" My temper rose. "It's more than just the animals. So many animal thefts are bound to draw notice. People could discover the Sidhe are behind these incursions."

"So?"

"Your kind can't be allowed to know the faeries exist."

"What is that supposed to mean?"

"Look, everybody has some darkness in their nature, negative feelings about a failed relationship or a lost promotion—even the best people."

"Of course, but I still don't see a problem."

"The Sidhe could give them anything they wanted, grant any

wish no matter how petty or cruel—actually, from the faerie perspective the more petty and cruel the better."

"I don't think you're giving humanity enough credit."

I raised my brows. "You want some death row serial killer to know he could trade away his soul—whatever little he has left—for supernatural strength enough to escape and go on a bloody rampage?"

Dylan opened his mouth to object, but the wheels spun behind his eyes. He closed his mouth, wrinkles appearing on his brows until finally he spoke. "It's the Groundhog Day thing, no consequences."

"Oh, Dylan, honey. There'd be consequences. The whole world would be at risk if humans learned such powers were possible."

He stared into the middle distance a long time. His eyes flicked to me, sad and resigned. "You can't quit?"

I kissed him.

There was no magic to the kiss in and of itself, but as had often happened with Dylan, a simple soft kiss eased our tempers, quickly transforming anger into passion.

We just fit.

Our kissing migrated to the couch. His hands shifted down my body, exploring out of habit despite the new territory. A thought pulled me out of the kiss.

"Before we started arguing, you smirked," I said. "Why?"

"Thinking how cute you were, and, well," Dylan fidgeted.

"What?"

A sheepish grin spread beneath mischievous eyes. "That dating you means I get to sleep with other people without ever cheating."

I punched him in the stomach. He laughed, sweeping me up into his arms in an embrace that filled me with warm waves of happiness.

"So?" I gave him my most seductive smile. "Interested in exploring *all the* new me?"

A sly smile played across his lips. "Virgin territory as it were?"

"I love you." I smirked. "But you're such a dork."

Quayla

When I woke, I yearned to curl back up in the lingering warmth of sleep. My skin still tingled in the scent and afterglow of our union. It'd been a long night, but my new body was too new to wear down after only a day. Mortals preferred more sleep than my kind required, though I stayed abed longer whenever I could cuddle with Dylan.

I stretched.

My whole body still hummed from fresh exploration. My arm slid beneath the satin top sheet toward the mortal man that still wanted me. My hand slipped from beneath overlapped folds into a cold dent left in the old mattress by Dylan's absence. I indulged a small pout.

He's gone.

I rolled over.

Beside the alarm clock, Dylan had sandwiched a new phone between a charging pad and a blue gift bow. Warmth flooded me. Even mad at me, Dylan had listened and taken a special trip to see to my needs. The clock disagreed with my new phone over a few minutes, but both placed Dylan at work.

Dylan's going to be exhausted. I should have someone deliver some of that coffee he loves.

A thought sent my tongue along my lips in a gentle caress.

Maybe I should deliver it myself.

I stretched again, my motion kicking the sheet the rest of the way off. A sharp stab sent pain into my lower back where an old bedspring made a hobby of ambushing me at random. I shifted onto Dylan's side and stretched again. I cooed, luxuriating in my muscles' warm, after-pleasure glow.

Maybe I should explore marrying out of the Shield.

A giggle escaped me.

Maybe no one's tried and there's a loophole I can exploit.

I sobered.

Do I really want to give up everything I was created for? Everything I am? I love him, but is that love stronger than what I feel for the rest of Creation? Can I abandon all of humanity for one man who'll be dead before I know it?

Nature drew me from conflicted thoughts and cooling sheets. Exiting the bathroom, my eyes fell on new pants and shirts stacked atop my bureau and a reusable Walmart shopping bag. A platinum thermos canted on top of the clothes.

I am so spoiled.

I hurried to the still-warm thermos. Cracking the top filled the room with spicy Chai aroma. I hugged the tea to my skin, relishing scent and warmth and ideas for showing my gratitude.

A nasal tone intruded. "Can I nestle between your breasts, too?"

I whipped my head to one side. My gaze flitted over the room, coming to rest on a pixyish faerie, lying in missionary position atop some Disney Princess Barbie on a high bookshelf.

"That's disgusting, Grynnberry, in fact you're disgusting."

"Just copying you and your boy toy. Talk about make-up sex, wowsers."

"Why are you here?"

Grynnberry hovered off the Barbie in a blur of wings, stopping to push her spread legs back together and smooth her dress. "Maybe later, darling."

A growl undercut the one word. "Grynn?"

"She's a toadstool cap too tall for me, but hey," he smirked. "Any skirt for an itch, even a wafer, right?"

"You better talk fast, you little ingrate. You walked me into an ambush."

Grynnberry landed on my new clothes, licking lips as his eyes devoured me. He pressed a hand to his chest. "*Moi*? I never walked you into anything. I told you an Arch would open. It did, didn't it?"

"Yes, to the Wyld Wastes, not one of the Courts."

Grynnberry smoothed his long dark hair around his antennae. "Whoops. Everyone makes mistakes, but the tip was good."

"This was supposed to be my chance for a win no one else could lay claim to, but instead the," I made air quotes, "'valuable' informant I'm not allowed to have set me up for my biggest failure since being allowed back out in the city on my own. I died, Grynn."

"Hey, I came over last night to ensure you were reborn okay."

A flush edged into my cheeks. "Last night? When last night?"

"Early enough to watch that wafer propose—as if any one of us would ever consider giving up our lives for what they have." Grynnberry smiled. "Well, I might give up a few things for what he had last night. You're quite the minx for a little birdie."

"You little pervert."

"Hey, now. I sprinkled a little dust your way...right before you *really* started screaming, if you know what I mean." Grynnberry waggled his antennae. "You owe me."

I narrowed my eyes, a grin's shadow nudging my lips. "Not sure I agree, but for the sake of argument, what do you think I owe you?"

A lecherous smile filled his face, tiny sharp teeth out grinning a shark. "A nestle between those soft new breasts."

"Okay."

Grynnberry blinked. "Okay?"

I shrugged. "Well, if you're giving me time to think about it."

Grynnberry rocketed across the intervening distance, arms wide and grin wider. His flight left a contrail of sparkling dust colored like a summer sunset. The nymph expanded to human size, grabbed my ass and pushed his face between my breasts, giggling at a girlishly high pitch.

Lust slammed into me like a freight train. My every nerve lit up, and the scent of sex in the room redoubled.

My voice came out breathy. "Grynn?"

He grinned mischievously up into my face.

I blew in his face.

"Oh, you bitc—" Grynnberry's eyes rolled back into his head. He shrank back to pixie size, falling backward away from me like a tiny, suicidal action figure.

I caught him in cupped hands and walked him into the kitchen. It took me a moment to dig under the sink before I came up with a wide-mouthed cider jug I'd prepared in advance. I slid Grynn inside, gentle with his wings and closed it with a perforated metal cap.

I set the captured nymph on the counter and fetched Dylan's favorite coffee from the freezer. I set some to brewing in the coffee maker and headed for a nice, hot shower. Dylan's gift included a pair of blue jeans with flowers embroidered on the pocket and a soft t-shirt in my very favorite shade of teal. I slid the shirt on. The fabric's caress sent a tingle through my bare nipples then along my spine. They tightened in response to the pleasure and their excitement pushed against my top enough to show their arousal.

Probably what he had in mind.

I donned a clean pair of my drunk-shopping panties and slid into the jeans.

Bit tight, but at least I can close them.

Back in the kitchen, I found coffee and Grynn steaming. Threats, insults and jeers escaped the glass jug in a tinny ring. I transferred the Chai into my favorite mug and rinsed the thermos to carry Dylan his coffee.

I sat in front of Grynn's jar and sipped Chai. A malicious grin played across my face. I feigned sudden distress. "Oh, no, Dylan forgot to add sweetener."

I withdrew a honey bear from a cabinet.

"Heartless, traitorous, wafer-licking sadist!" Grynnberry jumped up and down in the jar until dust came nearly to his ankles. "I'm going to curse you and your Dylan with never-ending orgasms if you don't let me out right this moment."

I smirked. "Thanks?"

"You won't thank me when every touch, every shift of cloth sends your body through muscle wrenching pleasure. Every. Single. One."

I halted, examining my inadvertent nymph shaker.

Hmm, an endless supply of nymph sex enhancer...oh, I can just hear Vitae now. Using a Sidhe informant is bad enough, but if he caught on to me imprisoning the little monster for my own purposes, his head would explode. Besides, caging anything is wrong.

I popped the bear's top, swirling golden honey into my Chai. A web-fine string drizzled across my finger as I closed the bear. Bringing the honey to my lips, I sucked it from my finger with exaggerated pleasure.

"You win, you win, stop the torture all right?" Grynn folded his arms. "Hey, I still got to second base."

I sipped my tea.

Damn, too much honey.

"I said you win."

"You did."

"So let me out."

I smiled. "Why?"

"You can't hold me in here."

I tapped a finger to my lips. "I seem to recall that if you find a pixie trespassing and capture them—"

"That only applies to mortals and actual pixies," Grynn said.

I sipped my tea.

"All right, I'll give you something good."

"Like last time?" I asked.

"No, something not even I'm supposed to know," Grynn said.

"Go ahead."

"Let me out first."

I laughed.

"I swear on my best feature."

"Your silence?" I set down my Chai.

Should I trust him?

"Don't make me regret this." I reached for the cap. "Hold on."

I tilted the jug onto its side and removed the cap. Grynn squeezed out the top, his wings overlapped tight against his body. I watched, waiting for him to bolt. His muscles tensed to fly, but he relaxed. He expanded to full size, glamour dressing him in a tidy business suit as his wings vanished. He hopped onto one of my kitchen island's bar stools. "I was at a meeting with His Majesty Prince Vusolaryn and his knights."

"You said you weren't supposed to know this."

"I didn't say I was invited. Vusolaryn's meetings have some seriously good eats. If you sneak in after, you miss the good stuff."

"Fine," I sighed. "Go on."

"The Courts are majorly out of balance, Summer's winning and the Wyldfae are exploiting Winter's need to make their own gains."

"No. The Wyldfae wouldn't dare. They keep low when Seelie and Unseelie go at it. Besides, the Courts play their tug-of-war, but it stays close by its very nature."

Grynn shook his head. "Something's changed. Vusolaryn said there were whispers of the Unseelie doing something big."

"What?"

He shrugged.

"I need more than that."

"Sorry, they caught me. I had to leave."

"What did he say about the Wyldfae?" My stomach flip-flopped. "Wait, if you weren't supposed to hear, and they caught you, are they hunting you?"

"Nah, they're so arrogant they assume they caught me on my first attempt." He gestured dismissively. A lewd grin filled his face. "They caught me coming back in for my fourth haul."

"What if you're wrong?" I asked. "What if you're not safe?"

He glanced at the jug. "Could we arrange cable and an easy chair?"

Chapter Ten

Chasing Her Tail

Caelum

Caelum gestured across the dais to a middle-aged man leaning back in his chair. "...once again on behalf of Mister Heffernan and Circlestone, I want to thank all of our donors and volunteers for making this research project possible. Thanks to you, medical miracles are on the horizon."

The hall filled with applause. Caelum took an instant to soak it in with a rakish grin. He inclined his head to the audience and stepped away from the podium. He took his seat at the foot of the raised table and sipped the incredible Scotch served only to those seated with the CEO.

Smooth, oaky flavor burned its way down his throat.

"Mister Kite?"

Caelum smiled at the CEO's dazzling assistant.

She tucked away a wayward lock of hair so black it was almost blue, exposing more of her ivory skin. "Mister Heffernan would like a word."

"Is everything all right, Viviane?" Caelum asked.

"I think so..." She smirked, deep blue eyes glistening. "I mean, he's not likely to fire me."

Caelum laughed. "Charming."

She led him back up the table. Mister Heffernan turned away from a group of bluebloods as Caelum approached. He'd been intimidating seated, but on his feet, Dunham Heffernan loomed over Caelum—a huge, powerful man with an even more powerful voice.

"Thank you, Viviane." He directed his basso toward Caelum, extending a massive hand. "Mister Kite, a jewel for your already prestigious crown. I daren't call it a crown jewel lest you stop spearheading these research projects for me."

"Thank you, Mister Heffernan—"

The curl of a Celtic woad tattoo peaked from the collar of the CEO's tuxedo shirt. "Dunham, please."

"No risk there, Dunham. It's an honor, but really I just enjoy spending your money to help people."

Dunham laughed and slapped Caelum's back. "I've had my eye on you for some time, son. Keep up the good work and maybe we'll get to work more closely together—help all those that deserve it."

Caelum brightened.

"I look forward to seeing you at the picnic. Feel free to invite all your friends. The more the merrier," Dunham said.

"Thank you, sir."

"Mister Heffernan," Viviane said. "The mayor would like a word."

"Duty calls," Dunham said. "If you'll excuse me."

Caelum nodded.

Huh, rich philanthropist with a heart the size of his massive chest. Creator, I love this job. Why couldn't we have someone like Dunham in charge instead of stick-it-up-my-Vitae?

A call interrupted him before Caelum could dwell too long on replacing his Shieldheart with the CEO of Circlestone. "Quayla? Is everything all right?"

"I'm going back to Howell Mill tonight," Quayla said. "I'd like you to come with me."

"Does Vitae know about this?"

"No, and he won't unless you intend to tell him."

"He'll never stop crowing if you get caught out there again."

"That's why you're coming. Besides, I don't plan to get caught."

"Doubt you planned to die last time either," Caelum said.

"Stop being a prick, are you going to help me or not?"

"Well, with that kind of respect how can I say 'no'...wait...just a second, no." Caelum pantomimed, wiping sweat from his brow. "Wow, that was rough."

"Please, Caelum."

"Why are we going back to a crime scene while the cops are probably watching?"

"I need to figure out why the faeries are attacking shelters. I caught a glimpse of something strange but didn't get a chance to investigate—horde of grendlings stabbing me over and over."

"Fine, but we tell Anima too."

Quayla

I trudged up the stairs to my apartment. It'd been a hard day. Judith caught another discrepancy with my appearance—not that she cared. I'd run down a few contacts, but none of my faerie informants admitted having any knowledge of the attacks or their purpose. Mrs. Cox's voice filtered through the old wall, singing the same opera that always seemed to proceed a glut of baked goods.

I stepped into my apartment, leaned back against the door and took a long, slow breath. I reached for my seeds, finding several absent but none any more tainted than expected.

Going to have to track down Ralein soon.

My purse went onto the table by the door, a manila envelope poking out of its top containing my new IDs.

Still need to clean the old pictures out...after I talk to Dylan.

I pushed away the dreaded task for another more dreadful.

Might as well get started.

I stripped, leaving my clothes where they landed on my bedroom floor and dragged the rolling TV cart opposite the bookcase that hid my nest. I flipped through the romantic dramas shelved together rather than with the other blu-rays shelved in the living room.

I opened the book case, fetched a special silver-coated metal grate and placed it over my nest. I stopped, looking down at the almost depleted pool of my essence. I'd been taught other, faster ways to refill the basin.

I shivered at the unpleasant possibilities.

No, thanks. I'll do it this way.

I slid a movie into the player. The opening notes of Titanic filled my room with impending sadness.

I stepped naked into my nest and settled into a seated position atop the grate. Kate Winslet appeared on the screen and the tears started down my cheeks. "I hate this old movie."

Quayla

I pulled a U-turn and slid my Johammer in next to Caelum's motorcycle. Caelum stepped out of shadow dressed all in leather and shook his head as I removed my helmet. "You're one of a kind, little sister."

"Don't 'little sister' me. You're younger than I am."

He shrugged.

"Where's your helmet?"

"You dragged me out here so we can commit a B&E and you're going to lecture me about traffic laws?"

"Considering how people drive in Atlanta, you need a helmet."

"*My* nest is full," Caelum said. "Besides, what's the point of having a motorcycle only to wall off the wind from your hair?"

"You could still enjoy the wind and be a lot safer in a convertible," I dismounted.

"And wait in traffic? I thought water liked to keep it moving."

"Water isn't as restless as wind," I said. "Can we do this?

"Not restless, huh?"

We marched up the block across the street from the humane society complex. I reached into my essence, squeezing like I was going to transmogrify.

"You look kind of constipated," Caelum said.

I released my essence, dark water rippling outward to cover my skin head to toe. As soon as my essence settled, I punched him in the shoulder.

"Hey, take it easy on the leather."

"Why're you being such a pain tonight?"

"Besides the date I had to cut short so I could get slapped around by a moody walking puddle?"

"You're just jealous."

His tone sobered. "I am. You have no idea how lucky you are."

"Dylan's the best."

"No, well, maybe, but I meant the flexibility of your element."

I stopped, watching him for a moment. "Each element has its own brand of magic. None of us can bend the path of an arrow or a bullet, and Ignis is the only other shield who can compete with you when it comes to elemental destruction."

He eyed me in silence several minutes. "How shall we do this?"

I cradled a hand folded into a pantomimed gun in my opposite. I adopted a Russian accent. "With style, Boris."

Caelum raised a single brow. "Like moose and squirrel? I thought their names were Rocky and Bullwinkle."

I hit him again, and Caelum laughed.

"You're all masked up, and you've been here once, so you scout the cameras," Caelum said. "I'll take out the power."

"If we're killing the power why do we care about the cameras?"

"Just in case they have some kind of power backup."

We jogged across the street, splitting up on the far sidewalk. I edged onto the property, slipping from shadow to shadow. The scent of cooped-up animals twisted a tiny knife in my gut, but only faint taint added to my discomfort. A slow, methodical circle failed to discover any external cameras, but I did spot a red light from the inside camera watching the front door that had captured me when I'd tried to stop the grendling assault.

What I wouldn't give to be able to throw a little fire bolt like Ignis.

I pushed my essence through one of my hilts and waited. A boom like a shotgun blast shattered the night. Barking followed a moment later—a mix of excitement and challenge—as streetlights went dark and the red light on the camera died.

I slid my blade through the replacement deadbolt and pulled.

The door didn't budge.

I stepped sideways, squinting through the glass into the darkened entrance.

A wind swirled my face as an early warning before Caelum jogged up to meet me. "Problem?"

"Door's not opening."

"Good thing too," he gestured at pinpricks of light reflecting off glass on the counter. "Alarm's still on."

"Did you happen to see an alarm box?"

"No, it's probably cellular."

"Do you think it calls home when it loses power?"

"Only way to know is drop back and watch."

I gestured to the cut lock. "Pretty obvious we were here."

"Sure, if they do more than a drive-by."

I chewed my lip. There was a distinct possibility a patrol cruiser might make only a cursory inspection.

"I'll move the bikes," Caelum jogged away, leaving me standing before locked doors and slowly quieting barks.

I scanned the area, assessing each shadow. A deep, dark corner seemed the best hiding place. I stepped toward it when a prickle rippled my skin.

I retreated to a shadowy vantage across the street, the sound of my Johammer fading up the side street as I waited and waited. A police cruiser turned onto the street with lazy care. It pulled into the circular drive. It stopped, sitting under the awning for several minutes.

The car door opened. An old, thick-bodied officer circled the car. His head swept left and right, following the patch of light cast by his flashlight. The beam stopped in the dark corner I'd considered.

Too close.

He approached the door, speaking into a radio. I held my breath as he tried the door. He flashed the beam into the humane society for another few minutes before meandering back to his car. The cruiser drove away a few minutes later.

"Close one."

I nearly jumped out of my skin. "Curse it, Caelum. Don't do that!"

He chuckled. "That alarm called home when it lost power, but without power to the other sensors we should be good now."

We crossed together, heading straight for the door. My blade slid along the top and bottom of the door, cutting resistance four times. I cringed as I pushed open the door, but no chirp signaled the door opening.

Caelum sidelined to the alarm control. Sparks played about the fingers he used to caress the console. Its LED display went dark.

"Why did you do that?" I hurried toward the sounds of barking. "What if it calls the cops back out here?"

"Guess you'd better hurry th—hells that's a big cat."

I searched the surrounding floor, but didn't see a cat anywhere.

"She's got to feed that monster actual lasagna."

I followed his attention to the orange tabby picture on the counter that had distracted me the morning of the incursion. My lips turned down in a frown for the cat owner's loss.

Black ribbon's gone, label too, but why would they remove those? What's the point in memorializing a passed animal with no indication its dead?

"Weren't we in a hurry?" Caelum asked.

"You're the one that distracted me." I marched away turned toward the kennels.

Caelum adopted a decent impression of Vitae. "If you were a more dedicated shield, you would not allow yourself to be swayed from your mission."

I made talking gestures over one shoulder with an empty hand. I had to cut through the lock sealing off the kennels. It hadn't been locked the last time, but the grendlings had already been inside the humane society.

Animal scent hit me almost as hard as the countless barks and wagging tails. Dogs in all shapes and sizes looked up at me with soul wrenching eyes. Some jumped at their cages, begging for attention.

I wish I had the time to pet them all.

I navigated through the kennels to where I'd destroyed the Arch and lit the flashlight on my phone. Orange chalk colored the floor in a vaguely round smear. I bent closer.

"That picture of Garfield reeks of taint," Caelum said.

I glanced up frowning. "I didn't smell it."

Caelum tapped his nose. His attention shifted to the chalk stain. He frowned. "Is that a sigil?"

I followed his gaze. Squinting, I just made out faint lines of a poorly-executed sigil. Paw smudges and water damage obscured the inexpert marks.

"Amateurish at best."

"Yeah," I nodded. "Even grendlings draw better than this."

"I saw a bucket of sidewalk chalk at the desk," Caelum said.

"So, someone who works here drew the initial runes to open the way for the Wyldfae." The dots arranged themselves into a picture. "We need to chat with the dead cat's owner."

"Not sure overfeeding a cat is really in our jurisdiction."

"First time I came through, the picture said the cat was dead."

"Maybe they removed that to avoid discouraging potential adoptions."

"You smelled taint. I'm betting she's Fae Kissed."

"How do you propose we find her?" Caelum asked. "Normally, I'd suggest checking the personnel files, but they probably don't have paper copies. Can't check the computers with the power off, and we need to clear out before more cops arrive."

"All right, let's go," I said. "I'll just have to follow her home."

"Talk to Ignis or Terrance. Better they stake her out, so you're not seen."

"A smarter plan," Ignis said.

Both Caelum and I whipped around.

Ignis held up a portable police scanner. "It is time to go."

Chapter Eleven

Hard Choices

Quayla

After avoiding police attention, Ignis instructed Caelum and me to head home. He decreed he'd track down the possibly Fae Kissed woman, and that I wasn't to risk myself by staking her out near the Howell Mill Humane Society.

This is my tip. It isn't Ignis's investigation.

A trip to Walmart acquired several drones that fed video to my phone. I set up near the humane society at the Westside Cultural Arts Center, drones positioned to watch street access. When the humane society worker arrived, I marked her car with an essence seed and headed back to Ponds De Leon.

When I felt the seed move, I closed up the florist shop and felt my way to the woman's house. The trail led me to an apartment complex and a litany of curses.

If I'd just risked following her, I could've figure out her apartment or at least the right floor.

I parked my Johammer in an out of the way corner and approached the complex. I caught a whiff of taint, but it proved to be sulfur from the sprinkler system failing to keep the bushes from dying a slow death. Real taint met me inside the complex foyer.

Concentrated taint in the elevator sent my head spinning and gut roiling. Thick stench masked any chance to discern which floor the woman chose.

I sighed.

Only one way to do this.

Starting on the first floor, I strode up one hall, sniffing my way past door after door. A brown Berber carpet worn thinner along the center ran the interior hallway under bright LED bulbs that drove away all shadows. Small, recently dusted portraits dotted the hall.

When I finished that level, I climbed the stairs and went door to door again. Tension knotted my shoulders tighter and tighter the longer I searched. Alone, I had no way to ensure the woman didn't walk right out the front door while I tried to find her.

Eventually, I found an apartment that reeked of faerie.

More than one Fae Kissed seemed an unlikely occurrence, but I couldn't risk making an assumption that would end up causing a scene. When none of the other apartments proved contaminated, I went back to the door, raised my hand to knock and froze.

How should I approach this?

A cat's low growl escaped the apartment door followed at once by an indulgent soprano. "Are you hungry again, Bootsie? Give me a minute."

I decided on a course, drew a Karambit, hid it behind my back and wrapped on the door with my other hand.

"Just a minute."

The door opened a few inches, a bronze chain running across the short woman's forehead. Taint wafted out through the gap. "Hello?"

"Good evening."

"Can I help you?"

"I'm here about the deal."

The woman's brows pinched. "Deal?"

"The deal you made for Bootsie?"

The cat hissed in the background.

"I-I'm not sure w-what you're talking about."

I tightened my grip on the Karambit behind my back, pushing essence into the hilt in case I had to cut the chain. "Your cat, walking around no longer dead."

All color washed out of the woman's face.

"I know you made a deal to bring Bootsie back. If you don't let me in and tell me the who's and how's, I'll report you to," I put as much emphasis as I could into my voice, "the authorities."

The woman's eyes widened. She scrambled to remove the chain and yanked open the door. "No, please don't do that. I'll tell you everything you want to know."

Disappointment warred with triumph.

I emptied and sheathed my hilt before stepping into a world built for a cat. Freestanding play trees and scratching posts led to carpet-covered shelves mounted to walls. A mug tree sat on the breakfast bar festooned with cat collars. Where the space hadn't been built to accommodate a cat, pictures of the woman and her tabby covered nearly every surface. Despite inhaling deeply, I failed to scent a litter box beneath the taint.

"How did you find out?" the woman asked.

"That's not important. Tell me how it happened and who approached you."

She looked at her hands, a blush working into her cheeks. "I thought at first he was interested in me. He was so handsome. I should've known a man like that wouldn't be interested in a woman sobbing into her soup."

"Where was this?"

"Sweet Tomatoes, out on the perimeter."

"Did he openly offer to bring your cat back to life?"

She shook her head. She scooped up the tabby, clutching the cat to her chest like a life preserver. Tears streamed down her face.

"He sat down with me, asked me what was wrong, and he really listened.

"I've had Bootsie since I was a girl. My dad gave him to me for my twelfth birthday—before he and mom died in a fire. Bootsie's all I have left of my parents. When they died—"

Wracking sobs cut off the woman's story.

My own eyes itched. The woman reeked of taint and the cat more so, but I couldn't help wanting to cry with her. She was Fae Kissed. She'd made a deal with a Sidhe to bring back her cat—the most precious thing in the woman's life.

There was no way for me to know the price of animating a cat for the few years it had left. Weak and distraught as she'd been, manipulating a premium from her would've been easy.

I scanned the cat pictures looking for any sign of other friends or family. There weren't any. The woman's only source of love was the tabby, a last gift from her parents at the start of puberty.

If I get my hands on this faerie, I'm going to skin him alive.

When her sobs eased to a more controllable level, I sat on the foot stool across from her, leaned forward taking her hand. "What's your name?"

"Emma."

"I need to find this man. Did he give you a way to contact him?"

She shook her head.

"Did he tell you the marks he made you draw were for taking the other animals?"

Her head shot up. "That had nothing to do with me."

"Did you draw the marks in the play area?"

"Yes, but what's that matter? He just wanted people watching the dogs play to see his art." She held the cat tighter, but it didn't squirm. Her eyes narrowed. "You. I thought I recognized you. You're the one that did that."

"You made a deal with a faerie to bring Bootsie back to life with magic. That drawing opened a door for faeries to steal animals."

"No. I only thought he was dead. The man gave me a medicine to wake Bootsie up. You're the one that hurt all the animals." Emma lurched out the chair, the cat's bulk causing her to teeter. "I'm calling the police."

I interposed myself between Emma and the phone on her kitchen counter. "You work with animals, you know when they're dead."

"No," Emma pressed her face into the cat's fur. "Bootsie was just sick. He wasn't dead. He wasn't dead."

My heart went out to Emma. She had to know her cat died. She wasn't an evil woman who wanted to impose her will on others. She just wanted the companionship of her cat.

Unfortunately, when challenged she'd been all too willing to tell me the story. If she knew the faerie's name, she could give it to others that might have far worse desires.

Emma had to give up the cat as a sign of contrition, then Vilicangelus could grant her absolution, with luck excise the deal and then rewrite her memory.

I watched Emma with her cat for several moments.

There was no way Emma would ever surrender the cat, even if I tried to explain her cat wasn't her cat, but more likely a faerie spirit inhabiting the dead body. If she refused to repent of her actions, I had to kill her. A Fae Kissed could not be allowed to exist. The knowledge she had could lead to disaster.

I have to try anyway.

"Emma, did you tell anyone else about this man?"

"No."

"Did you get his name?"

"No."

I cursed inwardly. I could stake out the restaurant, but without the faerie's name I would be hard pressed to hold this event against him. At best, I'd have to catch him red handed dealing with someone else.

"Emma, you've made a deal with a faerie that could cost your immortal soul. You have to give Bootsie up. It's the only way I can save you."

Her eyes flashed up to me, all color draining from her face. She whipped around, putting her back between me and that cat, soundlessly shaking her head.

"Emma, you have to."

"No," Emma squeaked. "It doesn't matter what happens to me. I can't lose him again."

I drew my hilt, pushing essence through to grow a blade. I didn't want to kill Emma. She'd made a choice that demanded her death, but she didn't deserve it. She'd done what she had for love.

The tabby's yellow eyes fixed on me over Emma's shoulder, not the hard defiant eyes of a faerie but the pleading eyes of an animal that sensed a beating on the horizon.

I stepped closer, wringing the knife hilt I had to drive into Bootsie's skull.

I had to kill the possessed animal.

I had to kill Emma.

I have a duty.

I raised my knife.

I stepped, closing the last of the distance between us. One downward strike would slay the faerie abomination Emma held and hugged and soaked with tears.

I couldn't deliver the blow.

The cat wouldn't live many years longer. When Bootsie passed on, Emma would have time to repent of her actions. With enough time, she could still be saved.

It was my duty, but I couldn't end the sweet woman's life.

"Listen to me, Emma. I was never here. You must never tell breathe a word about any of this to another living soul. Never."

She nodded into the cat's fur.

I fixed Bootsie with my gaze. I didn't have to speak to the faerie in the fur. It knew I was supposed to kill it, and it knew what would happen if it pushed its luck.

I left Emma's apartment, drawing my phone from a pocket. I

got Ignis's voicemail—so much the better. "Ignis, it's Quayla. I checked on that woman from the humane society. I, uh, didn't find...what we expected. No need for you to worry about following her."

The elevator down reeked of taint that made me feel sick, but not as sick as I felt lying to Ignis. I'd failed at my duty.

Maybe Vitae is right about me.

Quayla

Overwhelming nausea woke me from a sound sleep. I bolted upright, preternaturally cold and skin crawling so horribly it left literal waves. I shot a glance at Dylan.

He grunted and tossed a little. He slept deeply enough that my sudden motion didn't wake him. The nausea vanished.

Taint, but come and gone that fast?

I threw off the top sheet and bolted to my nest. "Ani, I think we have a Veil breach."

"Confirmed," Anima said. "I detected a breach several seconds ago at the DeKalb Fur Family Hospital, but it's gone now."

"It's not gone, they destroyed my seed. I'm going to check it out."

"Should I notify the others?"

I glanced at the side table. The clock read a few minutes past three in the morning. "No, I can handle this."

"You said something similar a few days ago," Anima said.

"I didn't know what I was getting myself into." I fastened my jeans and scooped my backup Karambit hilts from the lingerie drawer. "This time I do."

I descended the stairs as fast as I could while taking care to land as lightly as possible, so as not to wake Mrs. Cox. I raced down the block, leapt onto my motorcycle and put on my helmet.

I hadn't managed to invoke my baby's purr before Vitae's voice exploded out of a disgruntled looking bronze angel. "Aquaylae, you will wait where you are until backup arrives at your location."

"Vitae, there's an incursion in progress. We have no idea what's happening, or who they're harming. There's no time to waste waiting while you divert someone here."

"Terrance wouldn't be required to deviate his route much to pick you up," Anima said.

"He's out in Dallas, almost half an hour away." I put my motorcycle into gear.

The engine died.

I shot the angel a dirty look.

The statuette glowered over folded arms, one raised foot frozen in mid tap.

"Mortals could be in danger," I said. "At least have someone meet me en route."

"No," Vitae snapped. "Your judgement can't be trusted in this."

"I'm a full shield, Vitae, not some green fledgling!"

"And if you were based here where you should be, you'd be central to all disturbances," Vitae shot back.

"Fine." I ripped off my helmet. "If I can't drive, I'll fly."

"Absolutely not," Vitae said.

"Shield Aquaylae, your form is particularly visible at night," Anima said.

Terrance's deep baritone escaped the statue. "Little sister."

I froze, essence already compressed halfway to winged escape.

"I will be at your home in ten minutes," Terrance said.

How?

"Please wait for me. I would rather no harm became you."

"I can look after myself."

"You proved that this week," Vitae snapped.

"Bide a few minutes. We can look after each other," Terrance said. "Unless you'd rather team up with our Vitae."

I shot the bronze archangel a nasty look. "Not a chance."

I leapt off of my baby. I folded my arms, not to warm myself in the muggy morning but to keep from flying apart—or just flying. I paced up and down the sidewalk.

I can't believe this. I'm a full shield. I called in the breach. I shouldn't be sitting here waiting for a babysitter. People could be dying right now!

A decades-old evergreen pickup, raised several feet off the ground, pulled to a stop behind Dylan's car. I glowered at the truck.

Terrance reached across the seat and rolled down the window. "Are we not in a hurry, little sister?"

Damn it, he's right.

Terrance pushed the door open as far as his fingers stretched. I jerked it the rest of the way and climbed Mount Pickup onto the old, duct-taped leather seats. Terrance's truck roared forward as I cast around for a seatbelt.

When digging into the seat didn't excavate one, I leveled an arched brow at him. "Where are your seatbelts?"

"They were not required when this truck was built."

"Were wafers walking upright?"

Terrance's laugh carried the warmth of rich farming soil.

"Aren't you our earth phoenix? Shouldn't you care about the environment?"

He pulled the truck onto Cobb Parkway. "I have cared for this Earth centuries beyond your time upon it, little sister."

"If driving this fossil fuel-guzzling monstrosity is how you've cared—"

Warning undercut his tone. "Take care, Aquaylae."

My tirade froze in my mouth. Terrance seldom if ever called me by my full name.

He pointed to a small dent just above the windshield over my seat. "That is where my so-named *monstrosity* cracked open the skull of a wyvern. My vehicle is built of steel and like myself is scarred from many victories over the Tainted Ones."

A wyvern?

"Were you alone?"

"Other than the beast."

I couldn't hide my amazement. "You slew a wyvern by yourself?"

Terrance chuckled as they drove up an onramp to I-95. "When you've served as long as I, you learn much about the limits of a given shield."

All by himself. I couldn't even handle a few grendling tribes.

"Still, it was reckless of me, little sister. A Shield contains five of us for a reason. Each shield brings complimentary elements. Our strengths protect weaknesses in the others." Terrance studied me several moments. "You needn't fight alone to prove your worth."

"Vitae treats me like an unskilled, untrained fledgling."

"Vitae has seen many years, many water phoenixes. He is correct in asserting that you have not shown what you are truly capable of becoming. More training, more working with the rest of us and more confidence in your true value will help—as would less time spent recreating with mortals."

I folded my arms and stared at a crack in the dashboard.

By time we arrived, an orange and yellow conflagration covered an entire city block. Firefighters worked in teams to halt spreading flames.

I pounded my fist against the dashboard. "We're too late."

Terrance rolled down his window and lifted his nose. "Faerie fire. These mortals are ill equipped to fight this battle. You must help them."

"Me? Not us?"

"The mortals wield water as their weapon, not earth. Have you never faced faerie fire?"

I shook my head. "Just the normal kind."

"Do you smell the taint in the wind? The shadow of their magic?"

I struggled to rotate the crank on my door that lowered the

window. Frustration at the foreign motion mounted, until I gave it up and threw open the door. I lifted my nose.

Thick taint left me choking.

"Yes, a very powerful Sidhe," Terrance said.

"I don't understand. First, they're abducting animals, now they're burning down shelters?"

"Understanding will come." Terrance gestured. "Help the mortals first."

The fire engulfed the shelter's block. Small fires had already spread to the closest building across the southern cross street. The fire department had the block surrounded, but even as I watched, two engine companies were forced to surrender their cornering positions and pull back another half block from the heat. Another two companies, supported by ladder trucks, held their position, spraying a four-story office building high and low.

With that much water in the air, I could transmog and smother the fire.

I grabbed the oh-shit handle, preparing my precarious descent.

Terrance seized my shoulder. "You needn't draw attention to yourself."

"You said I need to help them!"

"You do."

"From here?"

"Yes."

I barely restrained a scream. Outside my natural form, my aqua kinesis abilities remained extremely limited. "The only way I can put out that fire is—"

"Something spectacular, like swallowing the flames?" Terrance gestured. "Taking such action would reveal our kind to the world."

Well back from the firefighters, news vans parked interspaced by utility trucks.

I scowled. "We don't have time for this all this cloak and dagger. We need to do something now."

"The mortals have the blaze in check for the moment."

"That doesn't make this the time for a lesson."

Terrance pursed his lips. "Better the fire causes a little more property damage and you learn this lesson than the alternative."

"Better than killing the fire now and requesting a few rewrites?"

Disappointment crept into Terrance's gaze. "Yes, Aquaylae, either you or I could defeat these flames in a spectacular display."

Oh, blighted hells, he called me by my full name again.

My gut filled with hollow cold. I dropped my eyes.

Terrance drew my chin back up. "The power of our Divine Ones is not infinite. Every time we rely on them rather than doing our duty to protect the secrets of our existence, we risk Faery recruiting the one Fae Kissed that pushes their influence to critical mass.

"Be sure you are hearing me, Aquaylae." Terrance's expression sobered. "That is why we moved closer to the mortals. That is why we continue to insist living outside the sanctum is better. This world of billions and their access to instant communications makes the possibility of hitting critical mass that much more dangerous."

Terrance gestured, and I followed his gaze out the window to the mortal fireman throwing their lives into the path of a magical force they had no hope of stopping.

"Are there any among them that wouldn't make a deal with the faeries for the ability to stop this enchanted inferno from consuming the city?" Terrance asked. "If humanity learned of the power the Sidhe offered, that power wouldn't just corrupt the criminals. Our foes would usurp the souls of all of our charges. The Sidhe would pervert Creation to their purposes. They'd realize their revenge and whatever other motivations drive their need to usurp Creation."

I stared, seeing—no feeling—the weight of his words.

Chapter Twelve

Fighting Faerie Fire

Quayla

I returned my attention to the fire, searching the flames for ideas on how to satisfy Terrance's requirements. Taint undercut the thick smoke and acrid stink of burned plastics.

A loud crack snatched my attention to one side. Power lines fell from their former heights onto wet pavement. Thick, uninsulated electrical wires snapped and writhed, their melted ends resembling slender vipers' heads.

A moment later, the entire block went dark, killing the writhing of the downed power line and leaving only the fire and emergency vehicle lights to illuminate the scene.

My head shook back and forth. The mortals had no chance at all to prevail against the magical conflagration without our help. Terrance was right about revealing ourselves, but showing myself seemed the only way to extinguish the fire. This situation offered no alternatives, Vilicangelus or Summus would just have to track down and rewrite all the witnesses. "I don't have a choice."

"You do. Why can the mortals not slay these flames?"

"They're bolstered by magic."

"Correct."

"How am I supposed to steal magic from fire?" I asked.

Terrence turned fully toward me, brows knit until they joined together. The force of his personality hit me like an avalanche. "You are not a witch, Aquaylae, but neither are you stupid."

That's thrice. Did I piss him off somehow? Insulting his truck?

I liked Terrance better than any other shields, but he wasn't the only one getting pissed off. My reply sounded petulant even to me. "Then what am I exactly?"

"Young and lazy."

"I'm not lazy!"

"Your thinking is. You look upon this problem and search for the way Aquaylae might defeat the whole and save the day. You must think beyond ego. Find a solution that relies on cooperation."

"I don't care about being the hero!"

"All young do. They think how they are different from their elders but feel overshadowed and thus wish to stand out even more." He swept a hand toward the blaze. "This is not a problem for only Aquaylae."

I scanned the fire crews, concentrating my search around the chiefs coordinating the doomed battle. "I don't see Ignis."

Anima's voice drew both of our attentions to the bronze statuette with arms and wings outstretched. "Ignis is engaged with another Veil breach. Vitae has instructed me to remind you that you are forbidden from showing yourself."

I glanced at the news crews, then Terrance and then the figurine. It would be difficult, but surely two divine phoenixes could rewrite the wafers before word spread.

Unless the Sidhe are waiting in the wings to create a bevy of Fae Kissed. Is that what this is all about? Manipulating me into giving them converts?

"I can't. I don't know how to stop this without transmoging."

"If you do not, these flames will not cease," Terrance said. "The power behind them could consume the city."

"Then how do you expect me to contend with that kind of power?"

Terrance smiled. "By employing mind and essence without exiting my truck."

How in Creation do I do that?

A quarter of the southern block was aflame. Efforts to prevent fire from spreading to the office building kept the fire at bay, but the magical flames would not be denied forever. Hoses snaked through the dark, eventually latching onto hydrants to feed their sprays.

If I could get to the hydrants, I might be able to dope the supply lines.

The corners of my lips drooped.

I'd have to get to all of them, and Terrance won't let me leave the truck.

Another news van pulled to a stop. A flash of its headlights caught in mist spraying out of a hydrant connection valve. A rainbow flashed to life over the carpet of fog and smoke. It vanished a moment later when the van's headlights cut out.

Mist?

I scanned hydrant positions around us.

"What brightens your expression?" Terrance asked.

"Hush, I'm thinking."

Enough combined fog, mist and smoke surrounded the firefighters to camouflage an additional mist. Moving a thin cloud of my essence shouldn't take anywhere near the strength of moving enough water to extinguish the flames themselves.

If I can hold together a mist where water emerges from the nozzles, I might be able to enchant the whole.

I set a hand on my lap and cupped my palm. My offhand drew out a Karambit hilt. I bore down on my insides, squeezing a palmful of essence into my hand in the same way as I extruded the blade in my other hand.

I glanced at Terrance.

The intensity of his regard unsettled me.

I can't show him any weakness.

I hate severing my essence. That my life forces me to painfully cut away pieces of myself isn't exactly a great endorsement for life as a shield. I kept my cringe internal and sliced my watery knife along the open palm. A painful tearing severed the water from my body. A check ensured Terrance hadn't noticed my squeamishness as I raised my hand into the gap between door and truck.

This would be easier if Caelum were here.

I blew softly, my breath tingling along the essence.

A shimmering mist lifted off of my hand into the night. My breath didn't propel the cloud as much as offer me a mental lever. I dampened the glow around my satellite self, willed it dispersed enough to float, and concentrated on moving the vapor to the nearest hose team.

The focus required made the short journey feel like miles. Eventually, the cloud's edge cut across a hose stream. The blow of sudden pressure against me knocked the wind from my lungs. I grunted, gathering the scattered mist for another attempt.

Permeable, but strong, a mesh of mist.

My second attempt hit as hard as the first but braced for the impact I managed to slide my essence around the nozzle's mouth. I closed my eyes against the pressure of the pounding water and willed my essence to gift its magical nature to the countless gallons shooting out toward the fire.

Power washed out of me, stealing my breath. My energy plummeted at an alarming rate.

"It's working, little sister."

The pride in his voice made me grin.

Under attack by enchanted water, the formerly defiant fire weakened and fled. I pushed more energy out to my severed self and braced myself for more pain.

Extrude.

Sever.

Launch and shepherd the new cloud to another hose team.

Repeat.

Each subsequent team I helped fought the inferno further from Terrance's truck. With each mist, controlling them grew harder and more exhausting. Inserting the third into a stream nearly cost me all of them.

I pushed another puddle of essence into my palm.

"Do not over extend yourself."

I spoke through gritted teeth. "You told me I was more powerful than I realized."

"Muscles are not made with a single trip to the gym."

I glared at him and severed the fourth bit of essence. It took a lot of power and all of my will to move the last mist into position, but I'd be damned if I was going to let him think me weak as well as lazy.

An hour later, I slumped back against the truck seats.

The firefighters had gained the upper hand.

I'd done it.

"Well done, little sister." Terrance patted my leg.

I wanted to chastise him for his condescension, but the relatively small accomplishment had sapped all of my strength.

Terrance probably didn't mean it that way anyway.

"Anima, mortal authorities can handle things from here."

"Great work, Terra," Vitae said.

"Aquaylae deserves all the credit," Terrance said. "She thwarted this assault all on her own."

Both of us watched the statue as we awaited the next message relayed through the angel network. None came.

Ungrateful bastard.

Terrance turned over the engine.

I pushed strength into my voice. "We're not staying? What if the faerie responsible reverses what I've done?"

"I don't think he'll reveal himself to us. He's had his fun. Getting caught at mischief would undermine any reputation garnered from his attack."

I frowned.

Terrance's warm laugh returned. "You've dealt little with more powerful faeries in your years here, haven't you?"

"You guys wouldn't let me." Anger fueled my turn toward him. "Vitae insists I'm inferior while you and Ignis insist on taking care of the hard stuff without me."

Terrance frowned. After several streets worth of silence, his mouth twisted in mild disgust. "You know, I believe you are right. We do share fault in this."

Someone else owning up shouldn't have felt quite so good. The sudden rush of warmth bolstered me. My thoughts turned to the shelter fire.

How many animals died or were carried away and why?

"Terrance? Why would Wyldfae steal animals?"

"Besides for a snack?"

"They've taken a lot of animals for just food," I said. "There's more going on."

Terrance snatched glances at me while keeping an eye on the growing traffic. "Back at the fire, your elegant solution proved both your capabilities and your intelligence. It seems fitting to leave you to work out this problem for yourself."

"I know Vitae doesn't think the animals are important, but what if what's going on is bigger than it appears? What if I don't figure it out before it's too late?"

Terrance offered me a smile as he pulled his truck into a Waffle House. "Well then, little sister, if you think you need help rather than handling this on your own, I am glad to offer you any assistance you need while we eat. You need to replenish your strength."

Terrance forced me to eat before returning me home. We didn't come up with any answers before he dropped me off at my Johammer, but his support made me feel more capable of working out the problem. As the sun usurped his lover's control, Terrance wished me a good rest, pulled his truck around and headed back toward the city proper.

I turned toward the three-story walk-up, but hesitated. The

faerie had destroyed a lot of my DeKalb seeds and several of the others. I could set out an invitation for Ralein, but there was another, faster way to acquire his skills. All I had to do was find the Goblin Market.

I'll get answers about the animal thefts too, maybe even rescue some.

I dropped onto my motorcycle's seat. "Ani, do we know the present location of the Goblin Market?"

"You do not need to visit the Goblin Market," Vitae said.

"Why're you being an ass, Vitae? I'm just trying to do my duty."

Silence.

"No, Quayla," Anima said. "We don't know the Market's location right now."

Caelum will know.

I started my bike.

"What are your intentions," Vitae asked.

"I'm going to work," I snapped.

"You are not permitted to associate with the faerie without supervision," Vitae said.

Screw you too, Vitae.

The statue glowered at me.

Traffic had my thumbs drumming in minutes. Lingering anger and rude drivers raised my stress levels until I made an impromptu stop at a small local bakery. An éclair filled with heavenly cream, a hot Chai and three muffins distracted me from stress and sweetened my disposition. I stopped once to gift a last muffin to a homeless woman with cloth-wrapped feet, before arriving at Circlestone's corporate headquarters.

Circlestone corporate campus spread across a two-by-two block section of Atlanta, just north of downtown. Office buildings rose along the sidewalks, leaving the center for parking and a large park. I parked in a visitor space and crossed the park to the headquarters' entry foyer.

Wafers in business attire drifted across marble floors decorated with Circlestone's logo. They trod carelessly across the thick outer circle without stepping into the inner ring. Double lines split the inner circle, connecting the outer ring to an inner hub. Within the wheel's hub eight stones the size of grave markers surrounded a square of stone. Between the spokes eight larger stones mimicked those at the center.

A long line of mortals queued up for fresh coffee, checking email on their phones as they waited impatiently but queued so as not to stand inside the corporate logo.

I crossed to the information desk.

A woman with curlier hair than what had come with my new body smiled up at me. "May I help you?"

"Quayla Buckler here to see Caelum Kite."

"The purpose of your visit?"

"We're family."

Building security extended her hand. "If you would please fill out the visitor's log for me, I'll message Mister Kite."

A woman's voice caressed my ears. The tone floated on a rich texture normally associated with sultry movie stars. "We'll make an exception this time."

I shifted from the confused expression of the lady behind the counter to the confident smile of the luxurious voice's owner. An expensive skirt suit of seafoam green clung to her willowing but robust figure.

Wow.

Eyes the deep blue of Crater Lake in fall glanced self-consciously away. The fair woman seemed to master her confidence, pushing dark almost blue hair out of her face and raising intelligent eyes to meet my own. "Caelum is tied up in a meeting at the moment. He has another with Mister Heffernan directly after."

I chewed my lip.

I needed Caelum's help and getting to know the beautiful woman better wouldn't be bad either...if I hadn't been in a happy relationship with Dylan. "Oh, I guess there's no reason to sign in if he's too busy to see me."

"Nonsense, if you're willing to wait in Mister Heffernan's office, you'll be able to catch a quick word while Caelum awaits the boss."

"All right, I'm Quayla."

"I'm Viviane." The woman beamed. "I overheard you introduce yourself to security, and of course I know your name from Caelum's stories. Are you two dating?"

"No," I said. "Siblings of a sort."

Viviane led me to an elevator. Other employees stepped from our way, warmly acknowledging the attractive woman. Once inside the car, Viviane waved a security badge near a sensor and pressed the button for the top floor.

"Quayla is a beautiful name, what's its origin?" Viviane asked.

I shrugged. "I know it's old."

"Caelum didn't know either. He said he'd ask, well, I assume one of your parents."

"Father doesn't communicate with us directly very often."

Viviane smiled. "Family is never easy. So, what do you do, Quayla?"

"I'm just a florist."

"That's right. You did the table bouquets for this week's fundraiser. They were really beautiful."

"Thank you."

"You know, I'm just Mister Heffernan's assistant, but having your company on retainer sounds like good business, and we'd get to see you more often."

Butterflies fluttered through my stomach.

We?

"Ponds de Leon Flowers isn't mine," I lied. "I just work there, do arrangements and such."

Viviane smiled. "Then maybe we should steal you."

The elevator deposited us on an uppermost floor, though not

the very top as I'd assumed. Viviane led me to glass doors, scanning her security badge once more.

I stepped through the held doors. A long mahogany desk stretched across the far wall beneath the Circlestone logo. A robust blonde looked up from the desk's left half, showing off dimples. "You don't look like Mister Heffernan's next appointment."

"No, but close. This is Quayla, Caelum's sister," Viviane said.

The blonde leaned forward. "Really?"

A chirp wiped the hungry look from the blonde's expression. She leaned back, tapping her ear. "Mister Heffernan's office."

I glanced around for an unobtrusive seat. Freestanding glass islands haloed the reception area, each containing Celtic, Norse or Pict artwork. More art rested beneath the glass tabletops that separated comfortable-looking furniture. I settled into a chair which tried to swallow me in soft cushions.

"Quayla?" Viviane touched a small device on her belt. The twin mahogany doors to the inner office opened outward. "Coming?"

I checked the blonde for objection.

"No sir, we don't have any appointment openings left this year." She rolled her eyes, glanced at me and tilted her head toward the open door. "I can put you on our waiting list."

I struggled out of the chair and hurried to follow, entering a colossal office that stole my breath.

"I think it's a bit ostentatious personally," Viviane said. "Dunham could've gotten a decent portrait of a lake or maybe an ocean view and called the décor complete."

Priceless ancient weapons hung every few feet. Equally expensive art and open display stands cradling artifacts broke up the sparse executive space.

"Caelum will be with you in a few minutes. Make yourself at home." Viviane stepped through a hidden door behind a large desk.

The door clicked shut before I could object. I stood uncertain and unmoving. Beneath my feet, a thick Egyptian rug brightened the grey marble tiling the space.

Well, she told me to make myself at home. So long as I don't break anything, looking around can't hurt.

I eased toward the nearest artifacts, conscious of my still foreign balance.

A spoked metal wheel engraved with Celtic runes and pictograms drew my fingers. A soft tingle shot up my arms when I touched it, startling me. I jerked my fingers away.

A Celtic Wheel of the Year, but why does old magic linger within the wheel?

Markings to match the Wheel formed a circle on the slab behind the artifact. My eyes shifted to the wall behind the desk then back to the Wheel and accompanying ring. Together, they seemed the inspiration for Circlestone's logo. Even more symbols were arranged around the composite logo.

Symbolism gave way to runes as my fingers crossed to a second slab. Seven burial markers dominated the stone. One stood sentry at their arranged pinnacle. Two trios formed squat triangles below and to either side of their sentry, almost forming a vague mountain range. My fingers traced the runes carved into the topmost.

Father, water, unbalance and death. An ancestor?

I touched the other six in turn, unable to resist their eerie draw.

Brother, water, unbalance and death?

My eyes shot to the topmost, confirming the surprising epiphany.

You were all murdered, drowned.

My fingers traipsed to the water rune.

A deep basso brought me up short. "Captivating, aren't they?"

I snatched my hand back. "I'm sorry, Viviane told me to wait here for Caelum, I didn't mean—"

Circlestone's CEO loomed larger than even Terrance, with matching warm brown eyes that drove into me like spikes. A black sports coat and evergreen dress shirt slimmed the massive man without hiding his muscular build.

Voice, appearance, even dress all proclaim his power. There's warmth in his eyes though and a lust for life. Sharing this man's life would mean constant competition for his attention.

His open collar exposed a golden ring with matching chain resting on a bed of Celtic tattoos the dark of woad and thick curls of chest hair.

His laugh proved as powerful as the rest of him. "Stone's remarkably resilient, not that wind or water can't wear it down over time. It's a pleasure to meet you, Quayla. I'm Dunham Heffernan."

"I didn't tell you my name."

Dunham tapped his watch. "Viviane texted me you were here."

"Oh, right."

"Caelum will be here in a moment, but I wanted to thank you personally for what you've done for me."

I blinked at him.

"The flowers?" He seated himself on the edge of his desk. "Feel free to keep exploring. I should probably donate them, but I just can't bear to part with them."

I turned back to the burial markers. "I can understand. Where did you come by this?"

"I inherited it."

"Really?" I continued down the wall to a third display. A series of five standing stones rested against the wall atop matching base stones. Runes of a different style formed a wide base circle then wove their way up the standing stone's face. "Were you related to them?"

"Yes."

I glanced back to the burial markers. "I'm sorry."

"Why would you apologize?"

I shrugged. "Death is never easy."

"They died a very long time ago," Dunham said.

Viviane escorted Caelum into the office.

How did she get out there?

"Hey, uh, sis. I wasn't expecting you," Caelum said.

"Mister Heffernan was just telling me about his artifacts while I waited."

Caelum turned to his boss. "I'm sorry I'm late, sir. Cliff in accounting stopped me to talk about some numbers."

Dunham gestured. "Entertaining the young lady was most distracting."

"If you'll give me a moment to see her on her way, I'm all yours." Caelum crossed the office to me, eyes sweeping the burial wall. He lowered his voice. "What's going on?"

"I need your help," I whispered.

"I'm a little busy here."

"Fine, just tell me where to find the...," I glanced at Dunham. "...where to find the Market and I'll leave."

Caelum stiffened. "No."

I pressed my lips together.

He's not going to tell me openly? Vitae convince him I'm useless too?

I forced a smile and strode toward the exit. "Thank you for your time and hospitality, Mister Heffernan."

Dunham smiled. "We'll see you at our upcoming picnic I hope?"

"I did invite her," Caelum said.

"Good. Viviane will see you out."

I fell into step behind Viviane.

"Oh, Quayla, I never answered your original question." Dunham gestured to the burial markers. "I brought them over from their original resting place in Essex."

A sudden blizzard submerged me in ice. I glanced at the Wheel. A tenuous word fought its way free of my lips. "When?"

"They died in 1863."

The world spun around me. Emotions threw me up and down, left and right as if I were on the Batman ride at Six Flags. I held onto my composure with white-knuckled intensity and tried to reason my way off the rollercoaster.

Plenty of people died that year in Essex. This has nothing to do with Headingham.

I glanced toward Caelum. My fellow shield watched me with intense interest.

"Th-thank you again." I fled.

Chapter Thirteen

Seeking Answers

Ignis

Ignis walked up the apartment building's stairs. He hadn't followed immediately after the woman from the humane society. There wasn't any need. The likelihood that two Fae Kissed lived in the building to confuse the trail seemed pretty slim.

He entered the foyer, opening his senses. The taint from her lingered, concentrated at a bank of mailboxes before trailing to the elevator. Ignis strolled past the mailboxes, his gaze shifting to note the apartment number when the taint concentrated.

He crossed to an ashtray next to the building's entrance, pushed a finger deep under the sand and extruded a seed of essence. Rather than ride an elevator car filled with nauseating taint, he climbed the plain concrete stairs. The seed would warn him if she left before he reached her apartment.

Quayla had related her suspicions that the wafer had drawn the runes to open the Arch in exchange for her cat's life. She'd later recanted her theory, but something about the tone of the message felt wrong, making the duty before him more than a little unpleasant.

I can't imagine how sad must a person's life be that they'd sell their soul for a cat, but it's just the kind of sob story that would break Quayla's heart.

The taint concentrated on the door which matched the mailbox. A cat's low growl escaped beneath the door.

A sugary, high-pitched woman's voice followed from deeper in the apartment. "Bootsie? What's wrong, baby?"

Ignis knocked.

"Just a minute."

Ignis took a deep breath, settling on a story to gain entry.

A woman's face appeared beneath the door chain, her head topping out at five feet. "Can I help you?"

That she'd opened the door, even chained, rather than using the peephole spoke to the safety of the neighborhood. The wash of taint confirmed that the woman before him was potentially the most dangerous person in the building.

Ignis produced his badge. "Ignis Round, I'd like to ask you a few questions about the break-in at the humane society."

"Which one?"

"Howell Mill," Ignis said.

"No, the first break-in or the second?"

"The first," Ignis said.

"Well, I already told the cops everything I know about that horrible woman."

"Sometimes witnesses remember things after the fact. May I come in?"

"I suppose." She pushed the door closed and opened it again once the chain had been moved out of the track. "Come on in."

Ignis entered. The apartment had been set up to cater to the cat he'd seen in the humane society picture.

An angry hiss preceded an orange rocket streaking across the room. Ignis pushed the door shut hard. The cat stopped, looked daggers at Ignis and growled.

"It's all right, Bootsie," She pushed hair from her face. "Sorry, Mister Round, Bootsie, um, doesn't like people."

"I understand."

"Would you like to sit?"

"No, thank you."

The woman scooped up her cat and sat in a chair—her upper half nearly disappearing completely behind the mammoth feline. "I haven't remembered anything new. What did you want to ask?"

"I want to know where you learned about the faeries that made a bargain with you in exchange for your cat's life."

All color washed out of the woman's already pale complexion.

The cat bristled.

"H-how, w-what are you talking about?"

"The animal in your arms isn't Bootsie. It's a faerie inhabiting the body of your cat."

Bootsie hissed.

She hugged the cat closer to her. "N-no, that's not right. I've had Bootsie since I was twelve. I don't know who you are, but I don't want you here anymore."

Ignis closed the distance, towering over the pair. "You drew marks on the kennel floor. You let the faeries inside. You're the reason so many animals died."

Bootsie struggled harder to get away as the woman's grip tightened. She wiped tumbling tears off in the cat's fur. "I-no. It was th-that woman. The one who broke in."

"She was there to stop the faeries. Tell me the faerie's name that offered you the deal and anything you know about their actions and intentions?"

"I don't know what you're talking about. Just leave us alone."

Bootsie wriggled free and leapt away from Ignis and the woman.

Ignis sprang over a loveseat and snatched the cat up by the scruff of its neck. It twisted and curled, hissing and turning to slash Ignis with its claws.

The woman was on her feet. "Let him go. He doesn't like that."

Ignis whirled. "This is not your cat. Your cat died, didn't he?"

Her hard expression disintegrated. Her head fell forward, bob haircut curtaining her sobs as she nodded.

"Now that you've admitted he died, I ask you to willingly surrender him as recompense for what you've done."

"No!" She bolted forward and wrenched the cat out of Ignis's hand. "I love him."

"You loved Bootsie, not this thing."

"Get out. I don't want you here."

Ignis softened his tone. "If you aren't willing to surrender him, there is nothing more I can do to help you."

"I won't." She turned her back, shielding the cat from Ignis. "Not ever."

"You've obviously got a loving heart. Yours was a good and gentle soul, but you traded it away and the countless animal lives for this travesty of Creation. I want to help you, but you have to give up the cat." He placed his hands on her shoulders. "Please, let it go."

Her head shook back and forth, silent except for soft sobs.

So be it.

Ignis gathered his essence.

The cat went wild, howling, hissing and clawing at his owner. She struggled to keep a grip as if letting him go might cause her to lose him forever.

Ignis wrapped white hot wings around them and released his essence into them in a swirling firestorm. When nothing but ashes remained, he swept his wings once to spread the ashes through the apartment and transformed back to his human form. He looked down at the singed carpet.

She refused to repent. I hate it, but she left me no choice.

He turned to go, burning flesh and taint still thick in his nostril. He intensified his essence to burn away the smell, but when he reverted his essence to flesh the scent of faerie magic remained.

Ignis crossed to the breakfast bar. A tree mug supporting a 'free collars' sign held several dozen cat collars. Several others lay on their surface next to a glue gun, containers of glitter and a pile of fake gems. Ignis's nose itched.

He picked up a gem to find a mote of faerie essence hidden inside behind a thin layer of crafting glue. He exchanged the gem for one of the glitter decorated collars. The runes for a leech spell and several other incomplete marks scrawled around the collar's circumference.

Not so innocent after all.

Ignis cursed inwardly. He'd cremated Bootsie and its collar. There wasn't any way to tell after the fact if Bootie's collar had sported runes meant to catch the life leeched away from other animals by the partially finished collars.

He incinerated the lot.

Caelum

Caelum frowned at the closed door.

"She looked troubled," Dunham said. "I hope it wasn't anything I said."

"What? Oh, no, sir. She asked to borrow something valuable, and I told her no." Caelum turned back to the burial marker, hiding his uneasy expression by virtue of turning his back on Dunham. "You said this is from 1863?"

"Yes, why?"

Caelum frowned at the stonework. "The construction style is much older than that, possibly going back to Roman times."

Dunham brightened. "Are you a student of history, Caelum?"

Caelum chuckled. "Got a grumpy old teacher who always tried to shove that kind of stuff in my head despite my insistence no one needed to know such things anymore."

Dunham sucked his lip. "Need, no, but such knowledge offers us a glimpse into lives most can only imagine."

"Do you know how they all drowned?" Caelum asked.

"Your teacher was *very* thorough."

Caelum imitated Vitae. "Life is history reborn."

Dunham chuckled.

"So, what can I do for you, sir?"

"I keep an eye out for special talents. Most of my employees are out for an easy buck, looking for a way to get ahead through sidestepping work or rolling busses over their team members. You're a hard worker, the kind of employee I'd like to work alongside more closely—maybe see how you handle a crisis."

"With humor—some of it good, but I always battle through."

"Would you be amenable to travel?" Dunham asked.

Caelum frowned. "I'm afraid not. Fear of flying."

Dunham's brow rose.

"Nobody's perfect." Caelum shrugged.

"Very well, we could arrange for a private car to take you places."

"I can't be away for long. I have a practically ancient relative that nearly strokes out every time I even talk about going too far away."

"You're making it difficult to promote you," Dunham said. "Couldn't Quayla look in on this relative?"

"They don't get along."

He's going to promote me? To what?

Caelum looked around the office.

Too bad there's no way Vitae would allow me more job responsibility, let alone travel.

Viviane entered. She glanced at Caelum, peering into his eyes with an apprehension possibly connected to Caelum's proximity to the very expensive wall. "Your next appointment is here if you're finished."

"We haven't gotten as far as I'd have liked. Please reschedule Mister Kite for another visit." Dunham gestured Caelum toward the door. "Let's both take time to think of ways to achieve all we desire, and we'll meet up again to discuss our options."

Caelum let himself be led from the office, glancing back at the death mural. Dunham shook Caelum's hand once more. The CEO greeted his next appointment with handshakes and smiles. He disappeared with them back inside his office.

That's one incredible boss.

Caelum cursed under his breath.

I've got to catch Quayla before she gets herself killed...again.

The elevator took Caelum down to his office. He stopped opposite his very attractive assistant. "I've got an appointment with a perspective investor. I'll be back late."

She tapped her keyboard a few times. "I don't see an appointment."

"Last minute." Caelum hurried back to the elevator, lamenting that his assistant's value prevented him from including her in his series of lovers. There was something about her far beyond her outward appearance that convinced him they'd share a lot of fun before his real life forced him to let her down gently.

That's where Quayla makes her mistake. She's looking for happily ever after. Even if everything goes without a hitch, it still ends.

The elevator dropped Caelum in the lobby. He stepped into the foyer and lifted his nose. The scent of fresh coffee called him like a siren of the deep, but he abandoned his pleasures to chase Quayla's scent. At the parking garage, he declined to track her up to wherever she parked, circling instead to the complex exit.

Quayla's little white Johammer eased into view.

He waved her down.

She glared at him over her handlebars. He held up one finger and crossed to the first floor motorcycle parking. He checked to make sure his black case was still in the bike's saddle bags and slid his motorcycle up next to Quayla's electric jelly bean.

"I thought you weren't going to help me," she said tartly.

"You'd have gone anyway," he said.

"You're damned right I would have."

"I'm here to keep you from dying again."

"Damn it, Caelum, I'm as capable as you or the others."

"Maybe, but why chance letting Vitae lecture you again?"

A horn honked behind them.

"Where are we going?"

"Head to headquarters. We'll hoof it from there."

Quayla's eyes widened. "The Goblin Market set up right under our noses?"

Caelum smiled. "Not exactly."

Quayla

Caelum and I dismounted in front of a maintenance closet in sight of the elevator up to our Shield. He produced a key and let us in to a tiny room clogged with brooms, garbage cans and other detritus.

I frowned.

Caelum flashed me a smile and picked his way through the mess—feet never touching the floor. He pushed on a section of upper molding. A spring mechanism pushed out a short strip. Caelum pulled the disguised lever down. Clacks and clunks preceded the wall sliding out of view to reveal a small room stocked for launching a tactical assault.

"Caelum, why—"

He flashed me a grin and held up three fingers in a Boy Scout salute. "I solemnly swear—no...ah! Be prepared."

Caelum picked up a collapsible hand truck, yanked a lever inside the room and exited as the doors closed behind him. He cherry-picked his way out of the mess and closed the doors. "Come on."

"Where are we headed?"

"Georgia World Congress Center...more or less."

The afternoon air pressed against us. Unwelcome humidity wrapped the heat around us like a damp electric blanket. Caelum swirled a breeze across his face.

I lifted my brows. "Do you know how Vitae would react if he saw you do that?"

Caelum adjusted his voice into an eerie imitation of Vitae. "You are a shield, created with a duty. That duty does not afford you the right to waste your essence on something as insignificant as personal comfort. I expect you to grow up and have a stick surgically inserted in your buttocks this instant."

I laughed. "That last sentence was a bit off."

"I got the gist." Caelum smiled. "Besides, it made you laugh. Things back to normal with Dylan?"

"Yeah." Memory of his fingers exploring my new body birthed a smile. I chuckled. "He asked me to marry him."

Caelum's brows rose. "Really? What did you say?"

"I didn't, really. He thought marriage would free me from being a shield, like I'm here on a work visa or something."

"It doesn't work like that," Caelum said.

"That's what I told him."

Caelum's expression became distant, and we marched across Atlanta in silence. After my early morning and exhausting day, the heat combined to make our walk tougher than I expected. Even though perspiration was a waste of my essence, I allowed a light sweat to exit my exposed flesh. Caelum shifted his breeze to include me and turned us down a side street.

"That's the only problem with motorcycles," Caelum lamented. "No storage."

"I have some space." I eyed the cart. "How much do we need?"

"More than we could've moved on my bike and your little toy."

"Hey, my Johammer has as much horsepower as your bike." Caelum snorted.

"Be nice to my baby."

"Thanks, I'm good."

I punched the arm carrying the cart. "Take it back."

"If you insist." Caelum's wind withdrew from me as he

moved the cart into his other hand. "I love the wind on my face, even if I have to provide it myself."

"Can you imagine if we could just fly whenever we wanted?"

Caelum smiled and nodded. His grin drained away. "That's not the world we live in. Guess I'm just stuck walking to Market with a pretty girl."

"You can always buy a convertible," I said.

"We talked about this, I'm just not suited to waiting in traffic." He laughed. "This way I only suffer once in a while. We're here."

I examined the little hole in the wall grocery store. "Seriously?"

Caelum flashed me a smile. I followed him inside.

An attractive young blonde beamed at Caelum. Her Russian-accented voice was almost as beautiful. "You're Mister Caelum, da?"

"Yes. Please tell your father we're here, child."

Her smile soured when I stopped at Caelum's side. "Who is this?"

"My sister."

"Oh," the cashier beamed. "I will fetch Papa."

"Friend of yours?" I asked.

"Just a crush. She's too young."

"For now."

Caelum shrugged.

A man stepped out of the back. Grey frosted the spikes of his dark hair. He extended a hand to Caelum, and I noticed they shared height—though more muscles thickened the older man's frame. A doubly thick accent made his words harder to understand. "Mister Caelum, it is good to see you. Who is with you?"

"My sister. I thought you should meet. I may have to send her on occasion."

"Why not send her husband?"

An exasperated sigh escaped Caelum. "If only she had one, Nicolas."

"I have many nephews," Nicolas said.

"You wouldn't want her in the family." Caelum flashed me a grin. "She's kind of a wet blanket."

Nicolas rubbed his stubble. "You are sure? A good man can soften a shrew."

"I'm fine as I am," I said.

"I've come for another order," Caelum said.

"You are early. What do you do with all that sweet?"

Caelum smiled. "Share it with the little folk."

The shopkeeper said something to his daughter in Russian then disappeared into the back. She crossed the shop to the dairy case, then frowned at Caelum. "You're sure you want the soonest expired? It is a lot of milk."

"I go through it fast." Caelum converted his hand truck onto four wheels for maximum cargo.

She loaded two milk crates onto his cart. The beaming girl paid more attention to Caelum than the full and half gallons filling up the crates. Nicolas appeared, adding a dozen boxes of Bit-o-Honey candy bars. Caelum pressed six hundred-dollar bills into the man's hand.

"This is too much," Nicolas frowned.

"Stock up double for the next order. I have a feeling we're going to need it."

Nicolas scowled at the loaded cart. "I think you need a wife."

The girl brightened.

"No time to discuss that today. Maybe next time."

"I doubt Caelum's willing to settle on just one," I added in a tart tone.

The girl frowned.

Caelum shared an earthy smile with Nicolas and led the way outside. He turned up the street in the general direction of the congress center. The heavy cart rolled across uneven sidewalk. I managed to catch the cart the first time a corner ramp tried to spill the load.

"Thanks," Caelum said. "No matter how diligent I stay, I always end up nearly spilling the load."

"How often do you do this?" I asked.

His expression grew sly. "Only when necessary."

"Nicolas knew you pretty well."

"I visit the Market often, okay?"

"I'm not Vitae."

We continued on in silence.

Sidewalk artists and wandering wafers eyed our load and clothes with undisguised curiosity. He led me across the complex. A sweet lilt of growing things spiced the breeze. A sideways glance spotted Caelum's nose raised and eyes closed in pleasure.

I inhaled more deeply.

Don't have to be an earth phoenix to enjoy nature's scent on the wind.

Caelum brought us to a halt in front of a wide fountain just east of the Georgia Dome. I studied our destination. The center of the fountain was dominated by a statue of an impossibly agile man—particularly considering some of his stone attributes. He vaulted a stone ring like a gymnast's horse. At the fountain's base, a plaque named the statue, 'The Flair.'

"This is the entrance to the Goblin Market?" I asked.

"Yeah, the faerie like this statue enough to make it a semi-permanent door that opens if you know the magic words." Caelum flashed me a grin and cleared his throat. "I've got candy."

A psychedelic swirl of LSD inspired colors filled the ring. A wooden gangplank followed, sliding out across the fountain's top.

Caelum beamed at me. "Hold your breath, make a wish, count to three..."

He pulled our cart up the ramp and into the Goblin Market.

Bradley

Junior assistant coroner Bradley Sky hummed over the corpse on his table.

Bite wounds covered the animal shelter worker delivered that morning. He frowned at the body, sure he'd seen something similar but unable to dig out the memory.

He tapped the mute button on his headset. "Wake up. Desiccation around subject's bite wounds seems to have deteriorated abnormally fast. Discoloration suggests disease, but no disease I know of works so quickly—certainly not in a body without a functioning circulatory system."

Bradley frowned at the body. Something about the body felt off, but he couldn't put his finger on it. "Wound may have been contaminated by animal remains or some pathogen therein."

The door opened. A very attractive woman in professional attire strolled inside. Her eyes swept the room, taking in everything through oval spectacles.

Well, hello.

Bradley smiled. "Go to sleep."

"Pardon?" She asked.

He tapped his headset, activating the mute. "Can I help you?"

Her eyes locked on him with an almost physical grip. "I need your report."

"Sure, which one? Who are you again?"

Her expression darkened, accentuating the faint red highlights in her dark hair. "Detective Foxner, remember? I'm waiting on your examination results from those strange body parts."

He frowned. "What strange body parts?"

"From the Humane Society," Foxner said.

He knit his brows together. "From this morning? I haven't finished yet."

"No," she snapped. She visibly relaxed, dug into her case and pushed papers into his face. "No, Doctor. The Howell Mill break in, day before yesterday."

A spectral thought almost solidified before fleeing. "I don't remember getting anything from another animal shelter, and I think something like strange bodies from two shelters inside a week would stay with me."

"Another shelter got broken into?" Foxner asked.

He frowned at her. "Not that I know of, but this guy's nametag says he works at a no-kill shelter in DeKalb. Time of death is early this morning, but these wounds...I mean look at them. They look weeks along."

"You probably shouldn't sound so excited."

He shrugged. "He's just meat and a mystery."

Foxner darkened.

"Hey, they taught us to remain detached."

"As opposed to giddy?" Foxner asked.

"I love what I do. I get to solve mysteries without criminals shooting at me, and I can't do too much damage, so my malpractice premiums aren't as high." Bradley pointed at the corpse. "This one's a puzzler. I live for the weird stuff."

"No doubt." Foxner tapped the paper. "That is your signature, isn't it?"

He glanced at the large sweeping strokes. "Huh. I don't remember signing that, but yeah, that is my signature."

"Quite the puzzler."

"Yeah."

"How can you not remember? It was only a few days ago. You blathered on and on about trolls and movies."

"Trolls?" Bradley shrugged. "I'm sorry, detective, I just don't remember."

Foxner wrinkled her nose. "Blaming the fumes?"

He chuckled. "Give me a minute to check the slabs."

Bradley opened drawer after drawer, cabinet after cabinet. Something like an itch he couldn't reach scratched at the back of his recollection, but both his memory and Basement E remained empty of the evidence logged in under his signature. He scratched his head. "I can't remember signing for any of that, and it isn't here. I wish I could tell you something different."

She scowled, digging into her case once more. She handed him an evidence bag containing a bone dagger and a whole bone. She handed it over with another set of paperwork. "This ended up at my precinct by mistake."

Bradley signed the evidence transfer and frowned at the bag.

"Don't lose it." Foxner whirled.

"Detective? This says: bone weapon, two pieces."

"There's two pieces in there," Foxner said.

"Two *whole* pieces and there seems to be some biological material on it. Shouldn't that be on the description?" Bradley asked.

"Obviously, people make mistakes."

Bradley scratched his head. "Yeah, about that, can I take you out to dinner to make up in some way?"

"Just don't lose this," Foxner said. "And get me an analysis...fast."

"Are you sure—"

"Doctor, you're not my type."

He blinked. "What type aren't I?"

"Female." She glowered at him, practically daring him to comment.

"Well, you've got me there." He patted the bag. "I'll get right on this."

A smile slowly filled her face. "Thank you, Doctor."

Chapter Fourteen

Goblin Market Rewards

Quayla

Color exploded in every direction, spinning gossamer walkways five stories high. Silk and finer fabrics formed gangways and hammocks, shops and bowers suspended in a handful of millennia-old trees. Sprites chained to one another by spider silk lit the walks in fluttering lines. Musical whistles rose and fell in the distance.

Three gruff voices spoke in unison. "Pay the toll."

A satyr-like creature and his two larger brothers all extended hands.

"Toll?" I asked.

Caelum held up a hand to forestall me and handed three candy bars to each. Their gruff billy goat features transformed into the youthful delight typical of billy kids. He smiled encouragement back at me, but the encounter left me frowning.

He led me to one side. "What is it?"

"There's never been a toll before." I gestured upward. "And sure, the Market changes, but it's never looked like this. How do we even get up there?"

"Vitae's kept you on too tight a leash," Caelum said.

"Not the way he tells it."

"Let me guess, on your past visits the Market looked like a weekend swap meet decorated by some bigwig's no-talent, color-blind mistress?"

"Yeah."

He patted my shoulder.

I slapped his hand away. "Don't condescend to me."

Caelum held up both hands. "Isn't water supposed to be calm, easy going?"

I glared and tapped a foot.

"Right, we're enjoying a whitewater, raging waterfall kind of day. You only saw the tourist version." Caelum swept the scene with a hand. "This is the *real* Goblin Market where natives come to play. It doesn't offer the same protections to visitors, so rein in that temper and remember to keep things calm and polite."

"How did you get in here then?"

He waggled a candy bar. "I'm a charming soul."

"You bribed your way in."

"We are talking about faeries here. The lesser Sidhe have no easy way to get into Creation. They live for experiences and making deals. I bring some of those things into their reach."

"All right, mister smarty pants, how do we get up there? Climb a tree?"

He rolled his eyes. "So gauche."

"Well?"

Caelum patted his pockets, turning the exercise into something of an amateur magic show. When my expression promised an imminent tsunami, he withdrew a silk handkerchief from his back pocket. He unfolded it once, twice, a dozen times until it reached the size of a small area rug. The silk carpet shimmered in a constantly changing rainbow, gathering the colors around it like a greedy toddler and swirling them around before seizing the next. He rolled the cart onto it and took a seat. "Coming?"

"On that flimsy thing?"

"Silk might look pretty and delicate, but it's actually quite tough." He beamed. "Like me."

I folded my arms.

A thought widened his smile. He leapt to his feet and extended a hand. "Do you trust me?"

I knocked away his hand and seated myself on the carpet. "You watch too many Seelie movies."

Caelum laughed. He settled into his seat and whistled. The ether-silk rectangle rose at his command, changing directions as Caelum changed tones.

We floated among merchants hawking wares or themselves in equally persuasive tones. I scanned the shops, searching out Ralein.

Will he even be here? What if he only sells to tourists?

A first-tier shop offered an army of knee-high versions of Cousin It all lined up on wooden shelves braced against a tree trunk. Each rank seemed shelved by hair color in ascending heights without regard to fat or skinny. A half-elf—a half-sized miniature of larger elves—appeared almost at once, decked out in white and silver silks.

"Shield Caelum, it is good to see you again. I trust your apartment is tidy to your satisfaction?"

"It is, Oshyn."

"You let brownies clean your apartment?" I gasped.

"I assure you, we do a first-rate job, Shield Aquaylae," Oshyn said.

"How do you know my name?" I asked.

"Being acquainted with those assigned to the Shields near all the Market entrances is good business," Oshyn quieted the tittering brownies. "Besides, the way Grynnberry tells it, you could use our services—particularly in your bedroom."

I darkened.

Grynnberry and I are going to talk.

Caelum pushed two gallons of milk at the half-elf. "For an introductory cleaning of Quayla's place."

"I don't want them cleaning my apartment, besides how would I explain that to Dylan?"

"Your mortal paramour would never see us," Oshyn said.

"Exactly," I said. "He'd think I was sick or having an affair."

"Or he'd expect you to clean up more often," Caelum added.

I was already on thin ice. While Sidhe like Grynnberry were happy to trade intelligence for little pay outs rather than causing genuine mischief to the wafers, I didn't know Oshyn or his brownies. "Thanks, but still, no thanks."

Hairy shoulders fell like an inverse wave.

"Fine, keep the milk. A gift to the crew for all their good work."

The brownies perked up, but Oshyn's expression grew fearful. "Shield Caelum, a gift—"

Caelum held up his hands. "You're right, but perhaps a trade?"

Oshyn relaxed. "A barter, yes, advance payment for—"

"Actually, we need a little coin of the realm," Caelum countered.

"And some information about the animal abductions," I said.

Caelum and Oshyn both frowned.

Oshyn turned his body to exclude me from their conversation. "Blood, berries, dust, or...gold perchance?"

Caelum laughed. "Do I look like a peapod pixie to you?"

"Shield Caelum has proven himself as shrewd as he is generous."

"All the above—except keep the gold and add some magic?"

Oshyn eyed the cart. "I cannot provide trade for so much treasure."

"Start with the milk—not including the two gallons negotiating advance."

Oshyn stroked his ears in turn. "Yes. I can part with a little of each but must keep some for trading."

"Excellent." Caelum flashed me a smile.

Quayla

I perused a pouch filled with loose berries and crystalized spider silk balls. "But you paid for the milk and candy."

"I still have most of the candy," Caelum resumed whistling at a different octave. The carpet banked a steep leftward spiral ascent. "The milk isn't that expensive."

I eyed the little containers filled with blood—hopefully faerie blood, pixie dust, and throbbing magic. "Where are we going?"

"*The* place for making deals."

"I thought we'd run through the market. They might be selling the animals."

"This is better."

"We're going to a bar, aren't we?"

"Like I said, better."

Above the silken catwalks, the venerable branches cradled a palatial wooden tavern. A sign swung before the entrance, displaying pixies in their cups—literally. Their carpet orbited the spacious tavern. Table-crowded balconies filled with faerie folk. Seelie occupied the eastern terraces, and Unseelie crowded the west. Behind the tavern, a deck, half the size of either balcony, teemed to overflowing with small tables crowded by Wyldfae.

I pointed. "Down there."

Caelum shook his head. "That's not the best way to get what we need."

"What's wrong with the direct approach?"

"Once you've had more experience, you'll see that the obvious path isn't the path of least resistance when dealing with the faerie."

I'm not much older than he is.

I shot him a dirty look. "Fine, where do we start?"

Caelum landed us on the tavern's doorstep, pulled the cart to one side and folded up our transport. "The faerie courts are like siblings. If you want dirt on one, you just tempt the others to tattle."

"But they're just going to lie to us."

"You know they say the faerie cannot lie," he smiled.

I snorted. "Not directly."

"Right, so our job is to trade drinks for lies, then cross reference them for the truth we need. Simple enough."

"If your mind twists like a tornado."

Caelum bowed and gestured me to the door.

I stepped inside.

All conversation stopped.

Seven steps descended into a wide central floor. Seven tables, accompanied each by three stools, filled the space. Several tables had a fourth and even fifth member standing, despite empty stools at other tables.

Unlike the outer seating, the central space mixed Seelie, Unseelie and Wyldfae as well as a smattering of fantastical creatures and the occasional human. Most of the standing patrons loomed, their dour expressions marking them as muscle of one kind or another. A group of Fae Kissed Picts clustered around a table, their priest conversing in low tones with a beautiful Seelie elf. Another table boasted a drinking game between a Viking, a Celt and a young sorcerer who'd apparently taken fashion tips from a science fiction convention when picking his burgundy and silver attire.

And we can't touch any of the wafers as long as they're here.

Caelum somehow picked up the loaded cart by himself and lowered it to an ogre checking weapons. The mammoth Unseelie scratched her head, scraping knuckles on the ceiling as she considered Caelum's cart. A box of Bit-o-Honey turned uncertainty into a rotted grin. She took Caelum's black case then hefted his cart to her side of the check counter. She shook a shaker-contained sprite over Caelum's belongings before handing over the imprisoned Fae.

Caelum whispered to the little creature as he returned. "Let's get a table. Little Wullie here hasn't eaten yet today."

As we descended, I glanced right and left. Larger dining areas to either hand were occupied by Seelie or Unseelie and no one else. A small arched doorway on the bar's right dominated the central room's back wall offered stairs which presumably led to the small area set aside for Wyldfae.

"Patience." Caelum pulled out a stool for me with his foot and took another at the empty table.

I wasn't tickled that Caelum chose the least defensible table in the place.

I don't favor sitting dead center among all these faeries...key word being dead.

Caelum had another whispered conversation with the sprite and extended a hand. "Could you pass two elderberries?"

The sprite's glow brightened in anticipation.

I handed over two, and Caelum slipped them into the shaker without letting the sprite escape.

"Now what?" I asked.

"We wait."

"For?"

Caelum shrugged, fanning candy bars out across the tabletop. "Our food?"

"What are those for then?"

He winked. "Dessert."

I folded my arms and glared. I'd gotten what I asked for, more really. Caelum had helped me enter the Goblin Market. He'd gotten me into the real thing, though there was no way to be sure the other hadn't been real and this one some holiday version.

Wouldn't put it past Caelum to lead me on just so he could have a drink.

"You should leave." The suave, dour voice brought my head around.

"We haven't received our meal yet, Knight Dolumii," Caelum said.

A velvet cloak covered the broad-shouldered elf in a great swath of deepest violet. Long hair cascaded over his shoulders like ebony quicksilver. Moonlight silver tinged vibrant skin tones of the Greek isles, marking him a Knight of the Unseelie court. He turned more fully toward Caelum and slid a hand within his garments. Shifted fabric revealed ornate raspberry and midnight armor gilt in silver filigree. An indigo glove rested cross body on the hilt of a dark sword, index finger tapping a guard of tormented faces cast in bluish-silver.

"Unless you wish to add to my guard, you will depart unsated."

My eyes darted from his face back to the hilt. The face he tapped shied away, mouthing in silent torment.

I rose, slipping fingers into the guard rings on my hilts. "We're here on business, Knight."

One corner of his lips rose, pushing a fine, ebony brow higher. "This isn't your world, bird. You have no jurisdiction here."

"You want us to leave, how about you tell us which of your kind have been abducting animals and why?" I asked.

"Such reasons are too numerous to list. Age would slay you before I finished enumerating the reasons to claim only the two-legged animals."

Caelum rose. "Knight Dolumii, the Grotto is neutral territory bound by peace bond."

Dolumii smirked. "True. No faction of *faerie* may accost another."

Caelum pressed a hand to his chest. "I'm shocked, so noble a knight without the talent of words? Perhaps I could read you the rules."

Dolumii darkened. His grip tightened and his sword slid out an inch.

The timbre of my voice rose. "There are no wafers here to prevent us from taking our true form. Draw that blade further and face a tempest of wind and water."

No sound gave away their movement, but a prickling of the

little hairs on my neck compelled me to look. I detached my eyes from their lock on Dolumii. Fae stood within both east and west dining areas, all eyes on their table.

Dolumii licked his lips. "I doubt you'll survive accosting me."

Caelum leaned in. "Maybe not, but we'll be reborn."

"You perhaps, but what about your complacent companion?"

Air fled my lungs. My nest was low, not so low that I might not be reborn, but that Dolumii knew the state of my nest left me uneasy.

Could be a bluff. He might be...Grynnberry. He's seen my nest, and the brownies have been in Caelum's apartment.

"I don't know, a century lounging in an egg might well be worth ridding Faery of your like," Caelum said. "Care to try us or will you be the one to leave unsated?"

I watched the elf like my smaller bird of prey cousins. I reached into my core, gathering the energies to fill my blades or transmogrify into a phoenix.

A bandaged grendling shambled down the stairs in a group of his fellows. His eyes locked on mine.

"You," I hissed.

The grendling bolted back up the stairs, knocking around his companions in his haste. I bolted after him. I grabbed foul, tangled grendlings and threw them from my way.

"Quayla!" Caelum called.

I crested the stair, searching right and left. To my right, the grendling bounced downward branch by branch. Teeth latched onto my thigh.

Finding the teeth part of a seldom seen female grendling cost me a moment's hesitation. Nausea and foulness radiated up my leg. I seized a handful of oily black hair and leapt over the railing toward my fleeing quarry. My essence shot into a Karambit and out as a glistening blade. I released the grendling's hair, trusting the foul thing's teeth to keep the Fae tick from being dislodged, and passed the blade to my off hand.

We hit hard, pain jarring up my leg as teeth tore muscle.

Impact added to my downward thrust. My impaling knife sank hilt and blade into the grendling's head. Grabbing hair and skull as I leapt for the next branch, I tore the grendling's locked teeth from my flesh.

The next landing hurt more than the last.

The fleeing grendling bobbed left and right through smaller branches, nearing the silk causeways.

I squeezed my essence, pushing it out from my center to fill in the missing chunk of flesh and muscle. Healing while running turned my mad chase into leaping and limping pursuit.

Blighted hells! I'm losing him.

Rather than follow the grendling's path through tangled branches and foliage, I bound left and leapt from a bit higher. My essence burst forth, consuming clothes and flesh, knives and hair. Light blazed a corona around me. I shrieked a battle cry and swept my wings downward for a few beats more height.

I folded my wings and dove.

Another screech forewarned my prey of imminent death.

Keep control. I need him alive.

He leapt the last distance to the silk ways, head yanked around and eyes wide with terror.

Wind swept through my wings and rattled feathers.

Coursing blood pounded against my ears like surf the shore.

The Goblin Market folded up like a startled anemone.

Furled silk rolled together in knots and twists, cocooning my prey only moments from my beak and talons reaching him.

I pulled up, back winging hard. Phoenix eyes—model for the eagle—scoured the Market for the slightest sign of my prey.

The Market countered.

Silk shifted and swirled, blocking my line of sight at every angle.

"It's no good." Caelum floated next to me on his silk carpet, alone save the small pixie shaker cradled in his folded legs. "You'll never find him now."

The Goblin Market unfolded once more. My quarry had

escaped. The traders had vanished. I couldn't understand why it would open back up empty until my eyes saw an elven knight step out of a shimmer veil.

The new elf seemed fairer than Dolumii. Chestnut waves framed bronze skin. He held a slender golden sword. He swished it up in a salute, light catching the pumpkin orange guard and causing the embedded eyes to squeeze tight against the flash.

"Quick, land here and change back," Caelum said

I screeched an objection, bobbing up and down in the air and searching the horizon for my quarry.

"Quayla," Caelum snapped. "Now."

I hesitated. Whatever Caelum's reasons, he had them, but dropping wingless atop a floating sheet of silk seemed dubious at best. I did it anyway. The silk sagged only a little, but enough to cause a stumble. I tumbled off the carpet, pushing my essence together for another transmog.

The knight bounded from silk way to pavilion to sky, catching me mid fall. He alighted on another way with a feather-light touch and set me on my feet. "Lady Aquaylae."

"Uh, sir knight."

He bowed, flourishing his arms. "Gherrian, Knight Champion of the Seelie Court."

Caelum landed. "Why do we warrant a visit, Knight Gherrian?"

The elf smirked. "Be it an occurrence far and between, away and beyond, I must concur with Knight Champion Dolumii. You are not within your kingdom and your dispensation as sheriff bears no authority in these shires."

I blinked at Caelum.

"We're out of our jurisdiction and instructed to stop poking the beehive."

Gherrian laughed. "Perhaps better worded if only for your succinctness."

"Someone in Faery is killing and abducting...our subjects. We are here to find the culprits and bring them to justice."

The elf shook his head. "Better to seek the Sovereigns and beg a boon. None will stand aside from your way in this, not after you assaulted a faerie in the Grotto."

"No." I shook a finger at the knight. "She bit me. I didn't kill her until we were beyond the railing."

"Your word against witnesses."

"They're ly—"

Caelum slapped a hand around my mouth. "Very well, Sir Gherrian, we depart in peace."

Gherrian produced Caelum's folded cart and held it out. "The sprite, please."

Caelum frowned at the empty cart, but traded the sprite for it, nonetheless. Knight Gherrian marched us to the gate. The three billy goat guards eyed me darkly.

The smallest addressed Caelum. "Your toll is thrice and thrice again for many tomorrows."

"Understood," Caelum scowled. He gestured me onto the little bridge. "After you."

I returned his dirty look with interest but marched onto the bridge.

"Shield Aquaylae?" Knight Gherrian asked.

"What?"

Gherrian slipped out of sight through a Veil, but his voice carried. "It would be wise to mind your nests better in future."

Chapter Fifteen

Faerie Fairplay

Quayla

Vitae paced back and forth in a corporate conference room housed on the first floor of our headquarters building. "You two are out of control."

Behind him, an elf of indistinguishable court perused his nails, disdaining to take part in the noisome scene.

Caelum shook his head in an attempt to head off my rebuttal.

I can't believe he's just going to stand here and take this. Vitae isn't any more important than we are.

The elf folded his hands behind his back, stepping between us and Vitae to glower down his long nose at us despite his inferior height. "You attacked a faerie citizen within our sovereign borders without leave to be present."

Vitae scowled. "What do you have to say for yourselves?"

Caelum stole the initiative. "We were given leave to enter the Market after paying the toll."

The elf barely hesitated a breath. "The Market's current sovereign insists she did not grant you entry. Further, neither Her Highness nor her servants granted you permission to traffic addictive substances or—"

"What addictive substances?" I demanded.

"Edenberries."

"What?" I gaped. "We got those berries from one of your merchants."

"Likely story," the elf said. "It's an established fact that your residence harbors a garden full of Edenberries."

I opened my mouth, but Vitae snarled over me. "Be silent, Aquaylae. You assaulted innocent diners on peace-bound, neutral ground."

"That grendling wasn't innocent," I objected. "I caught him stealing kittens in the Howell Mill humane society."

The elf examined his fingers. "I do not believe you can accurately label claiming animals humanity has abandoned as theft. Besides, animals are not protected under the Articles of Ararat, so your objection to a Sidhe shopping for his evening repast isn't actionable."

"Those grendlings assaulted me when I ordered them to stand down. Their actions fell under the Articles' rules for protecting Creation. The grendling in the Grotto fled apprehension."

The elf's brow rose. "You can prove it was the same grendling? You have images? Witnesses?"

The more of the elf's matter-of-fact tone escaped his lips, the closer my fingers grew toward steaming. I turned to Vitae. "The kitten room has a webcam. Ask the Isaac to produce the video."

"You will keep a civil tone, Aquaylae."

"I didn't attack anyone inside the tavern. Blighted hells, I didn't even defend myself until I'd leapt the barrier."

Vitae scooped up and brandished a handful of ornate, vellum-wrapped scroll rods. "That's not what these say—I have here no less than half a dozen official complaints about you two."

"What complaints?" Caelum asked.

Vitae glanced at the elf. When he disdained to comment, Vitae answered. "You insulted a highly placed Unseelie Knight, refused to turn in weapons in a peace zone, bribed officials, assaulted innocent Fae, caused an affront and forced closure of the

Goblin Market—someplace you don't have any business entering."

I goggled at him, eyes flicking from Vitae's cold rage, the gesticulating scrolls and the elf's cruel smirk.

"They're demanding your head," Vitae said

"Give it to them," Caelum said.

The elf's smirk grew into a barracuda's grin.

"I didn't do anything wrong," I objected.

Caelum shrugged. "They kill you, you're reborn, matter settled."

Vitae darkened.

"Oh no," the elf chuckled. "I'm afraid the debt she owes our Courts isn't so easily settled. After Shield Aquaylae is publicly executed and reborn before both Courts, she will pay penance in apologies for her sins against the faerie."

"Sins?!" I grabbed my hilts.

Vitae and Caelum took hold of my arms.

"A verbal apology will be required while you display your contrition by washing the feet of both sovereigns with your unspoiled essence."

My world did a plausible imitation of Six Flag's Georgia Cyclone.

The phoenixes on either side of me tightened their grips. My eyes traced the veins in the elf's throat.

One talon stroke and — "And of course, I'm afraid we must demand reparations for damaged merchandise and sales lost on account of her actions."

"The Market closed before she reached it," Caelum countered. "Besides, you withheld considerable wealth in honey candy, milk and local currency when returning my belongings."

"Forfeited for your violations in the Grotto."

I shoved Caelum sideways enough that the incredibly agile phoenix nearly lost his footing. Vitae had a moment's warning, but I still managed to shake him off. I shoved a finger into the elf's chest. "I. Did not. Attack. Anyone. Inside the Grotto."

Caelum and Vitae managed to pull me back before the elf bled all over the expensive carpet. He dusted off the place where I'd touched him, disgust bending handsome features.

He addressed Vitae. "We will expect your formal answer before sunset on the morrow."

"You can have my answer now," I said.

Caelum tightened his hold. "Take a breath, little sister."

I jerked free of Caelum's grip. "Don't you little sister me. I didn't do anything wrong, and I am damn well not going to be the main event for some dog and pony show."

"We await your reasoned reply, Shieldheart." The elf bowed himself into the building foyer and vanished before I could get my hands on him.

"I've had enough tantrums," Vitae snarled. "You are moving back into headquarters so I can keep an eye on you."

Caelum cut across me. "She doesn't answer to you, Vitae."

"I was talking to both of you."

"To hell with you," Caelum said.

"I am the Shieldheart. I am responsible for this Shield and that means you have to do as I instruct." He glowered at me. "In order to mend relations, you will apologize as required by the Courts."

I lowered my voice. "Why wait until your next death, Vitae? Go get the spare stick out of your nest and shove it up your ass now."

I stormed out, not stopping my headlong march until I reached where I'd parked my Johammer in the garage.

Quayla

I slammed my apartment door closed without regard to the lecture Mrs. Cox would deliver the next time we met in the halls. I stormed into my bedroom, furious to the point of tears.

I stripped naked.

Dark oaths spilled from my lips.

I flopped onto my nest grate and ground the play button on my remote. The paused tearjerker resumed.

I didn't want to sit in my little alcove and cry. I wanted to sink my talons into faeries or, lacking a more suitable subject, Vitae. Humans never dealt with the kinds of obscene ludicrousness in their jobs. They never faced unreasonable employers or had petty know-it-all bosses intrude on their private lives.

They've got it all, and what do I have? Some old buzzard telling me to make nice and let the faeries chop my head off. I don't even have my own name.

Steam wafted off of my skin.

I ought to go back there and piss in his nest. It couldn't make him any worse. Better, maybe I'll just quit. What's the worst they can do to me? Hunt me down? Give me True Death?

Nausea extinguished my rising temper and plunged me into icy sewage. A seed within blocks of my apartment registered a powerful Veil breach.

Holy Hells, that's a lot of taint.

My seed went silent a moment later, and the taint vanished.

"Quayla?" Anima asked.

"Yea—"

Another massive wave of taint entered the next nearest seed.

What the hell could cause that much taint that fast?

"Shield Quayla, two potent faerie forces have breached the Veil in your area."

"Yeah, I felt them." I leapt from my nest. Uncertainty dragged my eyes back to the basin. The remaining essence level knotted every muscle with dread. "I'm on it."

It's going to take weeks of tearjerkers to refill my nest.

I dressed in a rush, slipped my backup hilts into belt loops and grabbed my purse in a headlong rush out the door. I practically flew down the stairs.

Mrs. Cox emerged from her apartment. The little old lady's voice had steel in it. "Young lady, I want a word with you."

"No time, Mrs. Cox. Yell at me later."

I threw open the door hard enough to rattle the imbedded glass. I turned toward my parking space ready to buy myself a few more steps by leaping the stairs.

A shrill whistle ripped the air.

I jerked toward the sound to find the escaped grendling, trousers around his ankles, waving his moldy, mulberry ass in my direction.

"Well, I never!" Mrs. Cox exclaimed. "I'll call the police, see if I don't, you hooligan!"

Unease slowed drawing my hilts. "Get back inside, Mrs. Cox."

The grendling leaped around, taunting me with waggling genitals and a singsong voice. "Yoohooo, little birdie. You can't touch me."

Squeezed essence slid through my hilts. I gritted my teeth against coming pain. "Wanna bet?"

"That's no way to act in public. The authorities will deal with you!" Mrs. Cox rushed into the building, much to my relief.

I charged three steps.

Mrs. Cox's shriek brought me up short.

The bay windows fronting Mrs. Cox's apartment exploded. Brick and wood, glass and doilies flew everywhere. Beyond the dust, a half-ogre stood in Mrs. Cox's living room—one hand clamped over my landlady's head and shoulders. His other hand shoveled baked goods into his mouth.

He grinned a rotted, frosting-coated smile. "Hello, little birdie. Their majesties send their regards."

Quayla

I turned my head toward the offending grendling. A wide, sinister smile split his face.

I whipped the knife in a quick spin by its finger ring as I swept my arm his direction. I simultaneously halted my arm at the swing's pinnacle and snatched the hilt to a stop. The blade of my essence tore painfully away from the hilt. An S-shaped blade of shimmering essence spun through the air and split the grendling's face, perpendicular to his shock-faded smile.

I turned back toward the ogre and pointed a newly extruded blade. "Drop the muffins and let my landlady go."

"Call the police, dear," Mrs. Cox said through a gap in the massive fingers. "They'll take care of this hoodlum."

Dylan's car pulled in.

I ignored him. I had no time for distractions. My mind raced. I had to figure out how to best the ogre before he hurt Mrs. Cox. "When it comes to his type, Mrs. Cox, I am the authority."

The ogre chortled.

"You're a florist, dear," Mrs. Cox said. "I think forget-me-nots and daisies are more your speed."

I smirked, sweeping my feet through the fluid, focusing forms of Hep-Silat, an ancient martial art taken from Indonesian origins by Egyptian sailors and reborn to honor the river god Hapi. "By the Undying Light, I order you to release that mortal and either surrender immediately or return to Faery with all haste."

The half-ogre chuckled. Mrs. Cox hung onto the ogre's sausage fingers for dear life as he shook her by her head and shoulders. "Play nice, little birdie, or there are melon chunks on the menu."

I slid a hand behind my back. Slight finger motions whipped the Karambit into a rapid spin. I pushed more of myself through the hilt. A quick jerk brought the blade out from behind my back. Fingers snapped down on the hilt. The water blade tore away from my already torn essence with a ripping sensation twice as painful. The new S-shaped blade stretched as it flew, severing the half-ogre's hand at the wrist.

"Quayla, stop!" Dylan yelled.

Mrs. Cox dropped to the ground, grey hair coated in gloopy dark ick. She turned toward the ogre and kicked its shin.

I didn't hesitate.

I raced toward the Wyldfae, forcing another blade from my hilt. I leapt onto the front stair. A bounding round kick off the banister spun me into a fluid whirl of gleaming blades. The Wyldfae swung wildly with both fist and stump. I flowed around its lumbering blows, darting in to slice again and again.

A fist drove me onto Mrs. Cox's blood-slimed carpet. The blow shattered bones that remained lighter for flight even in human shape. Brittle bones shattered at the point of impact. A birdlike shriek escaped me.

The half-ogre reared back to kill me.

I have to hurry back and save them even if my nest is too low for another rebirth. Can I talk to Ani if my nest is empty?

Dylan leapt onto the ogre's back, stabbing into the side of the Wyldfae's head with his keychain Swiss Army knife.

We needed help. I fumbled with a silver chain, struggling but failing to draw a silvered feather pendant from the neck of my shirt.

The ogre roared, somehow swelling in size. His head brought ceiling pieces down.

An ogre hand seized Dylan's torso and squeezed.

All thought of calling for help vanished in Dylan's agonized cry.

"No!"

One of my arms refused to move, bellowing agony instead when muscles tried obey. Even with the cat out of the bag, I didn't have enough time to transmogrify into pure essence and rebalance. The connected forearm was shattered so badly that it flopped like a noodle from my elbow down. The ogre was out of reach of my working arm, so I kicked upward with the only leg not in pain. My heel slammed into the ogre's groin.

The faerie bellowed. He doubled over and dropped Dylan in favor of cradling his genitals.

Mrs. Cox seized a nearby baking pan covered in muffins. She slammed the cookie sheet into the ogre's face. "That's for stealing. That's for accosting me and Quayla, and that's for messing up my hair."

"Dylan, Mrs. Cox, run." I hooked my working leg behind the ogre's ankle.

"We can't leave you alone with this thing," Dylan leapt out the destroyed wall, and grabbed a metal trash can lid.

I jerked myself upright and threw my less-damaged arm in a wide arc to impale the creature's femoral artery. Snapping sounds and pain exploded from my shoulder. My blade sank into the meat of his leg but missed the target. Impact shot fire up my arm. Dark spots swirled before my eyes.

My bladeless hilt clattered to the floor.

I could barely summon air enough for pleading whispers. "Help...we need...help...Ani...Vili..."

Dylan hopped onto the banister and jumped back into Mrs. Cox's apartment. He brought the lid down onto the bent ogre's head with both hands.

"Cox...Dylan...," I wheezed, unable to take a full breath. "Go...please."

"He ate my muffins."

Without enough air to convince Mrs. Cox or Dylan, I tried to transmogrify. Reaching for my essence sent spikes through my eyes. I tried to fight through the pain but even the smallest wisps of essence slid from my attempts to harness it.

I gave up on rebalancing and turned my attention to summoning help. "Dylan...please...my necklace...then...get her...clear."

Dylan dug a hand into my shirt.

"Mister Silus!" Mrs. Cox scolded.

He yanked the pendant from my shirt.

I gasped for breath. "Vili...cangel...us, Vili...cangel...us—"

A bright light filled my eyes.

Hope spiked through me like blessed morphine.

A shadow stepped in front of the light.

Tears collected in my eyes, girding themselves up to leap to freedom.

Terrance

A huge bellow proceeded Terrance. He drew earth from beneath him, swelling until he rivaled the Sidhe's bulk. He crashed through the door into the apartment and slammed bodily into the ogre. The impact sent the Wyldfae sprawling through the demolished wall and onto the trash cans.

The ogre screamed in pain.

Terrance leapt down onto it. He pummeled the ogre with spiked gauntlets of jagged glowing quartz and obsidian. Crystal and lava rock hammered the Wyldfae backward into the street one blow at a time. Foul blood coated Terrance's cestuses, taint sinking sickness into his flesh.

Quayla blinked. "Terr...ance?"

"Dylan, move little sister away." Terrance dodged a blow and slammed crystal into the Wyldfae's face.

"Do I know you?" Dylan asked.

"We know you." He took a blow from the half-ogre, sliding backward a stride and using the space to answer back harder. "Get her to safety, the old wafer too."

Mrs. Cox gave the ogre's severed hand a disgusted snarl and kicked it into the street. "Wafer, dear?"

"Safety?" Dylan asked. "I thought Quayla could heal herself."

"She must be too badly inj—"

The half-ogre took advantage of Terrance's distraction, delivering his own hammer blow into the earth phoenix's gut. Terrance grunted, but answered back just as hard. The ogre—no doubt deciding his ambush had been routed, snatched up his hand and bolted up the street.

Terrance looked as if he might pursue for a three count. A soft growl escaped Aquaylae's shield brother, but he leapt into the broken apartment and bent over her.

"Dylan...knows, but Mrs.—"

Terrance put a finger over her lips. "I will handle things. This is going to hurt." Terrance scooped her up. "Dylan, lead."

She cried out.

I am sorry, little sister.

Each jarring step up to her apartment poked a yelp from her lips until the pain overwhelmed her and she fell still. Terrance laid her on her couch. "Dylan, fetch a pitcher."

Quayla's paramour returned with a plastic pitcher.

"Fetch water from her nest," Terrance said. "Do not let your skin touch it."

Mrs. Cox frowned at him. "She's not a bird, why would she have a nest? I'll call an ambulance."

"I'll see to it, ma'am," Terrance said. "Can you fetch washcloths?"

"Oh, of course." Mrs. Cox exited the apartment.

Dylan returned with the pitcher, handing it to Terrance before closing the door behind the landlady. He went to Aquaylae's side as Terrance dribbled essence into her mouth. The expression on Dylan's face emphasized the things Aquaylae had told them about the mortal. Terrance agreed with Vitae that mortals shouldn't be aware of their existence, but it was hard to fault Aquaylae's choice.

"She'll be fine," Terrance reassured.

"That thing crushed her. She can't breathe."

"Her essence will heal the lung punctures. She needs time to regain her strength."

"Maybe we really should take her to the hospital."

"You're an engineer, correct? A man with an analytical mind?"

"Yeah," Dylan said.

"Analyze what happens if she's taken to a hospital."

"They take her in, run some tests...tests will tell them something's different about her, won't they?" Dylan asked.

"They will."

Aquaylae's eyes flickered open. Seeing Dylan added pleasure to her weary expression. Her gaze travelled higher and higher until it fixed on Terrance. "How?"

"Anima notified me of breaches adjacent to your apartment. After your incident in the Goblin Market, I feared the Sidhe might have their own justice planned. I'm glad you didn't have to die again."

"Maybe...better."

"Maybe." Terrance took the pitcher, tipped it slightly and dipped Aquaylae's uninjured hand into it. "Heal yourself."

Aquaylae shook her head. "Can't use...that, barely enough..."

"Can you transmogrify and rebalance?" Terrance asked.

Aquaylae shook her head. "Can't...focus."

Terrance's voice hardened, the basso echoing off the ceiling. "Then draw in this essence and heal."

Aquaylae focused on her fingers, drawing her essence back into her body. Bones rearranged with tearing, mind-numbing pain. The stabbing sensation in her chest eased and breath came easier. She drew essence until a salty crust dried on the pitcher's interior.

"Will she be all right?" Dylan asked.

"In time," Terrance said.

"That thing hit you too," Dylan said.

"My bones are stronger and I learned long ago to encase them in stone—something little Aquaylae cannot do," Terrance said.

Dylan frowned.

"We all have our talents." Terrance shrugged. "I'll notify Anima of our situation and request a rewrite."

He made it halfway to the bedroom when he froze. Aquaylae's sudden stiffening told him she felt it too, an Arch had opened nearby.

"Terrance?"

Terrance relaxed. "A departure I think. Rest, little sister."

Dylan took Terrance's place, kneeling next to Aquaylae and taking her hand as if it were most fragile china. "Rewrite?"

"Mrs. Cox will need—"

"What will I need?" Mrs. Cox asked.

"An undented baking dish," Aquaylae said.

"Look who's breathing better." Mrs. Cox wiped Aquaylae's forehead with one of her damp cloths. "We really should get you to a hospital."

"Terrance is taking care of it," Aquaylae said.

"Good, just rest now, dear. I told you to leave that hooligan be —not that I knew of your fancy knife skills." Mrs. Cox smiled at Dylan. "This is definitely a night I won't soon forget."

Chapter Sixteen

Mothering Earth

Terrance

Quayla slept beneath Terrance's watchful perch. Her breathing had steadied, the infusion of essence repairing the lung punctures she'd suffered from being moved after her bones had shattered.

"She should really go to a hospital, dear." Mrs. Cox frowned at Terrance hovering over Aquaylae. "Broken bones could puncture a lung. Maybe we should call her mother."

Terrance frowned. "She doesn't have one."

"Anymore," Dylan added. "No family."

Terrance cleared his throat.

"No blood relations," Dylan said.

"Poor dear and an orphan too." Mrs. Cox's frown brightened. "Guess you don't have to worry about a mother-in-law then, eh, boy? When *are* you two getting married?"

"Aquaylae needs rest," Terrance said.

"Thank you, Mrs. Cox, let's let her rest," Dylan said.

"Yes, yes, you're right," Mrs. Cox said. "Maybe. I'll fix up some soup and bring it by in the morning."

Terrance left Aquaylae to the lover and the landlady, crossing to her kitchen. A faint aroma of taint wrinkled his nose. The prevalent scent belonged to a nymph—vile Sidhe he hated for past incidents, but something almost hidden beneath the overly strong taint scented off. Either way, he couldn't fault her for having contacts in the Courts when he had some himself.

Opening the woefully stocked fridge offered little in the ingredients he required. The cabinets bolstered the meager makings with pinhead oats and honey. He could make do, but the thin offering would help Aquaylae little.

"Dylan?"

The mortal's eyes snapped up to meet his own. Anguish and anger lurked like caged beasts seeking prey.

"Show me little sister's bedroom."

Mrs. Cox frowned first at Terrance and then Dylan. "I don't think it's appropriate for any man to enter a single woman's bedroom, certainly not a stranger."

"T-Terrance is...family," Aquaylae whispered.

Mrs. Cox whispered, but not softly enough that her words escaped Terrance's hearing. "Honey, you're hurt, delirious maybe, and you might not be thinking straight. I don't think this man can be your kin. He's negro, not that there's anything wrong with that, but you can't be rel—"

"Aq—" Terrance cleared his throat. "Quayla has offered her blessing. Dylan, please show me."

Dylan crossed to a door and pushed it open. Before Terrance could reach the bedroom, Mrs. Cox rose, and faced off against Terrance despite at a considerable height deficiency. "This is my building, sonny, and—"

Terrance placed his hands gently on her shoulders, lifted her a yard off the ground and set the disbelieving woman gently to one side before stepping through the door. Aquaylae's bedroom proved a mess. Two bookshelves bracketed a mirrored alcove barely glowing silver. He crossed to her nest with hasty strides only to stop short.

Oh, little sister.

He knelt down beside the stone basin. A shallow puddle of Aquaylae's essence offered nowhere near enough for even a single rebirth. "Summuseraphi."

"Get away from there," Mrs. Cox said. "You have no right digging through a woman's unmentionables."

Terrance glanced at the wrinkled hand clamped onto his shoulder. The landlady made every effort to pull him away. He let her and offered a smile. "You're quite right."

He allowed the smug old lady to escort him from Aquaylae's bed chamber.

Dylan's eyes met his return. "I hate seeing her like this."

Terrance surveyed the apartment. Pictures of Dylan and the former Aquaylae dotted the place, celebrating happy moments.

She's so young—like Caelum. She just hasn't learned the cost— may she never fully realize it. All the pictures must go.

He turned his attention back to Dylan's earnest expression.

Let his worry wane a bit, then have him dispose of them. No, better send him away and tend to it myself. Procrastination has already worsened this mess.

"I hate seeing her laid low, too," Terrance said. "Unfortunately, this is Quayla's fault."

"Well, if she'd called the authorities like I'd said, things would've been better, but you can hardly blame her for the actions of some ruffian," Mrs. Cox said.

"Not that," Terrance gestured to Aquaylae. "This."

Dylan scowled. His tone hardened. "How do you figure? You think she picked a fight with that bruiser?"

"No, that half-ogre ambushed her, that part wasn't her fault. I fear it did so as payback for her actions in the Goblin Market." Terrance rubbed his knuckles, one fist, then the other.

Perhaps I should speak to Yarque about this.

"Then how is this Quayla's fault?"

Before Terrance could answer, Mrs. Cox interrupted. "Ogre? Goblin Market? I knew it!"

Dylan and Terrance looked at her, the former in shock and

the latter with resignation. The old lady had needed a rewrite before, so he hadn't bothered to guard his tongue, but revealing the truth required Terrance to act with more haste.

"I think little sister's been remiss in tending her nest—possibly distracted by her relationship with you. If her nest had been full before yesterday's death, she could've healed this more quickly."

"Are you saying Quayla isn't human, dear? That she died yesterday? That she's some kind of bird?"

Terrance met Mrs. Cox's eyes. "Quayla's true name is Aquaylae, mine is Terra. We are both phoenixes."

"Well, that explains the hairdo." Mrs. Cox's eyes widened. "Wait, she's out of ashes? I thought phoenix were reborn from the ashes of their death. I'm sure I read—"

"Literary evidence is not truth. Aquaylae isn't born of flame. The ashes that give her rebirth are the waters of her essence."

"A phoenix...of water?" Mrs. Cox's astonishment twisted with disgust. "Surely you don't mean water as in making water."

"Tears," Dylan said. "She has to sit through marathons of sad movies atop her nest and cry to fill the damn thing up."

"That sound's horrible," Mrs. Cox said.

"That damned thing keeps her alive, and tears are hardly the most efficient method for refilling a nest." Terrance rubbed his knuckles, mumbling to himself. "She should've been taught better ways."

"Okay." Dylan threw up his hands in surrender. "But, how do we help her now? Can I donate blood or something?"

"She and I heal fastest of our Shield, but ultimately she must have time. We can speed things a bit if you are willing to take a trip to the store."

"Yes, anything she needs."

Terrance clapped him on the shoulder. "You're a good man. I need you to purchase raw liver, eggs, fresh spinach, onion, sunflower seeds—shelled, wheat germ and protein powder."

Terrance ran through the recipes in his head. "Oh, and canned puppy food."

Dylan looked up from the list he'd typed into his phone. "Puppy food?"

Terrance nodded. "Some prefer cat food, more protein, but I feel the higher fat in puppy food is more beneficial."

"She's going to eat all this?" Mrs. Cox asked.

"Essentially," Terrance said. "A healing slurry will build up her body, replacing essence faster. If Dylan can fetch what I need in quantity and with haste, we will be able to hurry her back to health."

"She needs to go to the hospital," Mrs. Cox said.

"Be quick, Dylan." Terrance snatched up the empty pitcher and marched back into Aquaylae's bedroom.

Mrs. Cox charged in behind him, a finger extended for waggling and her sharp tongue poised. The unobstructed sight of Aquaylae's nest stopped her.

"Phoenixes don't need hospitals, Mrs. Cox. They need special help." Terrance knelt next to the nest once more. "Summuseraphi?"

Mrs. Cox attempted to repeat her feat of pulling Terrance away. "Phoenix or not, a woman deserves her privacy, and I won't have you digging around Quayla's things."

"Summuseraphi."

"I don't hold with strange foreign languages, neither."

Terrance pushed the pitcher hard enough into the basin to flatten one side. He gathered as much of the remaining essence as he could, speaking the last call, "Summuseraphi."

Mrs. Cox stomped a foot. "I said, I don't—"

The bedroom filled with brilliant light.

Mrs. Cox bolted upright, backing away with her eyes as wide as they could grow. "Dear Heavens, an angel."

Summus smirked. "More or less. How can I assist you Shield Terrance?"

"We will need a rewrite and some building repairs."

Summus scanned the room. "Just the old woman?"

"Watch who you're calling old, young man." Mrs. Cox brandished her finger. "An angel should know better than to mention a lady's age."

Summus turned his back on her, facing Terrance. "I scent another mortal."

Mrs. Cox watched their discussion through suspicious, disapproving eyes.

"Aquaylae's partner needn't be rewritten at this time," Terrance said. "If you will see to this, I will tend Aquaylae."

Summus folded his wings, covering himself in a scratchy wool suit—probably based on Mrs. Cox's expectations. "Good evening, Hadley—"

"Angel or not, you've got no right addressing me in the familiar," Mrs. Cox said.

"My apologies, Mrs. Cox. Tell me about your evening."

Terrance left them to it, studying the apartment. Pictures of Aquaylae's last body and Dylan dotted the room. Each picture of her nearly glowed from the warmth and happiness she radiated in his presence.

A melancholy crept into Terrance and squeezed his chest. He had gone without a companion for centuries. Another agony wrapped itself around his heart, far, far worse than the melancholy.

I also haven't had to hold the hand of a loved one as they wasted away after sharing a life with them for all too short decades.

Terrance dug under the sink, brought out some garbage bags and doubled them. He set about collecting Dylan and Aquaylae's shared memories and dumped them into the bag.

Summus

Summus led Hadley Cox back down to her apartment. A blissful contentment radiated from her glazed eyes. She let him into her apartment. Half-ogre blood soiled the quaint abode, the stench of its taint overshadowing sweetness of baked Edenberries.

Edenberries, more commonly known in the mortal realm as elderberries, had never been meant for humanity. Early humans had been forbidden the favored fruit of Faery. Faerie kind convinced early mortals that such a prohibition was meant to horde the plant for only the angelic hosts. After the mortals capitulated to faerie encouragement and found themselves subject to Sidhe influence, the plant was stricken with a curse. The Edenberry plant and its fruit would sicken any mortal that consumed it raw. Cooking purified it from both the illness it delivered and its enthralling faerie influence.

The fruit still contained the seeds of the enthrallment originally added by Faery, but the all-consuming addiction worked only on the Sidhe themselves.

Summus turned to the missing bay window and shook his head.

Open for all the world to see.

He wasn't skilled enough to rewrite the architecture and listen to Hadley's account and rewrite her experiences. The longer her original memories remained, the more ingrained they became. The longer the scene remained open to public view, the more wafers he'd have to track down.

I could call Vilicangelus for help, but that hardly speaks well of my worthiness.

There was only one answer.

I must summon the putti.

Summus closed his eyes, focusing on his desire and slapped his hands together. An answering thrum signaled the approaching crew. He opened his eyes. Their arrival reached his ears—not a choir of cute little singing baby angels, but a raunchy joke and a lot of lewd laughter.

Six two-foot high little angels in construction attire wove

around each other on violent-orange wings. Heavy work boots thudded onto Hadley's well-tended floor. The first shoved a cigar into his cheek and pushed back a yellow hardhat with a halo drawn around its crown. Around him, the others folded orange wings around themselves into construction vests, assessing the damage.

Summus looked down at the little angel. "You're not supposed to smoke, Rusty."

"Up there." Rusty jabbed a thumb upward. "Bit different down here, birdie."

"Whatever, I need this building reconstructed as quickly as possible."

"Oh, look who's all high and mighty now that he's not all wet." Rusty canted his head back and forth. "And why ain't you doing it, all-powerful Divine One?"

"Get to work, all right. I need to focus on—where'd she go?"

Rusty pointed.

Hadley bustled around a kitchen stacked with towering mounds of elderberry muffins. She stripped all but seven berries from a plant sprig, arranged them atop the batter filled muffin cups and put the load into the oven.

"Mrs. Cox, what are you doing?" Summus asked. "I need you to tell me what happened."

"Just a minute, dear. The workers are going to be hungry, and Nana was quite clear the little folk were particularly persnickety about the customs of hospitality."

"They're not faeries," Summus said.

"Well, I can't have it being said that Hadley Sage Cox failed in her duties as hostess in this world or any other."

Work sounds stopped. Summus turned to find every tool held still and avaricious grins on every putti face.

"They're all glucose intolerant," Summus said. "Plus, they're too busy to eat."

Rusty's crew grumbled but returned to work.

Summus led Hadley out of her kitchen, but the only space

large enough was dominated by faerie blood. He sat her in a rocker and focused on the mess. He rolled his shoulders, then swept his arms back and forth collecting divine energy from his core. When his arms burned with power, he swept them together with a slap. Fire blossomed between his palms. He loosened his hands, releasing white fire to cleanse all that was tainted from the room.

A wave of exhaustion accompanied the released fire.

Divine flame swirled around the room. Small fires streamed from the main, gathering tainted fluids from the surroundings like little, burning sheepdogs. Rug and wall, furnishings and doilies, all were left pristine and undamaged. The moment all the taint was corralled, the white fire flared into a blinding inferno.

Fine golden ash settled onto the floor where the half-ogre's blood had pooled. Hadley got up from her chair.

"Hadley?" Summus said.

"What did I tell you about calling me that, young man?"

The putti snickered.

"My apologies," Summus said. "But, where are you going?"

"To get a dust pan. The floor's a mess."

Summus took her hand and moved her into the open area. He backed his command with his essence. "Now, tell me all that has happened this night."

She took him through her evening. The acuity of her memories surprised him. She held the evening's event with such precise recall that he picked up the full sensory memory without even having to touch her.

What an interesting little wafer you are.

Summus split himself from reality. Her memories slid around him like a floating ribbon. A rewrite had to be composed like a symphony. He had to draw new threads in the tapestry of time, creating new little pieces of reality to fit and engage the person being rewritten so that they could act on their own as the new time flowed around them.

Vilicangelus promised that Summus would grow more confident each time he rewrote something, but it still didn't feel natural to cut and reweave time and memory. Normally, one person was far easier to rewrite than a group. Rewriting a group meant each result from each person's reactions had to be carefully blended to ensure the new localized time didn't suffer from snags or broken threads.

Hadley Cox was the exception.

Her razor-sharp recollection required considerable care. There were no blurry moments he could easily massage into another shape. There were no easy blanks he could bridge with new experience. Hadley Cox had to have her entire memory painstakingly sculpted anew. Any inconsistency in not only the memories but how they were experienced could cause the tapestry to unravel— the least harmful result being to drive her mad.

He stepped to one side, snatching a muffin out of reality. He nibbled at first while he thought, but something about the baked goods drew him like gravity. He'd cleared an entire baking sheet before he'd realized it.

Wow, damn good. Can I think 'damn' without getting in trouble?

He resisted the desire to snatch another nearby platter and circled Hadley Cox, rubbing his chin.

What will you believe? Aquaylae mugged? You came to her aid? Terrance and Dylan arrive to drive them off? Maybe. It explains everything...except the missing muffins.

Summus absently reached into reality and plucked another. His grin shed crumbs. He snatched another.

Good Samaritans? Yes, that would appeal to your inner belief structure. The neighborhood helped too. You thanked everyone by sending them off with muffins. Once Quayla was moved upstairs, you came down for the wash cloths but realized you couldn't return immediately because you had muffins in the oven.

Summus licked his lips, cracked his knuckles and grabbed one more muffin.

All right. Here goes reality.

Terrance

Terrance marched the garbage bag down to Summus. Burgeoning day shone upon the door's glass oval. Time-accelerated construction sounds told him the new Divine One had called in a putti crew.

A wise choice.

He pushed open the landlady's door to find Summus slumped in a chair, being served muffins and milk by a beaming Mrs. Cox.

She turned her radiant smile on Terrance. "Thank you again for taking care of those ruffians. Can I offer you another muffin?"

Terrance took one off the offered tray. "Thank you."

He glanced at the putti crew. There were no muffins in view, but none of their shirts proved crumb free. They'd restored almost everything.

Probably stalling for more mortal food.

Terrance looked between them and Summus. He'd intended to ask Summus to rewrite the pictures, but the Divine One looked far too exhausted to even destroy them. Terrance stepped toward the work crew.

"Careful, dear. One of their rocks broke a window and I haven't had a moment to clean it up," Mrs. Cox said.

"I will be cautious." Terrance strolled through the curtain separating the putti from Mrs. Cox. He withdrew a smooth stone of amber from his pocket. He rubbed a thumb over the feather embedded in the otherwise flawless piece and handed the bag to the foreman. "Please take these with you and destroy them."

"Why should we?" Rusty asked.

"So I won't have to summon Vilicangelus to see to the task." Terrance smiled and spoke the Divine One's name a second time. "I'm sure Vilicangelus will be just as lenient about you consuming mortal foodstuffs stolen from Aquaylae's landlady."

The feather caught in amber radiated light.

Rusty snatched the bag from Terrance. "Fine. Fine. We'll take care of it."

"I believe you gentle-angels are finished."

The foreman glanced between the piles of muffins and Terrance's expression. "Right, union break's over, boys, put the finishing touches on and let's fly."

Terrance let them out as he exited Mrs. Cox's apartment. He headed back upstairs only to be met by Dylan's scowl. "What happened to our pictures?"

The earth phoenix endeavored to be understanding. "I saw them destroyed."

"Why?"

"The police are investigating the Humane Society incident. They have pictures of Aquaylae's former body—no matter how low their quality. No evidence can be allowed to remain."

"Look, Terrance, I appreciate you taking care of Quayla, but I *don't* appreciate you throwing away our things."

"You do not see the necessity?" Terrance said. "You who work in technology?"

"No. I don't."

"Tell me, Dylan, did Aquaylae not tell you we are enjoined to keep our existence secret?"

"She did, but surely we've outgrown all the superstition and panic. This is the information age."

Terrance stroked Aquaylae's soft, brown hair. "You did not tell him, did you, little sister?"

"Tell me what?" Dylan asked. "About faerie wishes destroying the world? That's pretty pessimistic. People aren't inherently evil.

"Didn't Aquaylae tell you that you'd have never met if she had not been burned at the stake?"

"She was what?!"

"It was some time ago. The details matter not. A few people learned about her nature and tried to slay her." Terrance looked up from stroking Aquaylae and fixed Dylan with all of his focus.

"Even good intensions enjoined with that kind of power can have destructive consequences. Are you *sure* her warnings were only pessimistic exaggerations? How many among your lofty intellectuals would make any deal to gain power offered by the faerie? What would they do to their neighbors with such power?"

Dylan dropped his eyes. "We talked about that. The more I considered it though, the more it seemed so far-fetched. Besides, you guys would be there to stop the worst of it."

"That is not our purpose."

Dylan raised pleading eyes. "Isn't that what you were made for?"

"No," Terrance said. "While we do destroy those the faeries corrupt when needed, our true purpose is to protect you from faerie, not each other."

"Why not?! You could save I don't even know how many lives."

"Free will."

"So, if we discovered the faerie, you'd just leave us in the dark clutches of Tinkerbelle."

Terrance sighed. "Dyssnie was a particularly crafty Summer Prince. In convincing generations of mortals that his Court was benign and the Unseelie villainous, he not only made our job that much harder, but staged a possible reality where your kind flocked to his Court with your wishes."

"Maleficent was an Unseelie? Jafar too? And Cruella?"

"No. Jafar wasn't his actual name, and he was Fae Kissed not Sidhe. Dyssnie's vilification of Maleficent was merely that of a spurned lover. Writers do enjoy particularly creative vengeances within their pages when it suits them. Nonetheless, my point stands."

"But Quayla said the Seelie were Summer. Wouldn't that mean there are good faeries, you know, summer—warmth and goodness?"

"She may have named them the Summer Court, but I seriously doubt she told you they represented warmth and goodness.

Think, Dylan. You are a smart mortal. Is winter any more malevolent a season than summer? Is fire any less dangerous than ice?"

Dylan looked away, folding his arms. "I still don't see how a couple of pictures could harm us. It isn't like you could remove the copies from the internet."

Terrance arched a brow.

"No," Dylan said.

Terrance shrugged.

Dylan leapt to his feet. "If that's true, you destroyed all the pictures we have left."

"You have your memories," Terrance said.

"Well, and the ones at my—you wouldn't," Dylan said.

"I am afraid yours were removed as well."

"This is ridiculous. They're not yours to take."

"What little sister possesses is the property of the Shield."

"Including Quayla herself."

"Yes."

Dylan's fists tightened until his knuckles turned white. "Maybe you have a claim on Quayla's things, but you don't have any right to what's mine."

"Like Aquaylae?"

"You're damn right. I'm not surrendering her or our pictures to a bunch of paranoid illegal aliens—"

"Technically, your kind are the aliens here."

Dylan blinked.

Three knocks sounded against the door.

Dylan cursed. "What else can go wrong today?!"

"Are you aware that many mythologies represent Fate as a particularly vindictive female spirit which delights in irony?" Terrance smiled. "Tempting her is ill advised, something you should remember if you escape her twisted sense of humor this day."

The next three knocks delivered more force against the old wood.

"You should also answer the door," Terrance said.

Dylan crossed to the door and opened it.

Detective Foxner glared through its frame.

Terrance chuckled.

No escape today.

"Can I help you?" Dylan asked.

Foxner spun a grainy video printout into Dylan's face without warning. "Do you know this woman?"

Her eyes hardened at whatever expression they saw cross Dylan's face.

"I-I'm sorry, who are you?" Dylan asked.

"Detective Foxner, Atlanta PD. I'm here to do a follow up interview with Quayla Buckler, but from your reaction I think I might like a word or two with you, Mister..."

"Snyder."

"Do you know this woman, Mister Snyder? A relation of Ms. Buckler perhaps?"

Terrance stepped into the conversation. "Perhaps I can assist."

Foxner's face swept upward to meet Terrance's calm expression.

Terrance snatched the paper from her hand too fast for her to react. "This image is poor quality and partially obstructed by a mask. I can see why you might wrongfully think there is a similarity. As for relations, I've known Aq—"

Detective Foxner's scrutiny intensified.

Terrance cleared his throat. "I've known Quayla for many years. She's an orphan, so while unknown relations are possible, I'm unaware of any living relation bearing this face."

"My." Foxner scrutinized Terrance's face, Dylan all but forgotten. "You are certainly a very helpful and informative person, Mister..."

Terrance returned the detective's scrutiny.

This mortal is quite perceptive and apparently good at her job. She has a scent here. Avoiding her queries will intensify the taint in her nostrils.

"Wall. Terrance Wall."

Foxner's brows rose. "Are you a spy, Mister Wall?"

"If so, it seems unlikely I would admit to such," Terrance said.

"Do you live here? You or Mister Snyder?" Foxner asked.

"I've got my own place, but I stay here a lot of the time," Dylan said.

"I'm merely tending poor Quayla. She was attacked this night near her front stoop," Terrance said.

"By who?" Foxner said.

Terrance smirked. "A hooligan, if you'll excuse me borrowing the term from Quayla's kindly landlady."

"Did she file a police report?" Foxner asked.

"She's been mostly unconscious since the attack," Dylan said.

"Miss Buckler or the landlady?" Foxner asked.

"Dylan, why don't you invite the good detective inside so she can take her ease while she inquires further? Do you have any medical experience, detective?"

"Some." Foxner stepped through the doorway at Dylan's gesture. Her eyes swept the place, falling last on Aquaylae's pale form. Swift steps took her to Aquaylae's side. "This woman should be in a hospital."

"She will survive her injuries," Terrance said.

"We can't take her to a hospital," Dylan said. "She's, uh, scientologist."

Foxner's brows rose in near unison with Terrance's own.

"Scientologist? Are you suggesting that belief system based on science would refuse medical care?" Foxner asked.

"Young Dylan means Quayla's of the Christian Sciences faith." Terrance chuckled. "An understandable confusion."

Foxner studied him. "*Young* Dylan? You're what, five years older than him?"

Terrance shrugged. "I have an old soul."

"Quayla's not really in any shape to answer questions, Detective," Dylan said. "And we—"

"We arrived late in the altercation," Terrance said. "Dylan was too consumed by Quayla's state to get a good look at the villain."

"What about you?" Foxner asked.

"Tall. Muscular. Quite filthy."

Foxner jotted on a small notepad. "Anything else?"

"I'm afraid I do not recall anything further."

"Did you engage the attacker in any way?" she asked.

"Mrs. Cox's baking dish is likely what drove him away."

"May I see your knuckles?"

Terrance shrugged and showed her his unblemished hands.

Foxner's jaw tightened. "Do you mind if I look around?"

Dylan shrugged. "Fine by me."

"Actually." Terrance raised a finger. "As Quayla is the only renter of contract, neither of us can grant you permission to examine her dwelling."

"You have a very odd mode of speech to you, Mister Wall."

"Old soul. If there is nothing else, Detective, I bid you good day."

Dylan let Detective Foxner out while Terrance checked Aquaylae once more. Shock could do many things, and while her current body hadn't actually suffered the shock of death, her soul had. He took the pitcher into Aquaylae's bedroom and scooped what little essence he could from the bottom of her nest.

Remiss, little sister, do you truly want to spend a century cooped up?

"She's gone," Dylan said.

"For now."

"Terrance?" Anima asked.

"Good morning, Anima. How may I serve?"

"Vitae wants you and Quayla at headquarters. We have a situation."

"Quayla's too weak to move," Dylan said.

"Who speaks?" Anima asked.

"Little sister's paramour," Terrance said.

"I haven't looked up paramour yet, but I don't think I like being called one," Dylan said.

"Is her condition such that she cannot be moved?" Anima asked.

"It is."

"I will inform Vitae. Stay with her on my authority until instructions change," Anima said.

Chapter Seventeen

Fantastic Nightmares

Quayla

My head slid up out of frigid water. A vast wasteland of ice and snow stretched out as far as I could see. I reached for the shore. Sight of my hand brought me up short.

My skin shimmered blue—the magical blue of my essence rather than that of cold. A hand stretched down into view. Fine, warm fingers wrapped around my own, not passing through the water but finding a firm grip.

"Up you get, Quayla."

I followed the hand, up a parka-covered arm to the hooded smile of a human-sized Grynnberry. I frowned at our surroundings. "But, I thought you're part of the Summer Court."

Grynnberry heaved me out of the water and held open a soft, white fur coat. I stepped into the offered warmth, sliding my arms inside with a sigh of pleasure. He closed the coat without even attempting to grope and handed me a pair of matching boots.

"This locale is of your choice, not mine," Grynnberry said. "Trust me, I'd rather we were on a nude beach in the Caribbean."

I bent to draw on the boots, erect nipples rubbing against the coat's interior. "Why would I choose someplace like this?"

"Asking a nymph to analyze your dreams isn't going to garner you answers about cigars sometimes being cigars. My kind knows what a phallus is for."

I slipped the second boot onto my foot, watery toes wriggling in the warmth. A frown dragged down the corners of my lips. "You can't be Grynn."

"Is that so?" Grynnberry asked.

"Yes. You haven't tried to grope me. You made no lewd comments about how the cold affected my nipples or even a sly innuendo about rolling around with me inside this fur."

Grynnberry shrugged.

"Wait, you said this was some sort of dream?"

"Not directly, but I suppose you could call it that."

I looked out over the vast arctic landscape.

Why would I dream up some place like this? And why would I include Grynnberry?

Grynnberry's voice entered my thoughts. *<Maybe you're wrestling with something and I represent your Id.>*

"What am I wrestling with then?"

Grynnberry scanned our surroundings. "Loneliness? Isolation? A sense of dread?"

Tears burned down my cold cheeks. As a water phoenix, I needn't have shed them, and yet I needed to let them fall.

"What if Dylan's right?" Grynnberry asked. "What if there were a way for you to walk away from the Shield and just be with him?"

I wrapped my arms tighter, stepping away from him with a shaking head. "There isn't. There won't be."

My footfall disturbed the snow, sending it up in a plume of ash. I bent. At my touch, the snow felt cold, but the texture wasn't iced flakes but gritty ash.

Grynnberry drew me up, interrupting my thoughts. "Are you sure there's no escape? Have you checked?"

"No."

"What about...no, you don't love Dylan enough."

Heat flashed through me. "If you're my Id, a part of me, then you know exactly how much I love Dylan."

"True, but I'm not sure it is really enough for you to do the one thing that would guarantee you could live out your lives together."

"And what exactly would that be?" I demanded.

"Reveal Faery."

I gaped at him. I couldn't believe any part of me would suggest such a thing. Revealing the existence of the faerie folk to humanity would upend the world as everyone knew it.

Any number of horrifying consequences could occur.

I looked out at the cold wasteland, a dingy grey falling over the snow as if plunged under cloud cover.

"True, Creation would change, but there'd be no need for Shields anymore," Grynnberry said. "You'd be free."

"Assuming the whole of us weren't just wiped out wholesale."

"God is love. He granted His new host a soul, didn't He? Why would He wipe out His Creation?"

If wafers knew about the faeries, we wouldn't need to protect the secret anymore. At worst, we'd end up policing the deals to be sure the faeries kept their end, but really, at that point, free will would come into play.

"If humanity knew, a single wish could let you and Dylan grow old together. You could be your own woman—no longer Shield Aquaylae, but perhaps Dylan's Angelica."

I turned my back on Grynnberry, looking over the cold sea.

"I'd be free." My hand came up grey with ash. "But at what cost?"

"Is any cost really too dear to realize true love?"

Detective Foxner

Sabrina Foxner scowled at the closed door.

Something here reeks to high heaven. These people are bending stretched truths almost to their breaking point.

She finished adding notes to her notebook as she descended to the first level. She knocked on a door labeled both '1A' and 'Manager.' A tiny old woman answered the door in flour-dusted apron and oven mitts. "Hello? Oh, police. Are you here about last night's hooligan?"

Sabrina smiled. "That is something I'm investigating."

"Come inside, Officer. I have fresh muffins. Would you care for some milk?"

"I didn't get your name." Sabrina entered behind the old lady to a thick aroma produced by sweet baked goods. A small island in the kitchen displayed numerous cupcake tins stacked atop each other. Empty thread spools separated each level. On the nearest end, dark berries mounded atop bowls besides plant sprigs—green leaves and reddish stems each wrapped in jingle-bell-capped silver ribbon with seven berries left on their branches.

"Mrs. Hadley Sage Cox, widowed *not* divorced."

"Mrs. Cox, what can you tell me about the assault last night?" Sabrina asked.

The little old woman shoved a plate of muffins and a tall glass of milk into Sabrina's hands. Juggling the food without spilling forced her to set her notebook aside onto a doily covered end table.

"They're still warm, elderberry of course, perfect for these dark times."

"Dark times?" Sabrina asked.

Mrs. Cox whispered conspiratorially. "Have you seen the likes they let into the White House? Something hoodwinked the voters, that's all I can say."

"Something?" Sabrina asked.

"Of course, something, certainly not someone. No one person could bamboozle so many people."

"Like what?"

Mrs. Cox shrugged. "The telebox? Music these days? Mushroom rings? That interwebs thing? Who's to say? Wouldn't have happened in my day, oh, no, we trusted in salt, sprig and silver to prevent things like this happening."

Sabrina scanned her surroundings. Nothing in the apartment screamed dementia. The carefully prepared bundles hung in every window and over every lintel. Bookshelves lined the room, piled with books, pictures and knickknacks but not a speck of dust.

"Eat, they're best when warm," Mrs. Cox insisted.

Warm, sweet perfection filled Sabrina's mouth. She'd skipped breakfast, sufficing with only precinct coffee, in her rush to come out here. She inhaled a third muffin before she's realized the first was done. So much bread should have filled her, but her eyes sought the stacked muffins in the kitchen when she realized her plate was empty.

Mrs. Cox swept the plate from her. "Drink your milk, dear, plenty more where those came from. Elderberries are best harvested around the fall equinox when they're at their most potent."

A chill sent gooseflesh across Sabrina's skin. "Potent?"

Mrs. Cox turned, beaming. "Their best flavor, dear. What did you think I meant? Old woman living alone doesn't equal witch, young lady. We did away with that kind of math in old Salem or so I hope."

Sabrina rose, forcing a small laugh. "No, I wasn't suggesting anything of the sort. After all, you don't have any cats."

"Filthy beasts, always give me hives and the sneezes."

"You prefer dogs?" Sabrina perused the bookcases.

"Birds really, but they're too noisy. Disturb my tenants."

A bureau covered in pictures drew Sabrina around the room. Toward the back, silver framed the man upstairs and a woman who strongly resembled the person who'd broken into the Humane Society. She snapped it up, knocking other frames in the process.

Mrs. Cox's voice floated out of the kitchen. "Careful now."

"Sorry." Sabrina compared the printout to the woman. Her

temper blew together like a winter thunderhead. She hurriedly stood up the frames she'd knocked down and brought the picture to the old woman. "Who's this?"

Mrs. Cox smiled. "That's my Quayla and her Dylan. They really should get married. I don't abide unmarried couples as tenants, but there's nothing I can do to stop him sleeping over."

"Quayla Buckler? 3B?" Sabrina asked.

"You run into the name Quayla often?" Mrs. Cox tried to trade the picture for another plate of muffins.

Sabrina didn't let her.

They lied to me.

"I need to borrow this picture, Mrs. Cox. I also need to see Quayla's lease."

Mrs. Cox frowned. "What for?"

Sabrina produced the printout. "This is a picture from a robbery two mornings ago. The woman caught on camera broke into a Humane Society. She stole and murdered animals."

Mrs. Cox snorted. "You think my Quayla did this? The florist who putters around on an electric jelly bean, murdered innocent animals?"

"Video doesn't lie." Sabrina picked a muffin up off the offered plate.

Mrs. Cox snatched it from her mouth. "My Quayla isn't that kind of woman. You will surrender my belongings and leave these premises, Officer. You and your accusations are no longer welcome on my property."

"I can get a warrant."

"Then do so."

Sabrina pulled her phone and aimed it at the frame. Mrs. Cox snatched the picture back, hugging it to her chest. "Good-bye, Officer."

Sabrina picked up her notebook and exited as asked. She stepped onto the sidewalk and called into the precinct. "I need a search warrant for apartments 1A and 3C at the following address."

Mrs. Cox appeared at the top of the steps. She marched down to Sabrina and shoved a red Solo cup into the detective's hand. "Finish your milk."

Sabrina frowned at her.

"Waste not, want not." Mrs. Cox spun on her heels and marched back inside.

Detective Foxner

Sabrina pulled to a hasty stop in the government center parking lot, her temper distracting her enough that she nearly ran her car's nose into the concrete railing. She slammed the door and thundered across the parking lot. The warrant was on the way, but the process had ground to a slow crawl for reasons her captain couldn't explain.

Damn coroner better have that report ready.

She badged into the building, rushed to the elevator bank and hit the down button. Doors opened to a handsome and probably useless man in a suit. He smiled on seeing her, opening his mouth in preparation from some probably unwelcome advance. She stormed inside and stabbed the button for Basement E. He exited on the next stop, eyes dark but never having spoken.

She stepped out of the elevator into white hall lit by flickering florescent bulbs, at least one of them almost as dead as the rest of the floor's contents. She threw open the door. "Where's my report?"

The ginger coroner glanced up and smiled. "Hello, Detective."

The young doctor looked particularly pleased with himself. Behind him a number of large glass jars had been added atop his filing cabinets holding odd body parts she couldn't readily identify. He picked up a purple folder from the corner of his desk as he rounded it. "Here you go."

She scanned its contents—mostly scientific—scowl increasing until one nonsensical word stopped her. "Troll?"

Bradley smiled. "Yup."

"Troll?"

His expression faltered. "Yes, troll. Surely, you've heard of trolls before. Like in Dungeons and Dragons."

Breathe. You can't hit the little shit.

She cracked her neck, trying to imagine calm, picturesque scenes that nonetheless seemed populated by bizarre severed bodies that'd haunted her nightmares. "I never played."

"Oh, fantastic game, really helps build imagination, problem-solving skills, even interpersonal skills—"

She glanced around the morgue. "Obviously."

His smile flickered for only a moment. "Okay. How about Tom Cruise? You look like a Tom Cruise kind of gir-woman."

"Tom. Cruise?"

"You watch movies, right? He did this fantastic movie way back before he became a raving egomaniac."

Sabrina folded her arms and narrowed her eyes.

"Legend? Come on, Tim Curry!"

She tapped her foot.

"Were your parents monks or something?"

Her control lost the war. "What the hell are you blathering about?"

Bradley took a deep breath and exhaled it slowly. "The bones you brought me are from the previously thought mythological creature known as a troll. According to available sources it's a large, generally malevolent beast which can regenerate from nearly any damage."

"Mythological creatures don't exist by definition."

Bradley rounded his desk once more, sliding out a filing cabinet drawer. He rummaged out of her sight until he brought out a bone in a tall glass jar and heavy rubber gloves. He set the jar on an examination table and opened the lid with exaggerated care.

"This is the whole bone you brought me." Bradley ducked under the examination table.

Sabrina reached for the open jar.

"Stop!"

"What?"

"That's very strong acid." He lifted a set of glass tongs. "You don't regrow skin—well, not in a way that would restore what you'd lose."

He took the bone from the jar, walked it over to a wash station and rinsed it thoroughly. "In myth, trolls regenerate, right? Only fire or acid stops them from regrowing anything lost in battle. Insidious creatures really, either they have no females, or they are insanely rare. Not that it matters. Chop a troll in half with a broad sword and you have to fight two trolls tomorrow."

"They regrow brains?"

"Not sure they've got much brain to regrow." Bradley smirked. "Guess I'll find out when I grow a whole troll. My containment ideas are still too weak, need more refining...few more tests."

He set the clean bone on the examination table, placed a face shield across his eyes and took the knob end of the bone off with a bone saw. "There. Now watch."

Sabrina watched, quickly feeling ridiculous. "Watch what?"

Bradley frowned, but it refused to stick long. He rushed to his desk and returned with a ruler. "Maybe this will help."

She watched.

I don't see anything.

"The end has grown a millimeter," Bradley said. "Technically they both did, but I've only got one ruler."

"Bullshit."

"Sorry, bone grows really slow, but it is growing."

"I don't have time for any of this bullshit, doctor. I need to know what happened in that building and your little chemically-induced hallucinations aren't getting me anywhere."

"Look, I could only guess about the lost specimens, but this has to be troll. What else do you know that can visibly regrow itself?"

Sabrina turned her back on him, hoping that not seeing his smug little insane face would help her not put a fist in it. The only piece of physical evidence she had left from the crime scene and the little nut insisted upon blathering about myth and movies.

Just call it a dead end and go see about that warrant.

"Thank you, doctor, for trying. Obviously, it's unidentifiable by medical science." She marched toward the elevator. "Good day to you."

Bradley

Bradley frowned after her. The bone had grown almost a centimeter and had started regrowing the knobby end. He slipped the larger piece back into the acid and resealed the container. He grabbed an 'out to lunch' sign from his desk, hung it on his door and locked himself inside. He pulled a small ice chest from the corpse cooler and laid out the mangy old cat that he'd picked up in an alley that morning.

He gave the cat a once over. The poor malnourished thing's fur fell out in clumps. He found no injuries on the body, but did notice a surgery scar.

She's chipped, but otherwise the body looks sound—must've died of old age.

Bradley couldn't have found a better subject if he'd bought it from the internet. If his experiment brought her back to life, the cat's old age would limit how long Bradley could work with her, but unlike his other experiments, the cat had an intact brain.

He removed the chip to prevent anyone tracking the animal and used a hypodermic to withdraw some troll marrow from the regrowing little knob. He injected the marrow into one of the cat's bones before moving the exam table closer to his desk.

His grin spread as the marrow replicated itself. As with earlier experiments, it melded with the body parts he'd injected and tried to regrow the host animal. An excited giggle escaped him.

He set a torch in easy reach then fetched a lunch bag from the cooler. He plopped down at his desk, eating liverwurst on crackers. While he waited for the dead cat to reanimate he examined the tracking chip. He slathered another Ritz and popped the whole thing into his mouth.

He chewed, salty meat underpinned with the slight sweet of the Ritz crackers. With a shrug, he pulled up the chip tracking database so he could add the cat's statistics with his experiment notes.

"Origination, Howell Mill Humane Society." Bradley scowled at the screen, mumbling dubiously to himself. "Age, eight...weeks?"

He glanced over at the twitching cat.

Must've mixed up their records. So much for that.

Vitae

I knocked on Aquaylae's door. The door opened, revealing her mortal paramour. "Can I help you?"

"Step aside." I shoved past the nuisance toward where Terra loomed over Aquaylae. A grunt of surprise and thud of impact suggested I'd used too much force. A twinge of guilt caused me to hesitate, but Aquaylae's condition drew me forward.

The mortal recovered fast enough to interpose himself. "Who the hell are you?"

It seems I did no lasting damage.

A sidestep allowed me to circle the mortal, but he seized my shoulder and turned me around. "I asked who you think you are."

I looked down at the mortal that'd diverted Aquaylae from her duty. Worry undercut his expression, but he faced me with strength.

Not a warrior, but would he go to war with me to defend Aquaylae?

"I am here to harm Aquaylae, how do you intend to stop me?"

The mortal looked to Terra who'd raised his brows in response. Dylan lifted his elbows away from his body, trying to appear larger. "I'll stop you."

Why in the name of the Light would Aquaylae defy me so vehemently for this ineffectual lump of clay?

"Of course you will." I pushed him from my way.

"Hey!"

I spun on my heels. "I am Vitae, Aquaylae's superior."

Terra cleared his throat. "Technically, Vitae, that designation belongs to Summuseraphi or Vilicangelus."

I ignored Terra and shoved a finger into the mortal's chest. "If you truly wish to help Aquaylae, go downstairs and bring up the stretcher."

The mortal squared off against me. "I don't answer to you, and I didn't invite you in, so how about you get out of our apartment?"

That the mortal would cover his weakness with impertinent bravado only lessened his overall worthiness. I narrowed my eyes, intensifying the glow of my essence behind my glare. "I was told you were worthy of Aquaylae, but instead I find a weakling so ignorant that he'd hamper the one capable of seeing to her well-being?"

The mortal looked over my shoulder.

Terra's basso answered his silent plea for help. "While I cannot excuse his rudeness, Dylan, I imagine Vitae's reactions are centered in concern for little sister's well-being."

"He can help her?" Dylan asked.

"Aquaylae does not have time for your mortal indecisiveness. If you truly care about her life, fetch the stretcher from the ambulance parked below, otherwise step from my path and stay out of the way."

Dylan stormed out of the apartment.

"That was manipulative," Terra said.

I dismissed the accusation with a gesture and marched past Aquaylae's sleeping form toward her bed chamber. "He won't remember this once he's rewritten."

"Little sister will object to you rewriting her paramour."

Aquaylae might well object, but I had both her best interests and the best interests of our Shield in mind. Our duty to protect all of Atlanta trumped her personal desires. The sooner she realized this, the sooner she might prove herself capable of rising to the occasion as a shield. Of course, she wouldn't accept the wisdom of my judgement because she wasn't capable of putting anyone or anything before her own desires.

A surge of fury met me just over the threshold to her bedroom. The untidy disaster substantiated all I believed of her. It provided all the evidence I needed that she wasn't taking her duties seriously. Moreover, the stench of taint clung to walls and carpet.

Living in filth, cavorting with Sidhe in her bed chamber...unbelievable, more it's unacceptable. Once she's safely sequestered, I'll need to inspect the others' residences too. This Shield must become what He meant it to be.

I strode to Aquaylae's nest and glowered at the remaining dregs of essence. "Terra?"

"I am here."

I started but recovered quickly. "Have you seen this disgrace?"

"I employed the remainder of her essence to speed her recovery."

All of it? Had she let her nest grow so low?

"Yes, little sister has been remiss, though not so much as your expression suggests," Terra said.

"What do you mean?"

"Anima logged numerous new seeds added around Atlanta a few weeks ago, shortly after Aquaylae reported a tip regarding the humane societies."

"What is your point, Terra?"

"I believe the level of her nest is a direct result of a hasty assembling of those additional seeds."

"Irrelevant. She's had more than sufficient time to recover such losses. Between her slovenly habits and your use of her remaining essence to stabilize her, she is no longer safe outside the sanctum."

"Vitae," All of Terra's exasperation was voiced in the single word. "Our Shield has decided against living in the sanctum."

I gestured at Aquaylae's nest "This is why shields belong in the sanctum, why there are rules—to prevent shields from running amuck, totally out of control."

Terra watched me in silence for several moments. "Vitae, life is not easily contained with the rigid framework you seem so fond of touting. I have stood shield between Aquaylae and harm. Even had I failed, her egg remains."

"Inept as Aquaylae insists upon remaining, Ignis insists she's discovered the edges of a greater plan. If our Shield is under siege, we cannot afford to be short any shield, not even an ineffectual one."

"Your evaluation is flawed, Vitae. Are you perhaps displacing your guilt over Mare into anger at her replacement?" Terra asked.

I opened my mouth, but Dylan marched into the bed chamber. "What's that about being under siege? What's going on? Does it have something to do with Quayla's death or the attack last night?"

"This mortal knows too much," I said.

"Bylaws permit certain exceptions," Terra said.

"At the Shieldheart's discretion," I snapped.

"That has never been enforced."

I gestured at Dylan. "Obviously, it should be."

"What the hell do you mean by that, birdbrain?" Dylan asked.

"How dare you?" I seethed. "You who live only because of our protection. You are unworthy of Aquaylae, and I forbid you to see her."

Terra's smirk vanished. He interposed himself. "Vitae, I think temperance might be the better—"

I closed the distance between us. "You are not Shieldheart. These are my decisions to make. You'll help me load Aquaylae into the ambulance and assist in the loading of her nest."

Terra stepped back and folded his arms. "Ask with respect, Shieldheart, or do your own lifting."

I considered Terra. He had long been the backbone of our Shield, more temperate than Ignis and more dependable. I inclined my head. "Forgive me, shield brother, my distress over our peril and Aquaylae's condition overmastered my control. I offer my apologies."

"And what about me?" Dylan asked.

I pressed my lips into a thin line.

"Dylan is correct, Vitae. If you owe me an apology, then you owe him no less."

I forced a smile. "I offer you apologies for the harshness of my words. Thank you for bringing up the stretcher."

I exited Aquaylae's bed chamber, eager to draw out Vilicangelus's feather. Summoning a rewrite to excise Aquaylae's weakness from our lives would hopefully focus her on what was truly important. She'd never hold a feather to Mare, but she might become a passible shield with enough discipline.

Removing the mortal would benefit her too, though I doubted she'd understand.

I'm saving her from watching Sidhe or old age take the mortal. The fulfillment of doing her duty will assuage the loss.

Chapter Eighteen

Broken Hearted

Terrance

Terrance set a restraining hand on Dylan's shoulder. "He is not himself. There's been great tragedy this week. We know your value to little sister. All shall be well."

"Why can't she just recover here?" Dylan asked.

"I can coat my bones in stone. A vitae can accelerate her healing."

"Is this about what Mrs. Cox said? About that thing coming here looking for her?" Dylan asked.

"Yes. Something stirs that must be addressed. Aquaylae's investigation cost her a life and almost a second. We cannot afford the loss of a second shield just to guard her here."

"Terra!"

Terrance's smile faltered. "My Shieldheart summons. Blend her drink afresh, that it give her strength for the move."

"She really didn't like it," Dylan said. "It reeks."

"Medicine should never taste like candy, lest we forget that being ill is not desirable." Terrance headed into the living room. Vitae stood imperiously to one side, arms folded and foot tapping.

Dylan took the blender's pitcher from the fridge. Two pulses combined separate layers before he put it in a travel cup.

"Load her," Vitae said.

"In a moment," Terrance said.

Vitae closed the distance between them, heat in his voice. "I should be in the Shield, protecting this city. Instead, I'm here because you ignored my instruction to transport her to headquarters.

Vitae pointed at Aquaylae. "She's laid out helpless and of no use protecting this city because she ignored my instructions to stay out of the Goblin Market and because, despite my strenuous objections, the four of you overruled me and moved out of the sanctum to where faerie can attack you individually."

Terrance raised his brows and canted his head at the couch.

Dylan woke Aquaylae, bringing the drink to her lips. Her nose wrinkled. She pushed it away. "Please, love. You must drink this."

"Stinks," Aquaylae said.

"Medicine shouldn't smell like flowers," Dylan said. "Otherwise you'd get yourself hurt all the time just for a whiff."

Terrance chuckled.

"Sometime today," Vitae said.

"Vitae?" Aquaylae sipped, her face scrunching up. "What is he doing here?"

"You're being moved," Dylan said.

"No." Aquaylae took another drink.

"This is not up for discussion," Vitae said. "You're injured, out of essence and Summuseraphi reported that the assault on you was premeditated."

"You'd be better protected there," Dylan said. "And the others could focus on why faeries are hurting animals if they don't have to guard you here."

"All right." She wrinkled her face but took another swallow. "As long as you're coming."

Vitae stormed forward. "Absolutely not. You're under house arrest, not on vacation."

"We're not allotted vacation." Terrance lowered his voice. "Look how she responds. It might be best for her healing—"

"I declared it not so," Vitae said.

"Very well," Terrance said. "I shall address this with Summus."

Vitae darkened.

Terrance raised his eyebrows. "There is time to declare again."

"The wafer's not coming," Vitae snarled.

"Mortal," Terrance corrected.

Quayla finished the drink. Terrance lifted her onto the stretcher. He and Vitae carried it down the stairwell. Dylan brought up the rear with a hastily-packed bag and a refilled cup of healing slurry.

Mrs. Cox exited her apartment. "Glad you decided to take her to the hospital." Mrs. Cox pressed a silver frame into Dylan's hands. "That officer seemed to think this was important."

Terrance scowled.

As much as I hate to agree with Vitae in this, such friendships are double-bladed with a treacherous edge.

Dylan thanked her and offered it to Terrance. "You'll need to take this. It's Quayla's after all."

Mrs. Cox kissed Dylan's cheek. "Smart boy, this one. You know, I know this preacher..."

Perhaps the other edge protects better than the first imperils.

Vitae

Terra drove away. Aquaylae's mortal nuisance hovered over her, fighting to get her to drink more slurry.

Drinking that shouldn't be a question. Recovering and returning to fighting strength is her duty.

I inclined my head to the mortal woman still trying to get me to taste her baked goods, stepped up to the ambulance and closed one of the doors. "Time to leave."

Weak as she was, Aquaylae held her mortal's hand, refusing to let him leave. I mounted the vehicle and pulled their hands apart, fixing Dylan with a glower. "Time. To. Go."

Aquaylae reached out weakly. "Dylan…"

I crowded the mortal out of the ambulance then jumped down. With my back to him, I slammed the door. When my turn brought me witness of his hangdog expression, I knew it was time to act. I lowered my voice, infusing it with finality. "You are not an acceptable companion for Aquaylae. You are distracting her from her duty and that will get her killed."

Dylan opened his mouth.

Power backlit my eyes. "There is no use trying to make excuses, *you* are the reason her death could've been final."

"I didn't—"

"I will not let one of my shields be destroyed by some frivolous relationship with a mortal who will shrivel and die in the blink of an eye." I shoved Aquaylae's phone into Dylan's hands. "A memento. Cherish it while you still remember whose it was."

The mortal stared down at the phone. Muscles along his face tightened and a reddish tinge crept up his neck.

"Take care with your tongue, mortal. You are fortunate I am leaving you with her memory for any length of time." With a softer countenance, I spoke as to soften his resolve. "This is what's best for Aquaylae. Do you want her to die? Would you instead make her watch you age and turn to dust in her arms?"

With that lasting image, I turned toward my Mercedes. I needed to get Aquaylae situated and see about checking the other shields' residences for signs of taint.

Dylan seized my arm. "I'm not going to let you just push me out of her life. I love her."

"Not enough it seems."

"I'd give my life for hers."

"You'd fight an impossible battle against powerful Sidhe? You, what most mortals would bully as an insignificant geek?" A derisive snort showed my contempt. "Geeks used to be carnival entertainers that bit heads from chickens solely for profit. You're just as greedy, one more selfish mortal unwilling to give up his toys."

"You're wrong."

"Deceive yourself all you like, *great warrior*, but you will not fool me. Be gone and trouble us no more. Defy me in this, and I shall hurry someone along to rewrite away every recollection of your life together."

Quayla

I awoke beneath a thick down coverlet in a bedroom frozen in time—a reminder of royal bedchambers and age-old mistakes. Four antique bed posts supported a looming canopy frilled in hand woven lace. Antique lamps half-heartedly lit the room from atop furniture shaped by the same hands as the bed. "Ani?"

"I am here, Shield Aquaylae," Anima said.

"Didn't I ask you to call me just Quayla?"

"Yes, but the Shieldheart disabused me of that practice."

I tried to sit up. Pain and a whirling room kept me down. I slammed both fists on the mattress at either hand and vented my frustrations at Anima. "It's not his name, it's mine...well as close to a name as I get to have."

"Did you wish something, Quayla?" Anima asked.

I want out of this bed for one.

The automata that ran our headquarters sounded almost hurt, though such a thing shouldn't have been possible.

I reached, but my essence refused to be caught. I furrowed my brow and focused harder. Pain seared though my head. When I failed, only one hope remained to me. "Is Dylan here?"

"Your former companion has been forbidden access."

"Why d'you refer to Dylan as former?"

"Vitae has ended your relationship with him."

A roaring waterfall filled my ears. I lurched out of bed on anger alone. "He did what?!"

Despite the frothing whitewater of my rage, my body was too weak to keep me on my feet. The world swam. My weight teetered onto my broken leg. Bones snapped. Pain lanced up my leg. Initial momentum carried me on as the leg buckled. I collapsed into the nearby bureau. Fire reignited in my chest, nearly eclipsing the pain in my heart.

I collapsed at the wall's foot, barely able to catch breath through sobs, pain and my once again punctured lung.

"Help is coming, Shield Aquaylae."

Tears blinded me. I shook my head, trying to force the words from thought into reality. "Just let me die."

Ignis

Ignis stood over Quayla's bed. He hadn't seen her when she'd first been relocated, but it was all he could do not to wince. "Why haven't you helped her along?"

Vitae glared through lowered lashes. "A lesson is called for. She brought this upon herself."

"She's young."

"It's about time she grew up. She's more than old enough to know better."

Ignis's temper flickered. "We've had a run of Veil breaches. The situation is deteriorating fast, and DragonCon will only make things worse. There's a feeling of oppression on the streets. Even the mortals are feeling it. We need her on her feet."

"The four of us can handle things," Vitae said.

"Vitae—"

"I am as capable of dealing with faeries as you are!"

Ignis held up his hands. "I meant no aspersions against character nor prowess, but you are the Shieldheart. Yours is the only essence that can transform the normal elements into something that can rejuvenate us."

Heat bolstered Vitae's tone. "My duty is to serve the Light. My duty is to guide and correct the members of this shield in service for His glory. I perform my duty gladly despite the fact that you all treat me like your maid—when you're not acting as if I am some kind of pariah. Is a little respect or consideration too much to ask?"

Ignis examined the old life phoenix.

Vitae had taken Mare's death hard. At first, they hadn't questioned Vitae's withdrawal. They'd given him the space he needed to heal. Vitae had emerged from his pain and thrown himself into books and duty. Poor Caelum had taken the brunt of Vitae's drive to form the perfect Shield—until Quayla arrived.

The water phoenix laid out between them brought on the rebirth of Vitae's pain. She'd needed nurturing, and Vitae had needed someone to blame. Ignis and Terrance had done what they could to help Quayla, protecting her from Vitae's temper by limiting the Shieldheart's opportunity to cast blame on her.

They'd tried to help Vitae too, but he'd resisted their efforts and found reason after reason to take issue with Quayla.

Their Shieldheart's loss had embrittled him. As the mortal world changed faster and faster, Vitae hadn't changed with it. In the last century of mortal changes, Ignis had been able to leave the nest, to interact with humanity. Such came with both good and bad, but Vitae clung to the old ways, keeping a lofty vigil separated not only from humanity, but from the others of his Shield.

Life is his element and yet he separates himself from the beating heart of our protectorate.

Ignis licked his lips. "What you ask is within your due. I'll speak to the others, but couldn't you heal Quayla enough for her to—"

Absolute certainty rang from Vitae's words. "What I do is best for her."

Anima claimed Quayla wished openly for death, and she lied to me about that Fae Kissed. I remember the misery of losing a love, but never did that pain escape my lips.

Even in sleep she looked tormented by pain and loss, ghosts and nightmares. His eyes flicked to the scowl on Vitae's face.

Perhaps we should have done more to protect her. Vitae may not be correct, but Quayla needs time to repair not just her body, but her heart.

"I support your decision, Vitae, and will lend my voice to yours, encouraging the others to abide by your wishes."

Vitae's shoulders relaxed. "I am heartened by your support."

"This decision requires you come down among the mortals."

"I am not some hatchling. I can fight just as well as you or Terra."

No doubt, but I rather hope time on the streets reminds you that we employ other skills than just fighting.

"Vitae, Ignis, I am detecting an incursion," Anima said.

"I will see to it." Vitae said

"Terrance is closer, Shieldheart," Anima said. "I merely notified you in accordance with your request."

"Understood. I'll handle the next one." Vitae watched Ignis for an objection.

Ignis offered none.

"Anima, when Terra is through, have him report here." Vitae eyed Ignis. "We can at least ease Aquaylae's discomfort and hurry her onto the path needed for her to see to her own condition."

Ignis patted Vitae on the back. "A wise choice, Heart of Our Shield."

Quayla

I sat naked in my nest, unable to stop the tears. Caelum's phone turned over and over in my hands, but Dylan refused to answer either my calls or texts. He even refused to answer my voicemail pleas to call me back. Fury dug nails into my palms deeply enough that I risked having to rebalance again.

How dare he? How dare Vitae? How could he be so cruel?

A single knock proceeded Vitae into my room. "Good, you're tending your nest."

I folded my arms. "So glad you approve, Judas."

"Wait, why are you doing it that way?" Vitae asked. "That's all wrong. You'll never keep your nest full like that."

How about you go stick fishhooks through your eyeballs?

"Tears are too slow. You need to extrude essence and separate it like you do when you hurl the blade of your Karambit daggers."

"That will leave me too weak to help with all these breaches."

Besides, that hurts.

"We will protect this Shield. You will focus on recovery. Drinking the bolstering slurry will help with weakness, but if you truly wish to speed your return to duty, you must do as I suggest. So, be about it." He strode from my room, closing the door behind him with a firm click.

"Be about it," I mocked. "Do what I say—unicorns fly out of my butt when I fart."

"Vitae did not claim that," Anima said.

Another Judas.

Where I hadn't been able to stop crying, Vitae's condescension and my answering anger dried my eyes. I stood, pulling myself up onto the crossbar to drip. "Suppose you're going to tell me how to do my job or go tattling?"

"I am only a Watcher. I'm not qualified to judge a shield."

"Well, neither is he." I stormed out. "Where is he?"

"Vitae is in the library."

I descended the stairs under a full head of steam. Unsteady legs and traitorous balance stole strength from my charge. I threw open the door. "How dare you order me around? How dare you say whatever you did to Dylan? How dare you—"

"Vitae, the sentry net has detected two, no, three breaches."

Vitae held a hand up in my face. "Status on the other shields?"

"Caelum and Ignis just reported sensing the breaches in their seeds. They're heading to the respective incursions."

"Terra?" Vitae asked.

"Terrance and Summus are still cleaning up a breach pair in the Mall of Georgia," Anima said. "Vitae, I have three more Veil breaches totaling six."

My pulse quickened. "Are any of them paired?"

"Yes. That's very odd," Anima said. "They're all paired—in geographically separate sectors of Atlanta—but all in relatively close proximity to one another."

Vitae stepped around me. "Notify Terra to pick up the fourth as soon as possible. I'll take the ones farthest from him. Whoever finishes first will meet up to help the others."

"I can help," I said.

"When you're done with your tantrum, you will tend to your nest." Vitae scowled at me. "While you remain injured and your nest unable to sustain another rebirth, I cannot allow you to leave the sanctum."

I threw my hands up. "Then what the hell am I supposed to do while you're all out fighting?"

Vitae snatched a book from the nearby shelf. "Educate yourself. Even you ought to be able to manage that while resting between meals and adding essence to your nest so you *can* be of some help."

Vitae sprinted out of the library, leaving me to my anger. I shrieked, almost throwing the book he'd foisted off on me.

Except damaging books reserves you a place in a very special hell.

"That book is quite interesting, Shield Aquaylae," Anima said.

I turned the ancient book over in my hands. Velum pages had

been hand laced between perfectly cut and oiled pieces of leather. The title had been burned into the leather in simple, understated letters: A Shieldheart's Guide to Nests.

I left the book on a side table and did my best to stomp back to my room on my wobbly legs. Vitae refused to allow televisions in the sanctum and I'd never seen a need to collect digital copies of my tear jerkers. Without a way to watch sad movies, I tried to remember them instead, but tears didn't come.

I tried thinking about Dylan.

Nothing I tried penetrated my anger and worry over being out of the fight when my brothers—even Vitae of all people—were embroiled in battle. I paced around my nest. Legs wobbled uncertainly with each step, but the motion eased my feelings of helplessness. Imagining different revenges against my Shieldheart kept the furnaces of my anger roaring.

Anima announced another pair of Veil breaches.

"Have the others cleared the other incursions?" I asked.

"They're still engaged," Anima said.

I snatched up my Karambit and dressed. "I'll take this one."

I charged down the stairs, jabbed the elevator button. Nothing happened. "Ani, I don't have my card. Activate this lock with my access."

The locking mechanism blinked red.

I scowled. "Ani, try it again please."

Red.

"Ani?"

A timid reply exited the nearest speaker. "Vitae suspended your access."

"I'm a prisoner?" I asked.

"You're in protective custody."

"And why didn't you tell me this when I asked you to key the locks?" I asked.

Anima's voice became smaller. "I didn't want you mad at me."

Every feather of my body felt as if it intended spontaneous combustion.

"I am sorry," Anima said.

It's not her fault. It's that damn, arrogant, know-it-all son-of-a-troll!

I paced the foyer, running through insults and options.

If I transmogrify, I could fly out of here.

I turned toward the stairs.

"Just so we're clear, it wasn't me who ordered all the windows and balcony accesses sealed," Anima said.

The shriek escaped my throat like a hunting cry. I stormed into the library, pacing its shelves like a trapped animal. Another Arch opened, but I remained trapped.

"I don't think your actions are very restful," Anima said.

"I should care why?" I asked.

"You should care because you need rest to restore yourself to fighting trim," Anima said.

Vitae has trapped me...for now.

"It seems obvious you are deeply troubled by your inability to assist your Shield brothers," Anima continued. "Your current actions may well be worsening your condition and delaying sufficient recovery to help them."

Blighted hells. She's right. I've no choice but to rest.

"I'm sorry, Ani. I shouldn't have snapped at you. I'm just very frustrated."

I turned to the shelves, scanning them for something that might lighten my mood. Shelf after shelf, I scanned titles. "Is anything here from this century?"

"Vitae finds no literary value in modern written works."

I held back another scream by mere fingertips. I grabbed the nest guide and flopped into a chair. Anima announced another breach. I turned the page with courteously restrained force.

Chapter Nineteen

The Deep Forensic

Bradley

Bradley rushed into Grady Memorial Hospital early the morning after his new cat became its new peculiar form of life. He'd concealed the makeshift cage of nested laundry baskets in a duffel, anxious every time the animal growled its meow. He headed to diagnostics, juggling duffel and package with badging the doors.

A short, plump figure in a doctor's coat met him. "This had better be good, Bradley."

"Better than your trip to the Shire in New Zealand." Bradley offered the package. "Your bribe."

The other doctor opened the box, eyes widening. "Holy shit, this is your entire collection. What exactly are you bribing me to do?"

Bradley lifted the duffel. "I need a cat scan."

"This is an MRI."

"Jesus, Tommy, it was a joke."

Tommy frowned. "I don't get it."

Bradley ducked into the MRI chamber and extracted the cage. Tommy leaned in closer. The reanimated cat hissed at him.

"It's a cat," Bradley said. "Cat scan? Eh?"

"Looks more like a Mogwai you fed after midnight." Tommy stared. "What is this thing?"

"That's the bribe. I need to run tests and I'd rather not answer questions."

Tommy glanced at the package. "You got it. Nothing metal in there, right?"

"I'm not stupid."

"You did score lower than me."

"In one class, and honestly who cares about sociology anyway?" Bradley asked. "Shrinks?"

"People that want to date."

They fell to reminiscing about medical school and weekends roleplaying while the MRI did its thing. When the conversation waned, Tommy turned up the morning news, a sappy grin pointed at the female anchor.

"Government officials confirm that the DeKalb county fire was yet another in a series of arsons fueled by gas lines tampered with to prevent safety cutoffs from doing their job."

Bradley scowled at the anchor. "That can't be right. Safety cutoffs are designed to be tamper proof."

"Valerie'd never lie to us. She's brilliant and beautiful and surely she fact-checks every report before delivering it." Tommy stormed over to the control console, jammed Bradley's flash drive into a port and transferred the test data. "Are we done yet, Mister Science, or do you need something more? Blood tests? A public inquisition?"

"What?" Bradley glanced from Tommy to the screen. He narrowed his eyes.

Is that? Ah, the girl from Tommy's lit course that was nice to him to get project help.

"No worries," Bradley said. "I can do blood tests back in my office."

"Morgue."

"Medical examiner's office."

"Morgue. People will be coming on shift soon. Did you want any more tests? Your CAT scan maybe?"

"That was a joke."

"If you say so."

"Fine, let's run it through. Be kind of interesting to see how she reacts to x-rays."

A concerned expression crossed Tommy's face, relieved by a glance toward his bribe. He led Bradley to an out of the way room, still dark and empty. The cat reacted immediately, howling like it was in pain. Tommy shut off the machine as Bradley rushed forward. The x-rays had burned the animal's skin. New skin grew back in thicker, scaly leather. The cat glowered at Bradley with malevolence befitting a much bigger cat.

"Hells, are those bone spurs growing out of its back?" Tommy asked.

"Looks like it. Still look like a gremlin to you?"

"More like a scaly Vapereon—without the blue," Tommy said.

An idea struck Bradley, provoking a grin.

"I hate it when you get that look. What do you want?"

"Think we have time to take Whiskers here down to radiology? I'd like to run a few more tests to see what other effects the x-rays had on it."

Detective Foxner

Sabrina pulled up in front of the apartment building. Numerous squad cars filled the small strip of parking spaces. She pulled the warrants from her bag. Anger clung to her, amplifying the day's heat. The judge had denied her warrant request to search Terrance Wall's residence, claiming she didn't possess enough proof to link Wall to Buckler as an accessory.

"I want four of you on the third floor outside 3C while I serve the landlady. Two of you go around and watch the back right corner to prevent our suspect from bolting down the fire escape. Be nice to the old lady. She's holding back possible evidence, but she's not involved, and she hasn't actually obstructed yet."

Sabrina climbed the stair, lifting a hand to knock on 1A. Mrs. Cox opened the door before she could, holding out an empty palm. Sabrina handed over the warrants.

"Thank you." Mrs. Cox perched reading glasses on her nose. "This seems in order, two apartments only. I'll comply, of course, no scofflaw—me or poor Quayla. You're barking up the wrong river, Detective."

"I'll be the judge of that."

"You'll be civil to my other tenants and if you break it, I'll be on the phone to Marge in a heartbeat."

"Your lawyer?"

"No, Marge plays bridge with the mayor's assistant's mother."

"I see. Anything else?" Sabrina asked.

"You're not getting any more muffins."

"I'll need you to hand over the picture you took from me."

Mrs. Cox smiled like the kindliest old lady that ever lived. "Returned it to its owner. After that? No idea."

You little—okay, you want to play hardball?

The detective turned to the four officers lining up to search Mrs. Cox's apartment. "Seems our evidence has gone missing."

Faces hardened.

"Please, find it. Remember, only items which include these three people." Sabrina held up pictures of Dylan and both Quaylas.

Mrs. Cox entered her apartment, planted herself in a rocking chair and folded her arms.

Sabrina climbed to the third floor. The sergeant supervising the second team frowned at her. "No answer."

Sabrina smirked. "Guess the landlady gets to come let us in."

She fetched Mrs. Cox and waited while the old lady flipped through a seemingly endless ring of keys for twelve apartments.

She tried each at least twice, refusing assistance with a merry if vindictive smile. "Oh, dearie me, I do hope I haven't misplaced it."

"Picture and a key?" the sergeant said. "Sounds like obstruction, Detective."

"Oh, no, officer. I'd never do anything to obstruct an officer executing his office." Mrs. Cox scowled at the keys. "Just give an old lady a moment to collect her thoughts."

As if you're not sharper than he is, you old fraud.

Mrs. Cox plucked a key at random and opened Quayla's door. She stepped in first. "Is anyone home? It's just me, Hadley, oh and the police."

Sabrina entered after Mrs. Cox. A cursory scan found gaps in the former furnishings. "Stuff's been removed."

"Oh, my," Mrs. Cox repeated. "You don't suppose those nice kids had a spat?"

Sabrina held up more warrants. "Doesn't matter. I've got him covered, too."

For a moment, Sabrina thought she heard the old lady curse softly. She let a smile blossom across her lips. "Okay, sergeant, this one's a full search. Find me something linking these people to our suspect or the break in. I'll be back after I serve the third warrant."

Sabrina drove across town toward Dylan's high-rise apartment, cursing traffic.

Why can't you people take a bag lunch?

Several squad cars waited for her. She considered getting the super before going up to Snyder's apartment, but he answered his door. "Good afternoon, Detective."

"We're here to search your premises." Sabrina handed him the warrant.

He didn't even glance at it, just snorted and waved them in. "Be my guest."

"I noticed a lot of things missing from Miss Buckler's apartment. Can you explain that?"

Dylan gestured to several boxes. "She dumped me."

"This girl dumped you?" Sabrina turned around a high-res printout of her suspect looking adoringly at Dylan.

"No," Dylan scowled at it. "Pretty bad Photoshop work, too."

"You're sure this isn't the woman who dumped you or is it this obviously in love woman didn't dump you at all?"

Anger darkened his features. He stabbed the printout. "As far as I know, *that* woman doesn't exist. And it wasn't my Quayla who dumped me as much as her...boss told me I wasn't welcome around anymore. Do you have any other questions, Detective?"

She brought out her notebook. "What's this boss's name?"

"We weren't introduced. Anything else?"

"Yeah, why's a clean-cut guy like you lying to me for some thief?"

Dylan snorted. "My Quayla, okay, the Quayla who used to be mine, isn't a thief. You're barking up the wrong river."

Sabrina narrowed her eyes. "Say that again?"

"You're barking up the wrong river?"

"Where did you hear that?"

"I don't know, why?" Dylan asked.

"Mrs. Cox said the same thing."

He shrugged.

"Maybe y'all colluded together, built a story to hide Miss Buckler's guilt."

"Think what you want." Dylan folded his arms and stepped to one side.

The search of Dylan's apartment turned up nothing. The search teams reported equal results when she returned to the suspect's three-story walk-up.

"Something's off here," the sergeant said. "No woman alive doesn't have pictures of her and her boyfriend."

"I don't know, Sarge," one of the younger officers said. "I hate pictures of myself. I could see avoiding the camera and just taking pictures of him."

"We found none of those either," the sergeant said. "And a

woman with her own mirrored dressing alcove is vain enough to have plenty of selfies."

Sabrina looked down. Quayla Buckler had broken the law. She'd lied to Sabrina. She'd used someone who was clearly head over heels for her and just thrown him away. She needed to pay. Sabrina held up the warrant for the florist shop. "Let's just hope fourth time's the charm."

Mrs. Cox stepped into their midst. "Are you done, Detective?"

"You in a hurry to see us go?"

Mrs. Cox made an exasperated gesture. "Of course, I am. I'm going to have to burn white sage all afternoon to remove the taint of your bad attitudes."

Detective Foxner

Sabrina hurried into precinct Tech Ops. The day had seemingly exercised a grudge against her. Long grueling hours searching had turned up nothing and kept her busy until the chances of catching Miri grew slimmer and slimmer. Sabrina tried anyway, hoping she'd beat the odds this once and find the tech still in, despite the hour. Light beyond frosted glass lifted Sabrina's spirit. "Good evening, Miri. Please make my day and tell me you have something I can use."

Miri turned toward her, dark curls crowding the edges of her oversized glasses.

If she just added a little makeup and downsized the glasses a bit...focus, criminals lying to your face.

"Yes." Miri turned back to her keyboard. Images popped into existence covering Miri's wall of screens. Dozens of pictures showed her burglar—without the mask—in crystal clear images alongside Dylan Snyder. Several of the images were overlaid by mathematical graphs of some kind.

"What am I seeing?" Sabrina asked.

"She's talented, but nothing is ever truly gone from the internet." Miri sipped out of a mug. "I've used date-time stamps, orbital charts and some algebra to compare the two women in question. They're not the same."

"Did she get the fastest plastic surgery in history?" Sabrina asked.

"Only if she let them chop half a foot off her legs. I suppose you could double check that with x-rays. Calculating heights and builds, they share similar overall mass, but their dimensions are too dissimilar to prove they were ever the same woman—even if they are using the same name and apparently the same man too."

"No chance of getting an order for an x-ray with what I have right now." Sabrina leaned closer. "Did you find any record of my suspect?"

"There are no matches in Federal facial recognition databases. As far as the Feds are concerned, your suspect doesn't exist, and this new girl always has."

"Fingerprint records?"

"Modified the morning of the robbery, but I haven't been able to dig down and prove that the modification wasn't something clerical like an address update."

"Backups?"

"Same modification dates."

"So, what am I dealing with, a super hacker animal extremist?"

Miri sipped her drink. "She didn't do the hacking."

"How do you know?" Sabrina asked.

Miri brought another image onto the screens. Scribbles covered the massive world map. A dot lit up in Washington D. C. followed by a line, then a dot, then a line over and over all over the world in a haphazard and seemingly random string of connections until the last dot lit dead center in Vatican City.

"She's a spy for the Pope?" Sabrina asked.

Miri shrugged. "Vatican denied any knowledge of her."

"Wouldn't they deny knowing a spy anyway?"

Miri shrugged once more and drank. "This is real life, not some Bond film, but aren't you church people supposed to tell the truth?"

"So, I've got proof my suspect was using the same name—"

"And man—talk about identity theft."

Sabrina cracked her neck. "So, we have no proof she ever existed outside social media pictures that you dug out of God knows where."

"I kept notes."

Sabrina paced. "Fine, you *and* God know where. The Humane Society folks found nothing missing except animals which are definitely not in her little apartment."

"None of the animals they listed have any market value."

"Right, so at best I've got B&E with a petty theft kicker. What the hell is going on here?" Sabrina said.

"Could be a cult, animal sacrifice, that sort of thing?" Miri said.

Sabrina leveled a dark expression at her. "Why is it every time I come here you suggest there's some blood sacrifice cult involved?"

Miri shrugged. "Probability says I have to be right sooner or later. Besides, they happen."

"Okay, is there anything else you can tell me about the new Quayla Buckler?"

Miri shrugged. "She works at a florist shop owned by a shell company whose officers don't exist, but all pay taxes."

Sabrina brightened. "Money laundering?"

Miri shrugged and sipped.

"Thanks, Miri. Anything I can get you?"

Miri pushed her glasses up, giving Sabrina a small, matter-of-fact smile. "I'm happy."

Chapter Twenty

War's Burning Heart

Quayla

I knelt beside my nest. The foul taste of Terrance's slurry lingered despite numerous rinses and two ginger ales. I extended a hand over the basin and squeezed my core tighter. As with arming my Karambit, essence pooled in my palm and hung in gravitational defiance. I pushed harder, expanding the mass in hopes enough would accumulate to drop away like rain collecting beneath a wind chime. When it didn't fall, I cringed in anticipation of the coming tearing sensation.

The Shieldheart's Guide had added to what I'd been taught in my initial training. Neither training nor the guide spared me from the tearing sensation which seemed to shred my heart each time essence separated from the whole, but the guide had revealed things my rushed initial training hadn't.

I pushed more essence from my palm, much more than I'd ever managed to force into one of my knives. I could've extruded essence from anywhere. The guide provided advanced methodologies illustrating nuances that theoretically enhanced my ability to transmogrify only part of my body into pure essence. It didn't provide a way to lessen the pain of severing a limb but it did offer a less painful way to rebalance my essence while maintaining my human shape in front of witnesses.

The thought alone made me shudder.

Tactical realities had forced me to hurl essence blades from my hilts, but I repeated the agonizing attack infrequently. Ripping a part of myself away from the whole just plain hurt. No matter how small, the loss weakened me. In my earliest training, it had made me dizzy, even starting with a hale and whole body.

Crying wasn't the most efficient way to refill my nest when it was badly depleted, but I'd gotten used to the painless method. When Vitae'd kept me under house arrest, he'd disdained any contact with me and made even stepping out of my bedroom miserable.

My only expenditures of essence had been to fulfill his demands that I provide seeds for the sentry net which he had both provided and placed for me. When Terrance or Ignis took me into the field—sometimes under vehement objection, they'd kept me from death. There hadn't been any hurry refilling my nest, and I was glad not needing to carve out chunks of my body.

I hate this.

I fought pain aversion and willed my essence to separate. Several cups hung from my palm like stubborn mucus—even when I tried to shake it from my hand.

"Perhaps if you cut it away," Anima said.

Anima offered no physical target, so I glared in general. I drew a Karambit and pushed essence into the hilt. The pressure of maintaining so much essence outside my skin made my head throb. It almost crossed my eyes.

I have to do this. I have to get out there, help the others and prove myself. Then I need to find Dylan. I need him. Besides the shop, he's all I have.

I hardened the blade in my left as much as I could, bringing its edge to my other hand. I touched the blade to the massive drop of essence, cringing at coming pain.

Even though my essence was liquid, it refused to part with an easy swipe. I sawed at it, forming serrated teeth along the blade's edge. Every cut felt as if I were sawing a sword through my chest. My essence clung willfully until the last glistening tendril severed. It fell, almost hovering as if it hoped to be scooped up and embraced once more.

Essence dropped into the basin like runny Jell-O, easily doubling the amount I'd collected after hours of crying over Dylan.

My eyes squeezed tight, a tear running from each corner. I collapsed backward and panted.

Pain won't stop me. Nothing will.

"Between the boost to recovery offered by Terrance's slurry recipe and repeating this feat every four hours, it should only take three days for you to return to fighting trim with enough essence in your nest for a single rebirth," Anima said.

I growled, too tired to hurl full insults.

"That's a substantial acceleration," Anima said. "Vitae will be pleased."

This isn't for Vitae, he can rip off his wings and jump from the balcony for all I care. I'm a shield...a good one.

I fell asleep on the floor, legs still folded. I slept poorly. Nightmares filled my mind with huge scissors and severed limbs. When I was reduced to a wingless torso, invisible hands hurled me from atop the building only to begin again. I woke in the dark of night. The sanctum felt oddly forlorn—dark, empty and haunted.

Anima lit a table lamp across the room, offering me enough light to see without blinding me. I rose, lip quivering at the sight of my nest. I blinked away tears and crawled back to my basin's side.

Repeating my earlier performance hurt more rather than less. Without my phone, I set the bedside alarm for two hours and crawled into bed. The higher quality but narrower mattress felt foreign. Dylan's absence left the bed frigid and forlorn. I curled into a tight ball and tearlessly cried myself back to sleep.

When the alarm dragged me kicking and sobbing from the warm covers, I cut away more of my body, reset the alarm and returned to my nightmares.

The third time my alarm woke me, my body refused to rouse. I fought its sloth toward my nest.

Concern underpinned Anima's rebuke "Quayla, you're severing essence too often. You must drink more of the healing slurry and rest longer."

Chilling the warm slurry didn't make it taste better, but the remains on my bureau had taken on a scent of rot. I crawled to the kitchen—dizzy even on hands and knees. I abandoned a fruitless search for junk food and claimed a container of slurry dated for use a day hence. I stuffed it into a shopping bag with a half-gallon of cranberry juice and dragged both back to my nest.

I choked down all the horrid slurry I could, failed to scour the taste away with the juice and pushed essence out through my palm. The mucousy glob refused to grow as large as the ones before. I severed it anyway and forced out a second.

"Shield Aquaylae," Anima cautioned. "You're going to bring harm to yourself."

Dylan. Freedom. Respect. Once I've reclaimed them all, maybe I'll leave and never return.

"I will be forced to notify Shield Vitae if you continue."

Like he cares. He'd be glad to replace me.

I cut away the second piece and crawled back toward bed. I didn't make it. I collapsed on the floor before I reached my cold covers.

Warmth suffused me when I woke. My fading dream claimed the warmth from Dylan. I turned over, stretching a hand toward my beloved. Questing fingers ran out of bed. I opened my eyes.

Ignis didn't look particularly mad, but his expression was definitely not happy.

He must've warmed the bed.

His expression filled in the pieces I'd cut away with guilt. He knew about the Fae Kissed. I couldn't look at him. I turned onto my other side, facing Terrance's sad disapproval.

I glanced toward my feet.

Caelum glanced up from his phone and flashed a smile. "You are in so much trouble."

I laughed. I couldn't help it even when the muscle motion hurt so badly.

"Little sister." Terrance laid a hand on me. "We are most displeased with you."

"You are not helping things like this," Ignis added. "Healing takes time."

I looked down at myself.

That's what Ignis is mad about?

I bristled. "I could be back on my feet if Vitae would get off his ass—"

"More needs healing than your body," Terrance said.

"And we are all in agreement with Vitae on this," Ignis said. "You haven't been paying proper attention to your duties or your studies."

"If we'd known you hadn't been shown how to refill your nest," Caelum shook his head. "Well, you should've told us you were struggling."

The warmth Ignis gifted my covers shot through me. "When should I have studied, Ignis? When Vitae snarled any time I stepped a toe out of my room? As for you, Caelum, my nest was empty because I had to rush a bunch of seeds and I know how to refill my nest, so why would I ask?"

"Then why didn't you refill it?" Caelum demanded.

"Doing it the fast way hurts. My essence doesn't like to be separated, it's the nature of—" I threw up my hands. "You know what, why am I even bothering to explain? None of you understand. You don't have to saw chunks of yourself away."

"I do," Terrance said. "And I have done so far longer than you."

"I bet it doesn't hurt you like it does me, because you and

Ignis don't feel *anything* anymore, just like Vitae. You're barely more than gargoyles."

Caelum smirked, but neither Terrance nor Ignis looked pleased.

"Vitae was right," Ignis said. "You're long overdue to grow up."

His words hit me like a slap.

"Ignis and I have grown weary of hurting while watching mortals dear to our heart pass from this world, little sister. That does not mean we do not feel."

"True, I don't sever essence very often," Caelum said. "But I keep extra on hand to ensure not being reborn is seldom a risk."

After all I'd been through, I couldn't resist lashing out. "I bet that's *really* hard for you, what do you do? Stand in your nest and tell jokes? Spout hot air while reveling in the sound of your own voice?"

Caelum darkened. "Maybe Vitae is right. If you'll do this to yourself just to get back to Dylan, maybe he'd be better rewritten and out of your life."

Caelum stormed out before I could say anything.

Ignis followed, pausing at the door. "When you are healed, we will discuss the lie you told me."

Terrance closed his eyes, head shaking slowly back and forth. "We are your family, Aquaylae. Like it or not, we will be together a long time, and our memories aren't short. If you want to be a productive member of this Shield—"

"Maybe I don't want to be in a Shield at all."

Terrance's eyes snapped onto mine and seemed to bore deep inside me. He studied my soul for an eternity, still as an old owl save the slowly drooping corners of his mouth.

He patted me. "Rest, little sister. Things will look different once you've recovered."

Terrance turned away.

"Terrance, please don't let them rewrite Dylan."

He looked back from the doorway, scrutinizing me once more. "I have heard your request. Rest."

I struggled upright. I managed to get to my feet and crossed to my nest. I looked at the still forlornly empty nest and then my skeletal limbs.

If I fill my nest any more Anima will inform them.

I turned aside for the library. My legs collapsed just over its threshold, but luckily Vitae wasn't present to lecture me. I crawled to his favorite armchair and collapsed in soft, encompassing leather. A book sat on his side table.

When sitting and panting grew too wearisome, I examined the new book.

"Primal Battle, A Primer on Essence Warfare," Anima said. "Vitae reads it often, apparently finding its contents interesting."

I frowned at the book.

Why would someone hiding in a library reread a battle primer? Does Vitae imagine himself some kind of warrior?

"Perhaps a bath might be a good use of your time?" Anima asked.

I wanted to be angry but didn't possess the energy. "Are you suggesting I stink?"

A bath actually sounds nice.

"I thought it might be relaxing."

"Thank you." I lurched out of the chair, the book coming along by the simple virtue of my never thinking to release it. A hot bath soothed me and the book—authored by a more impassioned Vitae than my own—proved curiously interesting as advertised.

Ignis

Ignis pulled up to the dilapidated strip mall, eyeing the burnt remains of an old church across the street. Faerie taint slammed into his nostrils the moment he opened the door. Fresh flame and the lingering warm aroma of old wood reduced to dormant charcoal rode just under the taint. He grabbed his bag, locked his Camaro and crossed to the obvious arson.

He walked the perimeter, making notes for his report and inhaling once more.

Unseelie? Maybe their Fae Kissed? Whoever it was lingered to watch it burn.

He shook his head, trying to ward off the rising heat in his core. The local fire house had recovered an old caretaker's remains from the rectory's ruins. It'd been a sad discovery, but they couldn't smell the lingering malicious delight of the murder that had preceded the arson.

He eased into the church, looking for the ignition point.

If they did this with spell fire, I'm going to have to fabricate something. Damned faeries, I hate lies.

The scent of Unseelie intensified inside the ruin, eliminating the possible involvement of Fae Kissed. There'd been a lot of them, or they'd come back to relive the murder like some sort of glamour newsreel.

A shift of ruin turned his head. An elven knight stood in ornate armor beneath the arriving wave of twilight.

Ignis's jaw tightened. "Which of yours did this, Sir Dolumii?"

Flaming hands seized Ignis's arms.

Efreet? What are Wyldfae doing working with an Unseelie knight?

Ignis addressed the efreet. "This action violates the Articl—"

"I set them upon the Betrayer's house. I killed the old caretaker," Dolumii said.

Efreet, I should've smelled them. Vilicangelus, hear my call.

Ignis tried to pull his arms free. "After you tortured him."

"Played, not tortured. Everyone likes to play with fire." Dolumii smirked. "I know you do."

Ignis reached into his core, gathering energies for a transmog. With the gaps in the burnt church and dim twilight making his flaming form all the more apparent, there'd be hell to pay.

Later and paid with Dolumii's hide.

His heat rose, but the efreet tightened their grip, growing stronger off his power while preventing his transmogrification.

"The wafers have a saying, fight fire with fire. Who knew they possessed wisdom?" Dolumii leaned in close, stroking the fingers of his gauntlet with magic that stretched them into a bladed claw. "Lore masters whisper that if you can rip out the still beating heart from a fire phoenix, it becomes an eternal flame—one that might prove able to control a phoenix. Shall we find out?"

They're stealing the energy before I can build it up to transmogrify. They're too strong to fight my way free. I must sacrifice this life and return.

"You know I'm coming back for you," Ignis said.

"Please do." Malicious delight twisted Dolumii's face. "Then we can try out my new toy."

Ignis focused on his inner self image, pouring all his strength into the mental picture.

Dolumii's hand drove into Ignis's chest.

Ignis fought to ignore the pain with every ounce of willpower, focusing on himself as his missing heart beat once more, before igniting in the elf's hand.

Vitae

An agonized shriek rippled through my study. An almost unintelligible word reverberated in the echoes of the dying cry. I bolted from my seat, setting my copy of Les Miserables onto the side table. My gaze shot to Aquaylae's statuette, but she was not the source of the cry. Eyes scanned the others, finding Ignis's ruby figurine folded in on itself. An odd pulsing lit the statuette in waves, nothing I'd ever seen. I sprinted to the control room.

"Vitae, a phoenix has fallen," Anima said.

My response came out an impatient bark. "Get me a location."

The map shifted to the far eastern end of our jurisdiction. A gaping hole deadened the sentry net around the area.

I cursed. "Where are the others?"

A quick scan showed the others further from whatever had cost Ignis his life. "Notify Summuseraphi."

I bolted for the exit, snatching twin canes from an umbrella stand next to the elevator doors. I rushed sideways into the parking deck, not waiting for the doors to open fully. A flash of light coalesced between me and my Mercedes. I bobbed my head in hasty respect and jumped into the car. "Ignis's last word was efreet."

Summuseraphi leapt into the other seat, fastening a seatbelt.

"Divine One, shouldn't you coordinate from upstairs?"

"This is the second phoenix I've lost my first month as your Praefectus," Summuseraphi growled. "Drive."

Dolumii

Dolumii bounced the burning jewel in his palm, willing it aflame and extinguished in delighted turns. He pulled a cell phone from his belt pouch, giving the instrument a dubious frown. He touched it in the sequence he'd been instructed.

A deep, powerful voice boomed one word. "Report."

"It is as bargained, mortal," Dolumii said.

"Leave the salamanders to face the Vitae."

"I do not trust these Wyldfae," Dolumii said. "And what if they send another phoenix rather than the Vitae?"

"Agents are in position to prevent that. I've fulfilled my end. Don't forget yours, *Sidhe*."

The device sparked, melting like snow brought to the desert. Dolumii shook the remnants from his fingers, drew his sword and reopened the rend he'd cut in the Veil. "Stay here and deal with the Vitae. Keep him as long as possible as you have bargained, Wyldfae."

He stepped into Faery.

Quayla

"Ignis has fallen." Anima's voice echoed out of my nest.

I froze.

As soon as I recovered, I lurched to a sitting position in bed, swung my emaciated legs over the side and placed Primal Battle on the side table. My thoughts raced a thousand miles an hour.

Iggy is dead? Wise, professional, experienced Ignis? How? Why?

I shut my eyes and reached out to my seeds. None of my seeds sensed new taint. "Ani, what happened?"

"Ignis did not report anything regarding an incursion. He did not transmogrify, but his dying word was efreet. Vitae and Summus are en route to investigate."

"Vitae *and* Summus?" I scowled. "That's not protocol. Whatever, I'm on my way."

"Shield Quayla, you are too weak. Please lay back down and continue your reading. I am sure they can deal with whatever slew Shield Ignis."

"They might need me."

"You are still not allowed to leave headquarters," Anima said.

I cursed, but I lay back down on the bed and stared at the ceiling.

I hate this.

Vitae

I screeched to a halt behind Ignis's Camaro. Throwing open my door and charging across the street, I barely avoided getting hit by a UPS van. Blazing firelight flickered in the early evening darkness within the burnt out church.

Fire? But Ignis is dead.

"Vitae, stop," Summuseraphi called from the Mercedes. "Don't you smell that?"

I ground to a halt in a gap in the church's wall. A pair of elfish figures reclined against broken furniture, their golden scaled doublets shimmering reddish in the small bonfire between them. They rose, stepping from either side into the bonfire. Flames shot skyward, splitting into two towering spirals firestorms. Massive burning wings spread as the spiral became serpent-shaped.

I froze, unable to move body or thought as I looked up at a threat greater than a bevy of Seelie knights. They swept their wings together in unison, filling my world with flame and death.

Blinding light walled me away from the pain.

I opened my eyes to find Summuseraphi's wings wrapped around me. The archangel leapt over me, a glowing spiked chain spinning in either hand.

The divine phoenix might've been young, but he was brave and quick on his feet. He darted around the towering efreet, lashing them in alternating blows as he danced out of reach of their strikes.

I collected myself, took control of my essence and shifted it through my fighting canes. Three-quarter moon blades of red-gold plasma wrapped around the ends of my fighting sticks.

Efreet, efreet, I must remember.

My blades carved deep lines into the nearest faerie. The efreet cried out. My energy plummeted without warning as the efreet's wound closed. A flaming claw raked me. The blow staggered me, but didn't immediately flare with pain. Agony engulfed me a moment later as the deep, charred gouges screamed their arrival.

I bit my lip and sliced the efreet's leg off at the knee.

My energy reserves all but vanished. My knees collapsed

beneath me, leaving me looking up as the efreet's limb reknitted and rose to stomp me.

Efreet can't do that.

Summuseraphi tackled the efreet at the last moment, my own efreet reduced to dying lumps of coal.

Coal? That's not possible, unless...

"Divine One, these aren't efreet at all, they're salamanders."

"I know that," Summuseraphi slashed an X across the fire serpent's skin.

Chapter Twenty-One

Assault from Above

Dolumii

An additional new moon appeared high in the night sky. Light pollution hid the gaping hole, camouflaged by roiling faerie fog from the wafers below.

An indigo-scaled wyvern slipped from within the Arch.

Sir Dolumii rode erect and resplendent on the beast's saddle. Shadowy colors swirled over his ornate armor as they winged their way toward city center. Dolumii turned the dragons' simpler cousin so that they circled the Shield building.

His wyvern drew in breath until the saddle straps creaked.

They flew low over the Shield's greenhouse.

Vitae

"Vitae!" Anima's panicked cry escaped the bronze angel on the Mercedes dash so loud it reached me from across the street. "We're under assa—"

Dolumii

Dolumii's wyvern let out the roar caged in its swollen lungs.

An ear-splitting shriek reverberated against high-rise buildings.

Glass in a three-block radius shattered, leaving the tougher glass of the Shield's greenhouse only cracked.

Power flickered and finally plunged the grid zone into darkness.

They landed on the penthouse patio and Dolumii dismounted. He closed his eyes and felt the area. The power outage was a bonus, but the true goal in the wyvern's cry was to knock out magic in the area. A smile played across his face.

Five gleams within the greenhouse and a sixth for the Shield-heart's nest confirmed that he'd knocked out the automata and any defenses. A seventh gleam came as a welcome surprise.

He patted the wyvern with an indigo glove and drew a dark sword bearing tormented faces cast in bluish-silver. The tormented opened their mouths, sucking the warmth from the immediate area.

Neither balcony nor patio offered direct entry into the greenhouse. Accessing the targets required he entered the sanctum then navigate a short hall intelligence suggested could be turned into a kill zone by the Shield's automata.

Dolumii sauntered toward the nearest door, footsteps crackling on broken glass as he stepped into the dark residence through an empty frame.

Chapter Twenty-Two

Shattered Shield

Quayla

I slapped my hands against my ears. Primal Battle slipped off my chest as the bedroom was plunged into almost total darkness. The runes drawn into my nest's basin pulsed a dim, steady rhythm.

Crap, what did the book say that means?

I reached for the Shieldheart's Guide before I realized that without a flashlight, I wouldn't have been able to read the pages even if someone hadn't removed the book from my bedside.

"Ani?"

No one answered.

A sudden foreboding wriggled down my spine with icy feet.

"Anima?"

The sound of boots crunching on glass reached me.

I looked at the glowing essence in my nest. There wasn't enough for another death.

What do I do?

Vitae

My opponent sprawled beside his partner's coal embers. His touch rekindled the embers back to life. They wriggled like a lizard's discarded tail, reforming into a tiny frilled salamander then reigniting in a blinding blaze—exploding in size and heat.

"Go," Summuseraphi said. "Defend your sanctum, Shieldheart."

I had to get back to headquarters. I had to defend the eggs. Between traffic and distance, only two methods offered rapid enough transit.

Transmogrify and fly, or...

I summoned all of my essence. Unlike the other shields, my essence could augment any element. Combined with already magical essence, my power could double or triple an equal amount of another phoenix's essence. I'd never tried with Vilicangelus, but as powerful as a Divine One could be, young Summuseraphi needed my strength more than I did.

I threw all of my energy at Summuseraphi, pouring out my life force to enhance Summuseraphi's already divine essence.

Too bad I cannot live to see what he does with it.

Summuseraphi exploded in size, gleaming ever brighter.

A salamander claw swept out at Summuseraphi's unguarded back. I knew death beneath the burning talons would be more agonizing than the others available to me, but I threw myself between Summuseraphi and the blow.

Dolumii

Another cry rent the night.

Dolumii's jaw clenched. He drew a sphere of dark, crackling energy from beyond the Veil.

A griffon's cry?

He scanned an empty sky and cursed softly.

How did they know? Better hurry.

Unlocking the door forced him to choose between sword and spell. He embedded his blade in the energy ball, opened the door and entered the upper foyer. The reek of phoenix saturated the place. He pushed it aside and reached for the outer doors leading into the garden tunnel.

An ornate blade nearly cut his hand off. "Stealing this Shield's eggs was not part of our bargain. I won't allow it."

Dolumii yanked his sword free and struck an *en garde*. He smirked at the Seelie elven knight. "You're merely upset to learn we thought to exploit the Shield's weakness before you, Gherrian."

Sir Gherrian smirked, shrugging one shoulder. He launched himself at Dolumii.

Swords clashed.

They dodged and weaved, slashed and circled.

Magically-enhanced edges cut through furnishings and fixtures.

Quayla

The ring of swords hitting one another reached me. None of the others used weapons with steel blades. Two—if not three—Sidhe factions were assaulting my Shield.

"Summuseraphi. Summuseraphi. Summuseraphi."

Nothing happened.

The calamity grew louder and closer.

He must be busy, leaving only me to defend our sanctum.

I forced myself out of bed, grabbing both Karambit hilts and staggered over to my nest. Stepping into the basin, I set both hilts atop the bureau, crouched down as low as I could inside my nest and concentrated the power within my frail body.

I released the gathered power. Waves of essence rippled through me, converting my human body into pure essence without allowing a full transmogrification to my true form.

I grabbed one of the hilts.

I held the knife backwards beside my throat.

I have to defend the sanctum.

A shimmering blade slid from the end.

I have a duty.

I braced myself.

I love you, Dylan.

Anima whispered out of nowhere. "Shield Quayla, stop, please."

"Ani?" The arm holding a blade to my throat started to shake. "But, the power's out."

"I am not a computer AI as is thought, though I often work within that system," Anima said.

"What's going on?"

"With the security system down, my senses are limited so far away," Anima said.

"But you stopped me, knew what I was doing."

"You are within your nest." Anima said it matter-of-factly, but the comment told me less than nothing. "You cannot slay yourself. The nest doesn't hold enough essence for a rebirth."

"Can you help? Call the others?" I asked.

"Only you are near angelic runes."

"Then I have no choice." I pressed the blade against my throat.

Dolumii

Gherrian tried a head cut.

Dolumii parried, seizing a dirk from his belt. He lunged with the dirk, trying to pierce Gherrian's gut. Gherrian retreated, spun to his left. He flipped his cloak up, fluttering the heavy velvet into Dolumii's face. Dolumii dove down the glass hall.

Gherrian's laughter brought him up short.

A griffon crashed through the ceiling and into the hall, screeching as its talons reached for Dolumii. A wyvern head shot in through the opened ceiling, snapping at the griffon. The griffon bowled over Dolumii, too intent on escaping the dead end to strike at its Unseelie enemy.

Gherrian got a low lunge in past the beast. Pain lanced up Dolumii's leg. He beat Gherrian's blade and sliced the dirk across Gherrian's face. Gherrian threw himself backward to protect his eyes. Dolumii pursued. Gherrian leapt onto the stair railing to avoid his griffon. Dolumii followed up onto the banister in pursuit. The two danced up and down the railing, swords flashing.

A disarm and riposte sent Dolumii's dirk down the stairs. Gherrian lunged once more. Dolumii beat the blade aside and answered with a quick thrust and then a ball of eldritch fire.

The spell blasted Gherrian sidelong off the railing through a set of double doors. Dolumii pursued his mortal enemy, unwilling to give quarter. Gherrian threw a dressing dummy at him, complete with a chalk-marked suit. Thrust and slice, spell against spell, they fought through a well-appointed room suitable for a gentleman. Their battle left Vitae's chambers suitable only for a formerly rich vagabond.

Emerald and purple blood flew, painting the room.

Quayla

"Please." Anguish riddled Anima's plea. "Quayla don't do this. There are intruders in the garden."

"I have to protect the sanctum."

"There isn't enough essence."

The cry of a dying phoenix delayed my stroke. A griffon cried challenge, answered by a wyvern.

My heart tore at the loss of one of my brethren. Grief steeled my resolve. "God willing, there will be enough."

The Karambit knife bit into my throat.

Anima wailed. "No!"

The world tunneled as I clung to a desperate hope with my dying gurgle.

Vitae

My new body exploded from a blood-filled basin in a swirling wash of burning red-gold energy. Plasma settled into naked flesh as I snatched fighting canes from wall mounts on either side of my nest. I shoved life energy through the canes as I connected their butts to form an Egyptian lajatang.

The bladed staff spun in my fingers as I turned toward the two battling faerie knights. Dolumii caught Gherrian through the chest with his sword. He kicked the other knight from his blade and whirled to face me.

Anger wrapped a fist around my heart. I wove the bladed staff back and forth in front of me, searching for the new body's balance.

Several things happened with no perceivable lapse in time.

An agonized griffon cry ripped through the sanctum.

A wyvern roared its frustration.

Another phoenix death cry pierced the air.

There is no time to acclimate.

I charged the Sidhe in a furious flurry of edges.

Quayla

My new body swirled up from an empty nest.

Thank the Light, I wasn't sure that would work.

I gulped air in near perfect darkness. Overwhelming taint turned first breaths into choking. I doubled over low in the basin. In front of me, my nest's runes throbbed dimly like their batteries were nearly dead. No essence remained within to glow.

"Anima?" I whispered.

A voice might have answered, but too softly to hear clearly.

My hands took a quick inventory of the new body. Cold shot through me. I was whole—two arms, two legs, ten fingers and toes. I wasn't the emaciated skeleton I'd been, but my new body wasn't nearly as athletic as the last two.

I must have positioned myself wrong. Not enough of my old essence fell into — The area around my nest was as bone dry as the basin. A crash of glass and twin bestial screams sent adrenalin through my body. I snatched up my fallen knife and grabbed the second from my bureau.

I managed a single step out of my nest.

A massive, invisible hand squeezed the breath from my chest.

All strength washed out of me.

The world swooped, spun and fell away.

The grip on me felt tighter than the half-ogre's but without the accompanying sound of breaking bones.

I mouthed silently, unable to draw air.

Vitae

Dolumii dodged my first strikes.

Two bladed edges against one, my attacks slowly mounted in advantage. A palpable redoubling of taint slammed into me, stealing my momentum for only a moment. A gleaming ball of eldritch magic swirled in to fill Dolumii's palm.

I launched a flurry of short slice-thrust combinations at the elf, meant to keep the intruder on the defensive.

The ball grew in intensity.

A shift in movement stole my attention for a split second.

Gherrian drove his short blade into the back of Dolumii's knee.

The ball of magic flared and flashed as Dolumii tried to keep the magic under his control through the pain.

I braced myself for a charge into the teeth of his magic, but uncertainty stole the initiative.

What happens if he loses control of all that energy?

Dolumii hurled his sword. I yanked the staff into two pieces, swept up both fighting canes and sidestepped—right into Dolumii's thrusting magic-filled hand.

Magical agony swallowed me—an amorphous violet, gelatinous hell. Screams ripped out of my throat, growing as primal as any bird of prey. I fought against the agony, concentrating my essence in hope that transmogrifying would break me free.

Beyond the magic, Dolumii struggled against an injured Gherrian while maintaining the torturous spell imprisoning me.

Another shape appeared in the doorway, a darker silhouette beyond the glowing violet. Blazing crescents of light gleamed in each of her hands.

Her whispered carried to my ears. "I'm here, Vitae. I'll save you."

She spun forward in a flash, launching shimmering blades.

No, the spell!

Time seemed to slow.

Dolumii's sword impaled Gherrian, knocking him backward into a slow fall.

The s-shaped blades hurdled end over end.

Dolumii's head snapped up.

His blade rose ever so slowly to parry Aquaylae's assault.

He missed.

Two blazing comets of power impacted Dolumii.

Aquaylae's essence flashed over Gherrian and into the elf knight whose magic engulfed me. In and of themselves, the essence blades didn't have sufficient mass to knock Dolumii backward, but the impact cost the elf his control.

My agony doubled as the spell flared out of control.

Aquaylae's essence reacted with the raw faerie magic like elemental potassium exposed to water. Dolumii's inner magic—linked to the magic run wild—went critical.

Dolumii exploded.

Armor, blood and bone shot in all directions. The sharp projectiles shredded my naked flesh. A humorous bone impaled my forehead, killing me for the second time that night.

Quayla

Magical backlash threw me through Vitae's doors—a hailstorm of vicious shrapnel close on my flight path.

I slammed into the stair's side, head snapping back against the wall. Novae of blinding pain erupted from the countless shards piercing my new flesh.

Darkness swallowed me in a single gulp like Jonah's fish.

Vitae

I coalesced in my nest once more. Only the dim glow of my basin's runes illuminated the otherwise pitch darkness. Nausea and vertigo shook me like a terrier. I kept myself upright only by reaching the bar crossing above my alcove. Breath came and went from my lungs in heavy gasps even though my new body shouldn't have been winded. I needed to check myself, but the incursion of not one, but two Knights of Faery took precedence.

I looked out my shattered window over a lightless city. I blinked several times to encourage my eyes to adjust. Dim shapes of blood and bone eased into my visible spectrum as I scanned the room. Both faerie swords gave off a pulsing magical glow.

I reached down for Dolumii's blade. The hilt writhed a moment, reshaping itself to the contours of my hand. I swished it back and forth, distracted by how right the blade felt in my grip.

An electrical shock lanced up my arm. The grip beneath my hand dug spiked into my palm. Vertigo assailed me once more.

<Vitae...>

All breath emptied from my lungs.

Mare's voice eviscerated me. *<Vitae...help...so much pain...>*

The blade adjusted to fit my hand again, cutting off Mare's screams. I tossed the sword onto my bed and stared at the cursed thing. It wasn't possible. She couldn't be alive inside the sword. She couldn't have been left for two centuries of torture because if it were true then we'd abandoned her.

Then I abandoned her.

Overhead lights flickered to life. I snatched up my fighting canes. If Sidhe remained in the sanctum, they would answer for more than just the invasion of the Shield.

"V-Vitae?"

The sound of the automata meant more than restoration of power, it gave me an ally I could count upon. "Yes, Anima, good. What is our status? How bad is the damage?" I tried to keep the eagerness from my voice. "Are there any more faeries present?"

"Not all my systems are back online yet," Anima said. "Was Quayla reborn?"

Temper flared at the automata's return to the familiar address. Before I could chastise it, I recalled the fourth shape in my doorway. At the time I'd thought Aquaylae had joined the fight, I'd even thought I'd heard her voice, but I knew both had to have been imagined.

Aquaylae was selfish and lazy. She didn't have enough essence to be reborn, and she'd never risk herself for the Shield.

I took a step toward the control room, but my head swam. Up seemed down, left seemed right. Nothing seemed certain. I had never seen the kind of marvelous, magical reaction that had killed me. I pushed the random thoughts away.

Could I be wrong? Did I hear her death cry when the spell exploded?

"Thank Him in all His Glory, she's laying outside your room."

"Anima what are you going on about?"

"Quayla killed herself atop her nest so she could defend the sanctum," Anima said. "I warned her that she didn't have enough essence, but she didn't listen."

"Typical."

"Oh, no. Vitae, the eggs are gone."

No. That's not possible. Both the knights are...dead. I need to see for myself.

I hurried toward the garden.

I stopped short in my doorway.

A woman lay supine against the stairwell wall. Shrapnel punctured her in countless locations and her head lolled in a crater dented in the drywall.

Could this be Aquaylae?

The naked woman seemed very thin. Short dark hair fell across her face in shallow waves that barely reached her chin. Small breasts, narrow hips, she looked more like an adolescent than a fully grown woman.

Irritation flashed through me.

I don't have time for this. I need to see about the eggs and then Mare.

I bolted for the stairs.

Anima spoke before I made the third step. "Shieldheart, Shield Aquaylae's nest is empty. She's injured. You must tend her."

"Fine." I rushed back down the stairs and threw the naked woman over my unclothed shoulder.

If this is Aquaylae, the fountain's waters will suffice to restore her.

Broken glass left a trail of my blood from the stairs to the fountain's edge. I lowered the bloody Aquaylae into the fountain's basin. A groan of discomfort escaping her lips became a sigh. She went still in the water, save for a shallow rise and fall of her chest/.

There, she's breathing, now to the business at hand.

I circled the fountain. As ripples from Aquaylae's motions eased away, I caught my reflection. My new body appeared shorter and finer boned. My facial features seemed more angular, but all together the handsome new body filled me with pleasure.

Eggs, right.

My circle brought me around the fountain one alcove at a time. Beneath each guarding putto our egg cradles gaped empty. My chest echoed their emptiness with hollow cold.

Only one alcove contained anything.

Fragments of Aquaylae's shattered egg traced the path they'd broken up. Larger pieces sparkled beside tiny shards in the fountain's bottom, purple in the blood-stained waters.

My eyes shot to Aquaylae's chest and my breath caught in my throat until her bosom rose almost unperceptively.

Light filled the greenhouse. "Vitae?"

I turned, groaning inwardly until I remembered Summuseraphi's assault on the salamanders. He'd proven an accomplished warrior. Of course, adolescents excelled at fighting. Warrior prowess didn't give him the wisdom of a Divine One. I bowed to our so-called Praefectus. "Summuseraphi."

Summuseraphi appeared worse for wear. His eyes fell on the empty cradles and then on Aquaylae. He hurried to her side. "Thank God, she's still breathing—though something about her looks off."

"Her mass is wrong, Praefectus, and her nest is completely empty," Anima said.

"How is that possible?" Summuseraphi asked.

"Without power for the recording devices, I can only guess her nest didn't catch as much of her essence as she'd hoped it would when she killed herself."

Summuseraphi pinned me with hard eyes. "She chanced suicide without her egg and with insufficient essence so she could protect the sanctum and you want her Destroyed?"

"She couldn't have known her egg was gone or she wouldn't have done so," I said.

"Are you so sure?" Anima asked.

"She's no Mare."

Summuseraphi slipped a hand beneath Aquaylae's head. "Vitae, add your essence to the waters."

"She's fine," I said. "We've got more important things to handle."

Blazing white light flared around Summuseraphi, writhing like a flaming aura. "I gave you an order, Shieldheart. Obey it."

I glowered but obeyed. I pushed essence out one finger, lowered it into the water and severed half of the offering by will. "There, now can we focus on what'd truly important?"

Summuseraphi's jaw clinched. "Tell me all that has happened since you left my side."

I gestured around us. "We were assaulted. Knight Dolumii and Knight Gherrian attacked our sanctum."

"Sensors are picking up evidence they were both mounted," Anima added. "No bodies were left behind, but I sense wyvern and griffon blood in addition to the Sidhe knights."

"Where are the others?" Summuseraphi asked.

"They are all engaged in Veil breaches, Praefectus. Caelum was ambushed on his way to a breach. He managed to defeat the faeries and continue on to the nearby breach, but he hasn't called back in yet," Anima said.

"Terra and Ignis?" I asked.

"Ignis was reborn and headed back to the site of his death."

"That's been dealt with," Summuseraphi said.

"It was not at the time, but I did tell him you and Vitae were handling it. I will brief him and the others once they are in communications range."

Summuseraphi frowned. "You don't have cellular capacity?"

"Vitae felt it prudent not to connect my systems with those of the mortals," Anima said.

"When time allows, I'll address that alongside my other concerns," Summuseraphi said. "What's the status of your Terra?"

"Injured and engaged with a third breach."

"Recall them all as soon as you get a hold of them," I said. "This is a full recall, Anima—nests and all. They're not safe living outside the sanctum."

Summuseraphi gestured. "Your sanctum doesn't seem that much safer, all things considered."

I bristled.

"Damn, you people require a lot of work." He glanced skyward. "Five rewrites and five deaths in less than a week. Ani, is that a record?"

"No, sir," Anima said. "Should I check what the record is?"

"Don't bother," Summuseraphi flopped onto a bench. "I have a feeling we'll be breaking it. Vilicangelus said the Shields in this territory would be little effort—practically managed themselves. How many Arches have opened since I started? Oh, right, you don't know because your web is full of holes."

"Have you notified Vilicangelus?" I asked.

"He's got his wings full, besides, I can manage this mess you call a Shield."

"I think perhaps you should reconsider, after all—"

Summuseraphi leapt to his feet, fire shrouded him once more. Light pulsed outward from his aura in waves that slammed against my body. "I said I can handle this."

Obviously not.

I took a reluctant knee. "I offer apologies."

Summuseraphi narrowed his eyes.

"Shall I set up a meeting with the Courts?" I asked.

"Why would we want to do that?" Summuseraphi asked.

I'm going to revenge Mare and get some answers.

"This Praefecture contains royal enclaves. We have two dead vassals. Their deaths and associated break-in must be formally addressed," I said.

Summuseraphi chewed his lip. "Do we want to inform them that we've lost our eggs?"

"One of them is already aware," I said.

Summuseraphi paced around the fountain, gnawing his lip. "Do we have any way to track the eggs besides proximity? Any evidence to suggest which Court took them?"

"Whatever took out power, took out our automata too," I said.

Summuseraphi's brows furrowed.

"All the sanctum cameras were taken out of commission when power in the surrounding blocks was disabled," Anima explained.

Summuseraphi cursed. He cringed, looking skyward. "Your anti-mortal leanings are costing this Shield, Vitae, but we'll have to deal with that too when time allows."

This is our new leader. God truly does favor the foolish things in Creation.

He stared out at the surrounding city. "The wafers will want an explanation. What in God's Creation are we going to tell them destroyed all the glass and knocked down power in a three block radius?"

"It was a wyvern's primal cry," Anima said. "The expulsion of magical sound designed to stun sorcerers and temporarily rob them of magical energy."

"I *know* what did it, Anima, but I can't tell the wafers—"

"Mortals," I said.

Summuseraphi stopped his pacing and glowered at me. "As I was saying, I can't tell the *mortals* that a wyvern did it."

"I stand ready to assist in whichever manner you desire."

If you ever come to an actual conclusion. Why ever did they promote this incompetent oaf instead of me? My failure? Well, I'll show them who is suitable and who is not.

Summuseraphi narrowed his eyes at me.

I stiffened.

Where did that thought come from? Of course our next course of action requires dutiful thought. I shouldn't criticize a Divine One. There are no individuals, only the Shield.

"Anima, run a search for possible causes the mortals might believe," Summuseraphi said, "and inform the Courts we're coming for a call."

"They will not willingly meet on such short notice," I said.

"Inform them that saying no is not an option."

Chapter Twenty-Three

Declaration of War

Detective Foxner

Sabrina waited in one of three uncomfortable precinct chairs outside her Captain's office.

Purposefully uncomfortable.

A smug detective from homicide with an all too cute pixie cut sauntered up to her. "Oh, how the mighty have fallen."

"Buzz off, Mary," Sabrina said.

"Not only are you only working burglary, but you're up shit creek without a suspect."

"I have a suspect."

"Not according to TechOps."

Damn Miri and her efficiency.

The extremely competent woman didn't only dig like she'd been born half Labrador, but she filled out all of her paperwork with better regularity than any clock Sabrina had ever seen.

"I've got her, I just can't prove it."

"Miri said they were entirely separate women. We both know you can tell the difference when you're sober."

"It's her."

"How? Magic?"

"You know better, preacher's brat."

Mary stiffened. Before she could retaliate, the Captain's door sprang open. "Gamete, don't you have a homicide to solve? Foxner, inside."

Sabrina followed him into the irritatingly untidy office. She scanned filing cabinets, half-stowed files, old mail and magazines, cigar butts and empty Coke cans.

This office would be pretty big if he actually kept it organized.

"Foxner!"

She whipped her head around, his walrus mustache still reverberated from the force of her name.

"You done woolgathering? Can we maybe have your attention on some police work today?"

"Captain, I've been—"

"Chasing the wrong woman."

"They've got the same name, the same man."

"So? This some sort of weird jealous obsession?"

Sabrina folded her arms across her chest. "I'm chasing a suspect."

"Sit."

She sat, refolding her arms.

"Look, Sabrina, you're not in homicide anymore—though why you requested the transfer I can't imagine. Like it or not, Burglary doesn't have the big budgets to focus on one suspect or one case. I need you off this and onto the next one."

"So we just let a chain of animal shelter thefts go?" Sabrina asked.

"You a pet lover? I've got two dogs myself. Love them more than I loved my last four wives, truth be told. It's horrible, but that's humanity. Your perp stole this poor woman's identity to lead you astray. Maybe it's even a frame-up."

"I have deleted pictures of Snyder with the suspect. I saw a photograph myself. They're related at the very least."

He sighed, his mustache fluttering. "Seven animal shelter heists, animals only, and you have one suspect that the Feds say doesn't exist. You've got no adoption records for a sister, no birth records, all you've got is a hippy florist and her dog of a boy toy, and some photo-shopped pictures. You may have been one of my best, but there's nothing even you can do with this one. File it under unsolved and move on."

Shock froze a retort on her tongue.

Unsolved? I've never filed a case under unsolved.

"That's an order, Detective. Out you go."

Vitae

Summuseraphi drove my Mercedes...badly, much to my discomfort and displeasure. He took us to the Central Presbyterian Church, parking and walking around the back to a trestle arch laced with too-dry vine roses. He extended both hands, an acorn and a small pinecone in either. The divine phoenix muttered, cursed, muttered again. The second round of cursing brought a thunderclap from the clear sky. Summuseraphi cringed, mouthing apologies and muttered once more.

A swirling portal eventually filled the archway.

Summuseraphi shrugged. "Pronunciation has to be just right."

I held my face in a passionless mask. "Of course."

Which anyone not an idiot could probably have managed on the first attempt without raising God's ire.

I followed him through the archway into a wide, cobbled hollow under a spring sky. A ring of cushioned chairs surrounded two curved tables and a small table at their foot. To my left, silk tents rested beneath tall pines—icy blue and dark raspberry, evergreen and white. On the opposite side, the silks shone daffodil and crimson, gold and orange.

Elven knights stood at either set of both tent entrances in the same—if slightly plainer—armor worn by the knights who'd assaulted our sanctum. My blood raced through my veins. My hands itched to draw either or both of the elven blades hung upon my hips.

All four knights reacted to my movement, placing hands upon their own blades beneath disapproving scowls.

A tiny tent on the far side opened to a rotund goblin in an Edwardian suit coat and vestment. His dark, greasy hair pulled back along his round skull into a black bow which poked out from his head half as far as his nose. Long narrow ears extended a middle distance between that of nose and ponytail. It shuffled along on patent leather clown shoes that fit its elongated toes.

"Greetings, Divine One, Vitae. You are welc—" The goblin's eyes fell on my swords. "Um, yes, welcome, you are welcome here."

Summuseraphi shook the goblin's olive hand, the faerie's long fingers almost wrapping around his hand a second time. "You honor us. May we know your name, Esteemed One?"

The goblin shrugged. "I'm nobody, just this year's token representative for my people in the Georgia Shire. Call me Thatch."

"The Divine One instructed the Courts to be here waiting," I said. "Why aren't they here?"

"Faery's folk aren't real big on being told what to do, kind of how we ended up here if you really think about it." The goblin cocked his head. "Pardon me for asking, Vitae. I've never had the pleasure—being a law-abiding merchant by trade—but can your kind do magic?"

"Not in the way I think you mean," Summuseraphi said.

"Hmm," Thatch said.

The goblin excused himself and waddled over to the Unseelie tent. "Pardon this interruption, Great One, but a council is called."

He repeated the performance at the Seelie tents. Thatch returned to us, gesturing into the center of the tables. "If you would stand there for council?"

"Haven't you seats we might use?" I asked.

Thatch cringed. "You're not important enough to warrant seats."

"Is that so?" My voice rose, and I reached for my swords.

Summuseraphi laid a hand on my arm. "We will stand. Thank you, Thatch."

Thatch took a seat at the tiny table and avoided eye contact with both phoenixes. After an interminable wait, I checked my pocket watch. Half an hour later—at least according to my watch—a tall young man in royal garb stepped out of the Unseelie tent.

It's about time.

He clapped his hands then disappeared back inside.

A flock of pixies in winter livery swarmed one table, laying a feast for eye, nose and palate. A summer flock appeared without invitation, laying out a feast like, but better, than the first. Winter added more scrumptious delicacies in more artistic layouts. Summer retaliated. For twenty minutes the contents of each table changed.

The Unseelie youth appeared at his tent entrance. "Sufficient."

Winter pixies fled with whatever they still held. A procession of men and women, some with elvish features, others huge versions of the pixies and another so unbelievably beautiful I felt as if I were trying to look into the sun.

A young woman in knightly garb led a procession from the Seelie tent. "Cease and remove yourselves."

I opened my mouth to object, but Summuseraphi shook his head. Summer's servitors left in a stream. One knocked a delicacy out of place. It swept back to restore it.

"Lady Esloah commanded you."

The pixie looked up at the voice, abject horror across its little face. It imploded with a small shriek.

My jaw clenched. I glared at a barely adolescent fairy in gossamer silks layered like flower petals around him.

Unseelie circled the tableaux. Seelie orbited in the opposite direction. Both groups wove in and out of each other, examining the table and pointedly ignoring us phoenixes, Thatch and the opposite party.

I folded my arms, careful not to move my hands near either sword as I tapped my foot. Words sprang to my tongue, held back by will that weakened at each tirade turned aside. At long last the circles stopped, the petal-wrapped youth coming face to face with one young woman too beautiful to look at directly.

"We win, Laryn," she said.

Vusolaryn smirked. "How do you figure?"

Her mouth quirked. "You got pixie on yours."

Vusolaryn turned, accepting a plain wooden cup from Lady Esloah. He presented it to the beautiful fairy woman with a slight bow. "Cup to you, Mariena."

Both parties reversed and took their seats.

Thatch stood. "Divine Phoenix, Summuseraphi, Shieldheart, May I introduce Princess Mariena of Unseelie and Prince Vusolaryn of Seelie, Royal mon—"

"Leaders," Mariena said.

Thatch bowed. "Your pardon, Royal Leaders of the Georgia Shire."

Mariena folded her hands. "This decade we're a republic."

Vusolaryn smirked at me. "We tried socialism last, but the pixies kept eating the best treats."

"The last Shire I guarded was a monarchy," Summuseraphi said.

Vusolaryn rolled his eyes.

"So our mothers prefer," Mariena sighed. "But that's just so last millennia."

"And it is our Shire," Vusolaryn turned to Esloah. "When's lunch?"

I stepped forward. "First off, Georgia is our Shield, not your Shire. Your shire abuts our Shield within *Faery*. You have no place and no right within our Shield."

Mariena's eyes fixed on me. Discomfort and arousal battled

for my foremost attention. "Oh, there's something *delicious* about this bird."

"I prefer warmer, more passionate fare," Vusolaryn said.

"Forgive our Shieldheart," Summuseraphi said. "He died twice defending our Sanctum from your knights."

Faeries fixed their attention on Summuseraphi, all signs of boredom gone.

"I would never condone an attack on a Shield Sanctum," Mariena said.

Vusolaryn darkened. "I certainly wouldn't deign to order such an assault."

"And yet I slew—yet Knights Dolumii and Gherrian were slain while assaulting our Shield," I said. "Behold their swords as proof."

All the faeries leapt to their feet. Outcries so clogged the air there was no way to unravel them. Thatch stood on his table, shouting to be heard until Summuseraphi quieted the crowd with a sudden blast of Light.

"Killing a Seelie Knight is an act of war," Esloah said.

"Same," an Unseelie prince spat.

Summuseraphi leaned close. "Perhaps I should handle things."

I shrugged. "Even you can't worsen this travesty."

Summuseraphi's expression hardened. He turned back to the assembled Courts. "Not only did Knight Dolumii and Knight Gherrian attack our Sanctum—"

"After slaying our Ignis," I added.

Summuseraphi inclined his head. "After Knight Dolumii ambushed and killed our Ignis, he and Knight Gherrian or their confederates made off with the Sanctum's eggs."

Both sides erupted in denials again.

Both sides demanded satisfaction against me.

Both demanded I return their Champions' swords.

Both insisted that if any of their subjects were present, they were only defending the Sanctum against their opposite Sidhe and both insisted they'd taken no eggs.

Summuseraphi defended me, refusing duels on my behalf that I'd have rather fought and trying to keep the discussion on point. He offered amnesty in return for the eggs despite my objections.

"You framed us," Mariena said.

"How dare you?" Vusolaryn asked. "This means war!"

"It certainly does," she said.

All pandemonium ceased.

Mariena and Vusolaryn smiled at one another and winked at me.

"Standard stakes?" Vusolaryn asked.

Mariena nodded. "First shopping rights to the Goblin Market for the next season."

"What about wafer deaths?" Vusolaryn glanced at Summuseraphi. "Unintentional, of course."

"Least deaths?" Mariena asked.

Vusolaryn glanced at Summuseraphi again. He gave Mariena a wink. "*Least*. Sprite laurel for a season?"

"And your best chef."

"For a season," Vusolaryn said.

They shook hands.

"War!" Vusolaryn and Mariena said together.

Both Courts stormed off to their pavilions with furious elegance, neither touching a single item of their prepared feasts.

"You did great," I said. "You just put our Shield in the middle of a meat grinder."

Summuseraphi glowered.

"No one died, that's almost a miracle," Thatch said. "If there's any way the Wyld can help recover your eggs, I'll happily provide it."

"Perhaps you could illuminate how Knight Dolumii's assault on our Ignis employed Wyldfae," Summuseraphi said. "Or perhaps why my Praefecture has been under assault by your faeries?"

I drew Dolumii's blade and shoved it just below the fork of Thatch's legs as I seized his shirt. "I want to know everything you know about this sword, *Sidhe*. What happens to those slain with it?"

Thatch's eyes widened. Waved his hands in the air. "I know nothing of this, nothing."

"Then maybe I'll kill you with it and you will."

"Vitae, I don't know what's gotten into you," Summuseraphi grabbed my hands, forcing me to let Thatch go. "But, we cannot shed Sidhe blood in this place without starting a major war."

All anger drained away, leaving me melancholy and disoriented.

Thatch scurried from my reach. "I swear, but I'll seek out the...well, someone. I'll find your answers, elf-slayer, I swear it."

Before they could respond, Thatch sprinted across the meeting ground and into his tiny tent. The sky flickered from day to night, filled with countless stars close enough to touch.

"Great," Summuseraphi said. "You just alienated our only ally."

Bradley

Bradley lowered the bizarre chandelier down around Whisker's cage. The drop-ceiling frame over which it hung groaned. The cat growled within the newly-reinforced cage. He considered lowering the chandelier all the way into place before feeding the cat, but making it wait for meals had doomed the last three cages.

"All right, all right. You're going to get fat, you know." He picked up a wire cage containing a plump alley rat. It hissed at him, glaring with beady eyes. Bradley dropped the rat into a kind of mesh airlock, ensuring the door double latched before drawing back the metal shield separating them.

The rat scrabbled to stay in the upper enclosure well away

from the growling cat. Whiskers didn't let it, shaking it free of its grip and shredding it with a choir of nauseating noises.

Bradley returned to his project while the cat daintily cleaned its long, bloody claws. It'd taken him two days to assimilate everything he could find on radiation, radiation detection and possible detection mediums. He'd scoured Atlanta and its flea markets for another two days, collecting an assortment of fuels and base materials to build the contraption that hung over the cat.

Someone knocked on his office door.

He threw a sheet over the cage. Whiskers voiced her displeasure with a low, highly unsettling sound.

Bradley opened the door. Delight filled him at the sight of overburdened gurneys. In the last week, something had changed on the streets. He'd received more deliveries than the whole rest of the year, all carrying mysterious lumps, covered by oddly-stained fabrics.

"It's not that exciting, Doc."

"Just love my job," Bradley said.

He hurried to the back of his office, rolling forward empty examination tables to take their delivery. The first orderly stared at the mad assortment of small glass globes, little lights popping in the swirling gasses contained by two of them.

"Um, Doc?"

"Gas spectrometer of my own design, though I included a few elements of scintillation detectors. All very experimental of course, cutting edge probably, not that I know anyone else who's working with such a thing. I might be the only one—"

"Whatever, Doc. What's it do?"

"In theory?" Bradley asked.

He nodded.

"It detects radiation."

The other orderlies hurried for the door. The first eyed the glowing orbs. "That sparkling means there's some kind of radiation? Here?"

"Of course, how would I test a radiation detector if I didn't have radioactive materials—"

"Thanks, Doc, lots to do. Just sign the papers and interoffice them to our department."

The orderly pushed his gurney away at a run.

Bradley shrugged, delighted that more than one of his gasses seemed to be picking up the radiation emanating off Whiskers. He pushed the examination tables to one side and returned to lowering the cobbled-together gas spectrometer into place.

Only one orb sparkled. He frowned at it.

Did it exhaust the gas that fast?

He leaned closer, checking the hand scribbled label decrying the orb's contents. A thought occurred to him. He dug under the discolored sheets, removing a limb so thickly tattooed and bruised, the skin resembled a moldy blackberry. He waved it near the detector. A second orb sparkled.

There must be more than one radiation involved.

Bradley clapped his free hand with the severed one. "Behold, Whiskers, a device to detect magic's flavors and colors."

Quayla

I woke in agony, not sure where I was, only that I hurt. I blinked up through the garden ceiling at a few stars strong enough to shine through Atlanta's light pollution. Flashes of magic and urgency exploded like fireworks between the booming throbs in my head.

"Ani?" I rasped. I licked my lips and sucked on my tongue to ease a dry mouth that should never have needed moistening.

"Shield Quayla! You're conscious," Anima said.

"Yay?" I moaned. "Status?"

"You saved the Shield, Vitae too."

Her words faded in and out. I think she said something about heroes, but I missed most of it from where I lay on consciousness's seesaw.

"Quayla?"

She's worried, not very automata of her.

A giggle escaped me. Pain transmogrified it into choking.

"Don't you realize what this means?" Anima asked. "You risked yourself to save the Shield just like Mare. You've proven yourself."

"Yay. Feels like I'm going to die like her now, too."

"Hold on, it'll be all right," Anima said. "The others are on their way as soon as they clear their breaches."

Whoever consciousness was playing with must have pissed it off because it jumped off the seesaw, took its ball and went home, dumping me into darkness's lap.

Bradley

Another set of bodies awaited Bradley in the hall when he unlocked his door after a lunch time trip for more gas samples. Most of the corpses died from the normal kind the other examiners sent down when they were too busy playing golf. He got old age, stroke, and gunshot—nothing unexpected.

The higher percentage of bizarre corpses continued.

He wheeled them in one by one.

His chandelier sorted them as they came in. If the little globes remained dark, he pushed the body into a bay he reserved for natural—as opposed to supernatural—causes.

He'd added more gasses to his overhead detector, coming away with three that seemed able to pick up radiations foreign to anything in his medical books. He sorted the bodies red, blue, gold and multihued where more than one radiation seemed present in the bites, burns or stab wounds involved.

Once sorted, he started on all the normal work. Regardless of cause of death, those that'd died of natural methods required none of the special editing when filing their reports. Caught in gang drive-by didn't raise any eyebrows upstairs.

Listing goblin bite as a cause of death had warranted him a trip upstairs where he'd been formally reprimanded for unprofessional conduct and allowing his fantasy life to intrude on official duties. Goblin bites became wild dogs and sword wounds became gruesome example-making knife play by some gang.

A small wand in his lab coat burned a hole in his pocket as he did the last evaluations on the poor woman whose buffet addiction had caused her to eat herself to a heart attack.

He took out a bulky device smaller than the chandelier. He'd cannibalized a universal remote bought at a flea market to join the other components. The number of batteries required unbalanced the device and made it unwieldy, but it was his first portable magic-o-meter.

I'll do better on Rattler generation two.

The device resembled a bulky baby's rattle. Three bulbs stuck out from its end, each filled with one of the gasses he'd found reactive to the radiation of the three types of magic he'd discovered so far.

I'll keep swapping gasses and use my Damocles Magic-O-Meter to ensure I find them all.

He lowered his rattler over the first body, a college coed whose lower legs had been chewed off. Blue lit bright as a magic missile.

Bradley scowled.

Too many blues. Whatever these things are, they don't respect us.

He moved to the other group. Red lit as he'd expected until the batteries died. He replaced them. The rattler was more sensitive than the big one, either because of a greater applied current, better proximity or the increased gas concentration of each globe.

Red Lights had killed almost as many as Blue Lights. Bradley didn't know whether they'd always killed this many—at least before he occupied Basement E, but it seemed clear something was going on just based on the uptick in bizarre body count.

He moved to the third group. Most of these dead were either blazingly blue with a splattering or red or vice versa.

Some kind of gang war.

The bodies weren't human. Their species wasn't as easy to identify as troll was, but they were some kind of fantastic creature. A few radiated hints of the much rarer yellow. Either yellow never died or cleaned up after their bodies better.

Best as I can guess without actually being present, it seems the golden yellow light must be the good guys. They're out there trying to stop red and blue all by themselves.

A grin spread across his face.

But not for much longer. Hold on, guys, help's growing.

THE STORY CONTINUES...

Keep reading for a sneak peek from
***Blood Phoenix Chronicles 2:
Ruled by Tainted Blood***

Thank you for reading *Ashes of Raging Water.*

Word of mouth recommendations and book reviews are insanely helpful, not just to other readers, but to an author's success. Moreover, we use these reviews to know what *you* want to read more of. Please consider leaving a short, honest review—nothing special required, just a sentence or two about how you felt about this book. I can't thank you enough.

If you loved this story and would like to stay up to date on the latest book releases, promotions, giveaways, and a free story, please be sure to become a member of the Delirious Scribbles Readers Group. [Your email address will never be shared, and you can opt out at any time.]

Begin your journey, just scan this image with your phone camera!

Keep reading for a sneak peak....

Sneak Peek:

Ruled by Tainted Blood

Ignis

A firestorm swirled Ignis back into existence. Flames reflected off the mirrored metal of his nest's alcove, redoubling the heat of his furious snarl. Ashes floated down around him, settling back into the basin of his nest. He stared into his reflection, eyes still glowing coals.

"How dare he? I'll hunt that infernal elf down if it takes—"

Anima's voice rose from his nest. "Shield Ignis?"

"What?" Ignis snapped. "I've got to get back there."

His Shield's automata sounded hurt even though she wasn't designed with emotions. "The Shieldheart and Summuseraphi are on route to the sight of your death. You are needed elsewhere."

"That son-of-a-bitch faerie ripped my heart out of my chest while I was still alive."

"I am sorry for your pain, but each of our shields has been ambushed and I'm seeing multiple coordinated incursions. Two shields and a Divine One for a single site is overkill."

Ignis pushed open the alcove. Lingering handprints glowed on the metal. He descended the rear access steps of his apartment building's ancient dead boiler. He yanked a pull chain. The handle warped, but a short deluge of scalding water from the newer boiler cooled his skin.

The putti had reworked the boilers so that neither could be removed without compromising building integrity and added an adjoining entrance behind them into Ignis's basement apartment.

A section of brick wall swung out of the way, admitting him into a large corner shower unit. A twist of a handle opened up shower heads above and around him, tepid water lowering his body temperature the rest of the way. He never used the hot water tap even in the cold of winter.

Ignis stepped out of the shower onto a fluffy slate grey rug and grabbed a matching if fluffier towel. He patted himself dry and took only a moment to double check his reflection. He was in a hurry to rip the Unseelie knight's head off, but haste was dangerous—particularly when combined with fury.

His glance at the mirror showed Ignis in need of a body-wide shave, but otherwise his basic size, shape and nationality had returned to a close approximation of his former self.

His focus in the final moments of his last life had informed the makeup of his new body. He'd learned the technique from an earth phoenix that had been positively persnickety about his appearance. It didn't always work. Little changes occurred no matter how much time he had to concentrate, but he never needed as many clothing changes as Aquaylae or Caelum.

Nobody needs as many changes as Caelum.

He dressed quickly and grabbed a spare hilt from his under-wear drawer. The foot-long ironwood rod resembled nothing so much as a thick, intricately carved flute. Nonetheless his weapon's flexibility served him better than Aquaylae's karambit hilts or even Vitae's fighting canes.

Ignis stepped out of his apartment building tense for a fight. One hand tucked inside his jacket, fingers wrapped white-knuckled around his hilt. Heat clung to his new skin, blood burning in his veins. Knight Dolumii had ambushed him with the help of some Wyldfae. They'd killed him, and Dolumii had stolen his heart.

If he thinks he's going to control me, he's got a lot to learn about fire.

Much to Ignis's disappointment, nothing so much as looked at him funny on his march to the bus stop.

Nothing waiting for me here because I was the first ambush.

Ignis took a deep breath, smothering the coals of fury that's started to outline his body in a nimbus of flame.

Calm, the flame of a scented candle or sandalwood and incense. Wildfires are destructive, and once unleashed control becomes problematic—not something anyone wants in a metropolitan area.

Ignis hated having to take public transit, but he wasn't comfortable storing money digitally and accumulating debt was out of the question. Without a banking card of some sort, he couldn't call one of the cab company replacements. He didn't have enough time to reach a banking branch to get cash for a taxi. He made it to the bus stop as the MARTA bus rounded the far corner. The dirty, dented bus pulled up stinking of natural gas. The door opened and a wave of taint rolled over him masking all other smells.

Ignis licked his lips, smiled and stepped inside.

So, who's today's contestant? Fae Kissed or faerie?

No one jumped him.

He scanned the half full seats. No one looked at him for more than a glance. No one failed to take that glance.

"Were you going to pay?" the driver asked.

Ignis slipped the bills into the reader labeled to warn him the unit didn't give change. The bus gave a small jerk as it lurched back onto the road.

Ignis stepped between benches and seats, keeping a hand on the guide bars to ensure his balance. He inhaled as he passed each passenger, envying Caelum his nose.

Old lady—no.

Two toughs—no.

Middle-aged waitress—no.

Corporate clone—no.

Each filled seat failed to intensify the taint, but the prickle along his skin identified the magic's origin as Unseelie.

Ignis closed to the final row of seats a somewhat feminine male doing his best to persuade the clothes off a teenage girl not long into her breeding years. Ignis inhaled the increased taint.

He dropped into the seat behind them and leaned his arms on both chair backs. "Unless you want to bleed purple for the young lady, I suggest you sit up straight and don't say another word until we step off this bus."

"What're you talking about?" the boy said. "Buzz off, creep."

Ignis grabbed him by the back of the throat. "You must be new to this Shield."

The girl paled, eyeing them both. "W-what's going on?"

"Everything will be fine, miss. He won't bother you anymore. The young gentleman and I are just going to get off at the next stop." Ignis let a flicker of his anger heat his fingers. "We need to chat."

"He wasn't bothering me," she said.

The young man jerked from Ignis's grip and whipped around. "I don't know who you are, but hands off or I call a cop."

Ignis frowned. He grabbed the boy's shirt, jerked him forward and inhaled.

"What the hell, freak?"

"What's going on back there?" The bus driver called.

"Everything's under control." Ignis pulled a wallet and flipped it open. At the distance, his fire inspector's badge did the job. He turned toward the girl. "Just questioning a suspect."

Her expression flickered. Then her whole image flickered.

"By the Undying Light," Ignis said. "I order you to hold and be known."

The girl looked from Ignis to the boy and back. "I-I'm not sure what you're talking about."

Ignis's eyes narrowed. "I think you do. After the boy's gone."

"Who're you calling boy? We're basically the same age."

Ignis smirked. "Would you care to repeat that? Are you telling an enforcer of law that you're a twenty year old male trying to seduce a teenage girl?"

"Um, well, I said basically the same, I-I'm seventeen, so—"

"ID, please," Ignis said.

A little ring heralded an impending stop.

"I didn't do anything. I've seen TV. You can't question anyone underage without a parent or guardian present."

"Show me your ID to establish your age, and I'll let you go."

"Screw you." The boy lurched out of the bench, grabbing a rail as the bus pulled up to a stop. He rushed out the door before Ignis could follow. Ignis didn't bother. He turned to the girl.

Her image vanished with a pop. A pixie scowled around a cigar that parted his salt and pepper beard. "What's the deal, bird? Do you have any idea how much fresh wafer semen goes for at the Goblin Market?"

"Ensorcelling a mortal's mind is a class-c infraction." Sightline blocked by the bus seat, Ignis slipped his spare phone from one pocket and an elderberry thorn loop from another.

"I didn't do a damned thing to his mind. I didn't offer him any deals. Hell, he was practically begging to put his little worm in my hand." The pixie grinned. "Besides, nothing happened thanks to you. No slime, no crime."

"You're wrong—plenty of slime in that seat." Ignis tossed the loop into the seat next to the little pixie.

The faerie leapt up, flitting away from the loop. He raised his eyes back to Ignis in time for Ignis to snap the surprise photo.

"Name, Sidhe," Ignis said.

"Cember, bird."

"This is an official warning. Leave the mortals alone and return home."

"I am home," Cember said. "Next stop."

Ignis tensed. "There's an Arch at the next stop?"

Cember's brow wrinkled. "Not that I know of, just my apartment."

"Apartment? You don't live in Faery?" Ignis asked.

"Cember fetch this. Cember do that. Cember lick my ass so I don't have to bathe. Thanks, but no thanks."

"How'd you pay for the apartment?" Ignis asked. "Fairy gold?"

Cember snorted. "Greenbacks, pal, and before you ask they were as genuine as spring rain. Earned fair and even, disgusting as that is."

"How?" Ignis asked.

Glamour changed Cember into a grizzled, middle aged man.

"I'm a private dick—surveillance, lost objects, just like in the Philip Marlowe books. Getting *very* candid pictures is easy when you can fly into the room with an invisible camera." Cember rang the stop request and stood. "I've been warned. I'm going."

"I don't like the idea of an Unseelie running around the city unsupervised," Ignis said. "What's to stop you from converting mortals?"

"I can glamour, okay, but wishes aren't my bag. Hell, who wants the administrative headache of keeping track of all those deals? Besides, if I were dealing, I'd have to answer to the Court, and that means losing my anonymity. Thanks, but no thanks." Cember headed for the exit.

Ignis didn't stop him. He retrieved the thorn loop and sat back in the seat thinking about the encounter. The bus pulled into Dunwoody station. He rode the escalator up to the train platform. Along the way, another taint played across his nose.

That lingering from Cember or something else?

Taint stench grew then faded.

Ignis followed, still itching to vent his spleen while waiting on the next train. A strange graffiti tag marked the foot of another stairway. The stylized goblin's head resembled a badly depicted house elf. Symbols rode a silver headband across the cocked head: a bag of gold coins and scales—typical of a Goblin Market; a birdcage; and a triangle composed of three smaller shards or possibly daggers. The bubble depicted around the head made less sense. Tiny marks shaded the bubble into a sphere. Violet and green goop graphically clung to its exterior.

That's pretty intricate. How'd they get this painted without getting caught?

Ignis cradled his face.

Glamour, you idiot, hence the taint.

He took a picture with his phone. The sound of an arriving train summoned him. He hurried back up to the platform and slipped into a car as the doors were closing. His body triggered a safety buzz. The doors opened back up. He'd claimed a seat and drew out his headphones before the doors closed and the train lurched forward. The new Sanderson audio book filled his ears, taking Ignis into foreign battlegrounds as MARTA whisked him through the city toward his Camaro.

Caelum

Caelum surveyed the carnage around his motorcycle. The dwarfish figures bled pools onto the parking bay floor, resurrecting the blood-red of their vests and berets. He'd been on his way to headquarters, stopping only to replace his empty clips.

He'd barely rounded the corner back to his motorcycle when the redcaps staged his second ambush that night. He piled their footman picks and Freddy Kruger gauntlets nearly to the top of his rear tire.

He headed over to the closet where he kept jugs of water, envying Quayla's ability to clean up so much more efficiently.

"What's going on—oh my God!" A woman shrieked.

Caelum whirled around and bolted in the direction of her scream. He threw his hand her direction, wind sweeping around her cry in an attempt to muffle her scream.

Probably too little too late like those first gunshots.

He bent the wind around her, sweeping air from the reach of her lungs. She gulped like a landed fish, grabbing at her throat. Almost a full minute later, her eyes rolled back. Her body followed suit.

Caelum's essence propelled him to double speed. A feet first slide caught her head moments before she hit the ground. Her head slammed a little too close to home, but he shook off the pain and lifted her from the ground. Wind fed and starved her, keeping her momentarily out while he rushed her to the stairwell.

Damn but it'd be nice sometimes to have Glamour.

Caelum laid her down and beckoned air to her lungs. She stirred almost at once. "What happen? Oh, God, dead bodies. There were dead bodies."

Caelum smiled. "I may not look my best, but I assure you I'm not dead."

"I saw...what happened?"

"You fainted, hit your head pretty hard." He flashed her a charming grin. "It would be my pleasure to escort the lady to a doctor."

"No, we need to call the police."

"For a little bump on the head?" Caelum asked.

A man's voice boomed deeper in the parking bay. "What the —hell, yes! I'm going to be rich!"

"Shit. It'd be so much easier being a faerie sometimes." Caelum pulled a small white feather from his back pocket.

The woman shrieked again as the down glowed to life.

"Vilicangelus, Vilicangelus, Vilicangelus," Caelum watched her staggering retreat transform into a shrieking sprint. "We're going to need some rewrites."

An indigo-scaled wyvern slipped from within the Arch.

Appendix A: Cast of Characters

Phoenixes:

Aquaylae (Quayla Buckler): A water phoenix assigned to the Atlanta Shield. Recently released from house arrest. Employed running a florist shop in eastern Atlanta. Dating Dylan Snyder. Preferred weapon: karambit knife

Caelum (Caelum Kite): An air phoenix assigned to the Atlanta Shield. Employed as Head of Charitable Projects by Circlestone Corporation. Preferred weapon: handgun or battle fan.

Ignis (Ignis Round): A fire phoenix assigned to the Atlanta Shield. Employed as a firefighter and arson investigator for the City of Atlanta. Preferred weapon: duo hilt bow and katana.

Mare: A water phoenix formerly assigned to the Atlanta Shield. Lost in a battle with Unseelie forced.. Preferred weapon: short swords.

Summuseraphi: A divine phoenix assigned as new praefectus of the shields of the southeastern United States. Formerly Lympha, Summuseraphi was recently elevated to divine status and placed under Villicangelus for training. Preferred weapon: chain blade.

Terrance (Terrance Wall): An earth phoenix assigned to the

Atlanta Shield. Employed at the Department of Motor Vehicles. Preferred weapon: cestus battle gloves.

Villicangelus: A divine phoenix assigned as overseers of the shields functioning in Southern Britain. Formerly overseer of the southern United States. Training supervisor over Summuseraphi. Preferred weapon: unknown.

Vitae: A life phoenix assigned to the Atlanta Shield as Shield-heart. Responsible for overall operations. Concerned about mortal deaths in her former shield, Vitae placed Quayla on house arrest. Preferred weapon: lajatang—bladed staff and baton forms.

HUMANS:

Detective Sabrina Foxner: Atlanta detective currently assigned to burglary. The former homicide detective is investigating the Howell Mill break-in.

Doctor Bradley Sky: Intelligent and enthusiastic junior assistant coroner working in Atlanta's morgue. His memory has been rewritten multiple times to remove discovery of the Fey.

Dunham Heffernan: CEO of Circlestone Corporation

Dylan Snyder: Quayla's bisexual boyfriend. Dylan is aware of Quayla's true nature. He's employed as an IT professional

Emma: Fae Kissed human who made a deal to resurrect her cat. Employed at Howell Mill Humane Society

Judith: Pessimistic and disinterested Korean college student employed at Ponds de Leon Flowers.

Mara: Employee of Camp Woof doggie daycare

Miri: Atlanta PD tech ops.

Mrs. Hadley Sage Cox: Quayla's sweet but nosey landlady. Superstitious with detailed knowledge of Fey folklore.

Nicolas: Owner of a hole in the wall grocery store near the Atlanta Sheild's HQ and Caelum's supplier for honey candy and milk used as currency in the Goblin Market

Pete: Owner of Camp Woof doggie daycare

Tommy: Doctor at Grady Memorial Hospital Long time friend of Bradley Sky.

Valerie: News anchor. Subject of lingering crush by Bradleh's friend Tommy

Viviane: Dunham Heffernan's executive assistant

FEY:

Grynnberry: A Seelie nymph. An informant that provides Quayla with intelligence.

Knight Dolumii: Knight Champion of the Unseelie Court.

Knight Gherrian: Knight Champion of the Seelie Court.

Lady Esloah: Knight of the Seelie Court

Oshyn: Half sized elf merchant in the Goblin Market. Provides brownie cleaning services.

Princess Mariene: Unseelie sovereign and royal court adjunct between the Seelie queen and the phoenixes.

Prince Vusolaryn: Seelie sovereign and royal court adjunct between the Seelie queen and the phoenixes.

Thatch: WyldFae representative for the Sidhe's Georgia Shire near Atlanta

OTHERS:

Anima: Monitoring entity assigned to the Atlanta Shield

Look for more great books like these at a book reailer near you and learn more at www.deliriousscribbles.com

Acknowledgments

Welcome to the end of the first Blood Phoenix Chronicle. This novel marks my tenth published novel and a long list of firsts. Ashes was my first attempt to join forces with other authors, my first try and completing a whole series before releasing any of it and my first attempt at rapidly releasing a series of books.

I've learned a scandalous amount about myself, my writing and subjects I didn't even realize I needed to know. Along the way I learned about Quayla's world too. Both of us thank you for reading our story. I know there were a few tense moments as well as some deliciously frustrating moments as well. There are plenty of questions left to explore even after hours and hours of enjoyable reading.

If you like Quayla and want more of her world or urban fantasy stories like this one, I ask you to add fuel to the fire by leaving a review.

A lot of people worked very hard to help bring you this story. Andrea Fodor spent countless hours designing and redesigning Quayla, her shieldmates and their phoenix forms for our covers. Thanks as always, Andrea, for putting up with how picky I can get.

On our editing, reading and proofreading teams, we had some heavy hitters this time around. Author Sam Gregory handled early edits. Authors L. V. Bell and Len Barry dealt with my mid-series rewrite-it-all crisis in addition to providing beta reading help. Author T. Allen Diaz not only put up with my neurosis and helped keeping me encouraged, he provided his firefighting expertise for scenes in Ashes as well as its sequels. I can't forget Larry Dixon (and Mercedes Lackey for loaning me her husband). Larry's guidance has been invaluable to keeping me grounded and moving forward. Billy and Rebecca, Scott, and Sarah also deserve thanks for various stages of reading and editing. Tina, well this one's dedicated to her for all the countless hours and rereads.

Lastly, thanks to Quayla and the whole Atlanta Shield. Usually, I'd be looking forward to continuing our journey in the sequels—except they've already been written. Well, see you in the future...

About the Author

Photo credit: Jim Cawthorne

Michael J. Allen is a star-lord, goofball, and USA Today bestselling author of character-driven, multi-layer, full-spectrum science fiction and fantasy novels - pretty much whatever madness sprouts from his head... (Learn more at www.deliriousscribbles.com)

Let's Connect

I love chatting with my readers, and hope you'll join my reader groups. If you'd rather stay up to date without joining in on the fun, there are plenty of ways to follow along.

— Michael J Allen

Reader Groups:

Discord : https://discord.gg/WeM4bwq
Facebook: https://www.facebook.com/groups/dsreaders
MeWe: https://www.mewe.com/join/dsreaders

Follow the Scribbler:

www.deliriousscribbles.com

amazon.com/-/e/B0096GEILG

bookbub.com/authors/michael-j-allen

facebook.com/deliriousscribbler

goodreads.com/deliriousscribbler

instagram.com/thedscribbler

twitter.com/Thedscribbler